Death By French Roast

ALEX ERICKSON

KENSINGTON BOOKS
KENSINGTON PUBLISHING CORP.
www.kensingtonbooks.com

First Printing: November 2020
ISBN-13: 978-1-4967-2113-6
ISBN-10: 1-4967-2113-6

ISBN-13: 978-1-4967-2114-3 (eBook)
ISBN-10: 1-4967-2114-4 (eBook)

10 9 8 7 6 5 4 3 2 1

Printed in the United States of America

Albie's brow furrowed and he leaned toward me. "What's all this about anyway? I doubt you're curious just because old Eleanor passed on."

"I'm interested to hear about her life, what made her the way she was."

"Why don't I believe that? Krissy Hancock on my

Books by Alex Erickson

Bookstore Café Mysteries

DEATH BY COFFEE

DEATH BY TEA

DEATH BY PUMPKIN SPICE

DEATH BY VANILLA LATTE

DEATH BY EGGNOG

DEATH BY ESPRESSO

DEATH BY CAFÉ MOCHA

DEATH BY FRENCH ROAST

Furever Pets Mysteries

THE POMERANIAN ALWAYS BARKS TWICE

DIAL 'M' FOR MAINE COON

Published by Kensington Publishing Corp.

1

"All life must come to an end. And for my mother, Eleanor, that time has come."

I lowered my head and wiped away a tear. Two rows behind me, a woman—Judith Banyon, I believed—sniffed. Other than the two of us, and Jane up front, all the other eyes in the place were dry.

"Mom didn't have many friends," Jane Winthrow went on. "She preferred it that way. She always said that there is only so much love to go around, and she'd much rather share it with a special few, rather than dilute it among too many people, many of whom might not deserve it. I didn't agree with her for the longest time, but now, I see that maybe she was right."

A quick glance around the funeral parlor showed me that no one else had shown up since Jane had started talking. My neighbors, Jules Phan and Lance Darby, sat a couple seats down, hands intertwined. They'd lived two houses down from Eleanor long before I'd moved to Pine Hills. They hadn't always seen eye to eye with her—no one really did—but they did seem sad to see her go.

Judith and Eddie Banyon, the owners of the local diner, the Banyon Tree, sat a few rows behind Jules and Lance. Behind them, a group of dour-looking men whispered amongst themselves. A man who often played Santa every Christmas, Randy Winter, sat to the front of the room, but he was lounging back, almost as if he was watching a play, rather than a funeral.

And that was it. Jane was Eleanor's only remaining family as far as I was aware. Eleanor, while a bit on the nosy side when it came to the neighborhood, had kept to herself in most matters. Her husband had died of an aneurism sometime before I'd moved to Pine Hills, so I'd never met him. Eleanor's only true friend I knew about was Judith, and last I heard, they weren't seeing each other as much as they once had.

I had a feeling health had a lot to do with that. Eleanor wasn't in the best shape, but I never realized it was so bad. Jane had shown up one day last week, and the next thing I knew, Eleanor was gone, passed away quietly in her sleep. Apparently, she'd known it was coming and had called her daughter so they could spend a final couple of hours together.

Jane finished up her speech with a few words of thanks and then turned to the casket. She laid a hand on it briefly, whispered something to her mother, and then she headed down the aisle, and out into the lobby.

One by one, Eleanor's few mourners rose and walked to the front of the room to view her casket. I remained seated and watched as Judith stiffly paid her respects. From the tension I saw on her face, I could tell she was just barely holding it together. Her husband, Eddie, looked sad, but wasn't in danger of breaking down in heaving sobs anytime soon.

Jules and Lance passed by, said their good-byes, and then when they walked back down the aisle, Jules gave my arm a squeeze. He didn't say anything; he didn't need to. I understood him perfectly. Eleanor had driven us both crazy with her constant binoculars-assisted spying from the armrest of her chair, but now that she was gone, we'd both miss her.

I rose, but before I could leave the aisle, two of the men I'd seen sitting together in the back walked by. They were older—one completely bald, the other with fine wisps of white hair that stood up every which way—and neither looked happy to be there. When I glanced back, I noticed the other men had already left. Randy Winter was also gone.

I waited for the two men to be done, rather than intrude, but neither of them said anything. They stood there, looking down at the casket, side by side, and then, as one, they turned and walked away. Both their faces were void of emotion, as if Eleanor's passing couldn't touch them. It made me instantly dislike both men, even though I didn't know a thing about them, let alone how they knew Eleanor.

With everyone else gone, I made for the front. The casket was open, and I noted Eleanor looked peaceful, which made me happy. She'd never seemed at peace while she was alive. I was glad she'd found it now.

"We had our differences," I said, keeping my voice low so it wouldn't echo in the now empty room. "But know that I never hated you. Not when you were peeping in my windows with your binoculars, or all those times you called the police on me because you misunderstood what was happening at my place. Rest well, Eleanor. You'll be missed."

And with blurry eyes and a sniff, I turned and walked away.

Jane was waiting for me by the door. Her smile was sad, but appreciative as she took my hands in both of hers. "Thank you for coming, Krissy."

"She was a good neighbor," I said, trying my best to be diplomatic, considering how often Eleanor had frustrated me. "I wish I'd gotten to know her better."

"We both know that's not true. Mother could be difficult at the best of times, and a downright terror the rest."

"Yeah, but she didn't hurt anyone."

"That's true." Jane was wearing a black pantsuit, which suited her. I couldn't imagine her wearing a dress, no matter the occasion. "Her life wasn't easy. She did it to herself, and I know that despite what she said, she missed having more people around her. She was lonely, and nothing I ever said helped ease that loneliness."

I didn't know what to say to that, so I merely nodded.

"I don't know why we bothered!" The shout came from outside. Both Jane and I moved so we could see what was happening on the other side of the door.

The group of older men were standing in a huddle, a few yards from the funeral parlor. The man who'd shouted was slightly younger than the rest, meaning he had all his gray hair, and he didn't have quite as many wrinkles lining his face as his companions.

"You'll be lucky if someone comes to your funeral, Arthur." This from a man with bifocals who was wearing a black suit and tie—an upgrade from the more casual attire of his friends.

"She hated every last one of us," the shouter—Arthur—said. "Do you think she would have paid her respects to a single one of us? No, she wouldn't have. She'd have spit on our graves before we were buried!"

"She had her reasons," the bald man said.

"They weren't good ones," Arthur muttered. He looked up, noticed Jane and me watching, and then turned and marched angrily away. After a moment, his friends followed.

Jane heaved a sigh and shook her head. "I can't believe they'd do that here. I was surprised they even came, to be honest."

"Who are they?" I asked. I didn't know them from around town, which wasn't saying much. Pine Hills might be small, and I owned and ran the only dedicated coffee shop in town, but that didn't mean I knew everyone.

"People from Eleanor's past," Jane said. "They—" She cut off as a man in a dark blue suit and a somber expression approached.

"Ms. Winthrow," he said, voice barely above a whisper. "If you have a moment, there's a few details we should go over before we proceed to the burial."

Jane glanced at me, but before she could speak, I waved her off.

"Go ahead," I said. "I'll talk to you later."

She started to walk away with the man, but paused. "I'm going to be going through a few of Mom's things once I'm done here. I ." She cleared her throat, and briefly, I saw a woman devastated before her mask was back in place. "If you have the time, I could use some help."

"Of course," I said. Going through her mother's things would be hard. She didn't need to do it alone.

"Give me an hour," Jane said, and then she headed into a side room with the man.

I drove home with a heavy heart. When I parked in front of my house, the neighborhood felt different, lonelier. Eleanor and I might not have been friends, but I'd always felt her presence nearby.

Her house looked strange knowing that she was no longer in it. It seemed smaller somehow, a shell of what it was. I wondered what would happen to it now, if it would be sold, or if Jane would keep it. I couldn't imagine anyone but Eleanor living there.

I spent the next forty minutes puttering around my house, cleaning with my long-haired orange cat, Misfit, trailing in my wake. He was rather demanding about being pet. Every time I paused, he would butt his head under my hand and then run his entire body across both of my legs. I had to be careful not to step on his long tail.

"I know," I told him. I knew the neighborhood would be more peaceful now without Eleanor calling the cops on me every chance she got, but oddly, I feared I'd miss it. I guess the fact that she was gone contributed to my somber, reflective mood.

Misfit meowed once, and then dug his claws into my leg to force me to pay more attention to him. I was happy to oblige.

When Jane's car pulled up in front of Eleanor's house, I was standing by the window, waiting. The sun was bright in the sky, the breeze cool. I crossed the yard and met her just as she unlocked the front door.

"I have a couple of hours," I said. "Then I'm due for work, if that's okay?"

"Thank you for coming," she said. "I should be fine to go it alone after the first twenty minutes or so. Starting is going to be the hard part."

We entered the house together, each of us braced for the oppressive silence that would follow.

The place was much like I remembered. The orange shag carpet was still dirty and faded, the television ancient. There were more newspapers stacked on the floor next to the blue armchair where Eleanor had often sat than the last time I was here, but that was to be expected. I'd learned then that Eleanor was a hoarder when it came to newspapers, and seeing that she'd kept at it, even as her health waned, made me feel somehow better.

"I'm not sure where to start," Jane said from the middle of the living room. "I mean, do I clean up the trash first? Or should I go through her clothes?" When she took a breath, it trembled. She was just barely holding on.

"What about the newspapers?" I asked, figuring that if anything, it might be the easiest. "What do you want to do with them?"

Jane picked up a stack and flipped through them. "It seems a shame to throw them all out," she said. "Mom took such good care of them." She set the papers on the recliner, and picked up a box sitting beside it. She ran a hand over the wood and then twisted the key that was already shoved into the lock. She lifted the lid and a sad smile played across her lips.

I was dying to know what was inside the box, but remained silent. Now wasn't the time to pry. If she wanted to tell me, she would.

After a few moments of quiet perusal, Jane removed a photograph from the box. She brushed her fingertips across it once, and then handed it to me.

The photograph was old. It looked like it was taken in the seventies, if the way the two people in it were dressed was anything to go by. The photo was of a man and a woman—the woman being a much younger Eleanor Winthrow. I recognized her features, but barely. Time had indeed been hard on her, and had worn her down to the bitter older woman she'd become. The man was taller than her by about a foot, and was extremely good-looking.

"That's Mom and Wade."

"Was Wade your dad?"

Jane surprised me by laughing. "No, Wade was my uncle."

"Eleanor had a brother?" I asked, looking at the photo again. Now that I knew they were related, I could see the resemblance. "I never knew."

"He died a long time ago." Jane took the photograph back. "He was the reason Mom started collecting papers. They'd always been close, and when he died . . ." She shrugged. "She sort of lost it."

"Did he get sick?" I asked.

Jane stared at the photo for a minute more before placing it back into its box. She turned the key and returned the box to where she'd found it. She then picked up the stack of newspapers from the recliner and carried them into the kitchen, where she set them on the table.

"I'm sorry," I said, following after. "I didn't mean to upset you."

"It's not that," Jane said. "I needed a moment to think."

"Still, I'm sorry. It has to be hard reliving any of this."

"It is." She turned in a slow circle, taking in her mother's kitchen. "It's much like it was back then," she said. "Everything is. After Wade died, Mom got stuck in the past. She didn't want things to change, refused to move forward, not until she learned the truth." She touched the stack of newspapers. "Now she never will."

Jane slid into one of the dining-room chairs and then motioned for me to do the same.

"You've solved a few murders in your time, haven't you?" she asked me once I was seated. She already knew that I had; she'd been around for one of them.

"A few, I suppose." Though, honestly, I was hoping to steer clear of any more suspicious deaths.

"Mom said it was a hobby of yours."

"Not on purpose," I said. "I tend to be in the right place at the right time." *Or the wrong place,* I thought.

Then it dawned on me why she might be asking. "Wade was murdered?"

Jane nodded. "It happened over thirty years ago. I think it was around 1985, '86. I was away at college, and honestly, back then, I wasn't too close with my family, so I hope you'll forgive me if I don't know the exact date."

"It was a long time ago," I said.

"Those men you saw at the funeral were Wade's friends. They didn't get on with my mother all that great, but knew her well enough. She always suspected they knew what happened to Wade, but none of them ever admitted to it."

"What do you think?"

Jane ran her hand over the table, then shrugged. "I don't know. All I know for sure is that one day, my uncle was killed, and the police never found out who did it."

A lightbulb clicked on in my head. "That's why she collected newspapers."

Jane nodded. "Mom was obsessed. She grabbed every paper she could and would scour them for information, hoping that something in one of them would tell her who killed her brother. It sounds crazy, but she believed it. I think she was hoping that the culprit would write in or something, like those serial killers you hear about who want attention." She laughed, and then motioned toward the hall, and the room that was filled with years of newspapers, stacked nearly to the ceiling. "He never did, obviously."

It made my heart ache to think about it. I might have treated Eleanor Winthrow with more understanding if I'd known what she'd gone through. That's not to say it made me approve of her spying on me, but perhaps I'd have stopped by more often to try to work things out, rather than just assume the worst of her.

"Mom spent years begging the police to do something, but what could they do? There was no evidence they could use, no witnesses. He was found off a trail, in a spot that didn't make sense."

"How so?"

Jane considered it a moment before responding. "It was an isolated spot. No one knew why he was there, and as far as I know, they still don't."

My interest piqued. There was a mystery here, and I was a sucker for a good mystery.

"Mom swore up and down the police were protecting the killer for some reason, though why she suspected that is anyone's guess," Jane went on. "She alienated most of the town with her accusations. It didn't help that Wade had started a controversy of his own before his death."

I leaned forward. "What kind of controversy?"

Jane fiddled with the newspapers as she answered. "As I mentioned, I wasn't around for it, so I got a lot of the details afterward. I'm not sure how accurate some of it is, mind you. I've heard different versions of the tale over the years, but nothing recently, other than when I talked to

Mother. Most of what she heard were mere rumors, and you know how that goes."

"Yeah." Rumor had a tendency to become fact sometimes, especially in a small town.

"My uncle was a few years younger than Mom, which put him in his thirties at the time of his death. The big hubbub started when it came out that his girlfriend was in her teens."

I couldn't help it; my eyebrows rose at that. "He was dating a teenager?"

"She was eighteen, I believe. Might have been nineteen, though the way some tell it, she was barely fifteen. I know for a fact that Wade wouldn't have dated her if she wasn't legal, so that's just hogwash."

"That's still a pretty big age difference, even if she was legal," I said.

"It was. And back then, people were more sensitive to that sort of thing, at least here in Pine Hills they were. The way Mom told it, Wade was harassed pretty badly, and his friends were involved just as much as everyone else. The girl was treated just as horribly, if not more so. You know how kids can be. School had to have been a nightmare for her."

I could only imagine. "Did someone kill him because of his relationship?" I asked, thinking that if the girl's parents disapproved of the two of them dating, one of them might have acted rashly and killed Wade for it.

"No one knows for sure," Jane said. "Mom thought so. She claimed there was no other reason anyone would want to hurt him, that Uncle Wade was well liked by everyone up until he started dating that girl."

I thought that it was a pretty crappy thing to do, to turn

on someone just because you didn't approve of who they were dating.

"What about the teenager?" I asked. "Was she murdered too?"

Jane shook her head. "No. Mom told me she still lives here in Pine Hills, but I can't fathom why she would. If she was treated as badly as I've heard, it would have made more sense for her to leave town and never come back. I know I would have."

"Do you know her name?" I asked, curious. If I knew her, then perhaps I could learn more about what made Eleanor like, well, Eleanor.

"I do," Jane said, rising. She grabbed a box of trash bags out from beneath the counter, removed a bag, and dumped the stack of newspapers into it. "Her name was Rita," she said. "Rita Jablonski."

2

"Rita?" my best friend, Vicki, asked later that day. "Are you sure she meant *our* Rita?"

"Positive," I said. I took a sip from my coffee before tying on my apron. "Apparently, our young Rita had a thing for older men back in the day."

"Wow." Vicki looked to her husband, Mason, who merely shrugged.

Vicki, Mason, and one of our employees, Lena, had worked the early shift at Death by Coffee, giving me time to go to Eleanor's services. I'd be working alongside Beth Milner and Jeff Braun until close, which was fine—I liked both of them—but I couldn't gossip with them like I could with my best friend, so I'd come in a little early so I could do so.

"I can't believe Rita's never said anything about it," I said. "She spends half her time egging me on to solve crimes around town, and she's never once brought up the fact she was involved, even indirectly, in a murder investigation over thirty years ago."

"Maybe she's forgotten about it," Mason said.

"Or she wishes she could forget." Vicki nudged her husband with her elbow. He grinned and then went to the counter to take an order from a regular with an allergy to cats—a sneezing Todd Melville.

"I feel like I should do something," I said, watching Todd. The man came to Death by Coffee nearly every day, but with his allergy, he looked miserable doing it. Even though Trouble—Vicki's black-and-white cat, who was also Misfit's littermate—rarely left the books section of the store, Todd's allergies made it a chore for him to order his coffee. I sometimes wondered why he bothered.

"Like what?" Vicki asked. "It happened a long time ago."

"I know, but I feel like I should, I don't know, check it out."

"You mean, investigate it?"

I gave a halfhearted shrug. "It sounds silly, but I keep thinking it might be a good way to honor Eleanor's memory. She spent her life wondering what happened to her brother. It caused her to become a hoarder and to pull away from society. If I could solve his murder, then perhaps her spirit might be able to rest peacefully."

Vicki regarded me a long moment before speaking. "It could be dangerous," she said. "Whoever killed him has kept it secret for over thirty years. They won't like you reviving it."

"There's no telling if he or she's still alive," Mason said, rejoining us.

"If the killer's dead, then I have even less to worry about."

"And if they're not?" Vicki asked.

"I'll be careful. It's not like I'm going to go door to door asking about it. I figure I'll talk to Rita and some of the people who lived in Pine Hills back then and see what they have to say. It might not amount to anything, but at least I'd feel like I'm doing *something*."

"Are you sure Rita will want you poking around in it?" Vicki asked. "She hasn't brought it up, and you know there's got to be a reason for that."

"If she asks me not to look into it, I'll drop it," I said, and I meant it. Over the years, Rita had become a friend, despite how often she got on my nerves. When I'd first met her, she was a nosy busybody who overreacted to just about everything. While much of that was still true, Rita's a genuinely good person at heart. When she wasn't trying to force me to do something I didn't want to do, I enjoyed spending time with her.

"Do Rita and her gossip buddies still go to that writers group?" Vicki asked. Rita's friends, Georgina McCully and Andi Caldwell, were two older ladies who might have some insights into what had happened thirty years ago.

"I think so," I said. "I haven't been there in ages, so I can't be sure."

"Maybe it's time you went back," Mason said as the front doors opened and Beth and Jeff entered one after the other.

They were closely followed by Mason's dad, Raymond Lawyer, and Raymond's girlfriend, Regina Harper.

"Uh-oh," I said, noting the look on Raymond's face. I could almost hear his teeth grinding from where I stood behind the counter.

Beth hurried to the back room, passing by the rest of us without so much as a hello. She looked stressed, and it was no wonder why. She used to work for Raymond at Lawyer's Insurance across the street. Raymond wasn't very happy she'd left his employ to come work for me, and he made sure everyone knew it.

Mason was the first to react. He left us to steer his father and Regina to a table in the corner, far away from Beth, who was hiding in the back. Raymond was giving him an earful, but thankfully, wasn't shouting.

Yet.

"Leave it be for now," Vicki said, resting a hand on my arm. I was trembling with anger and was dying to give Raymond an earful myself. "Mason will handle him."

"It's not right," I said, vainly trying to read Raymond's lips. If I made out one disparaging word toward Beth, I was going to leap across the room at him. "She doesn't deserve to be treated this way."

"Trust me, I feel the same way. But if you press him too much, Raymond is liable to explode. You know how he is."

Oh, did I ever. Raymond Lawyer wasn't a nice man. He only cared about himself—and maybe Regina now that they were a couple. He treated Mason badly, and never bothered to hide the fact he thought his son was wasting his life helping Vicki at Death by Coffee. He'd only gotten worse ever since he hooked up with Regina, who was his female counterpart—she was just as contrary and spiteful as he was. I've had nothing but bad experiences with the both of them.

"You should go," Vicki said, stepping in front of me so I'd stop staring at Raymond.

"Go where? I just got here."

"The writers group tonight. You should go and talk to Rita and her friends. It'll do you good, and I bet both Rita and Eleanor would appreciate that someone is looking into the murder after all this time."

Lena wandered down the stairs where she'd been shelving books. She glanced at Raymond, grimaced, and then joined us. "Everything's done," she said. Her hair was a bright purple, cut short, which was her preferred style. I couldn't imagine her with a normal hair color.

"Go ahead and clock out," Vicki said. "I'll see you tomorrow."

Jeff clocked in just as Lena grabbed her things to go. Beth had yet to return from the back, and I imagined she'd wait until Raymond left before she'd emerge.

"You go on ahead," I told Vicki. "I'll make sure Beth's okay."

"You sure? I could stick around if you want me to."

Since Raymond and Regina were here, I assumed Vicki and Mason had plans with them. At least, I hoped so. If they were here because of Beth, there'd be no holding me back.

"No. Go," I said, forcing a smile. "We'll be fine."

Vicki didn't look thrilled about joining her husband with his father, but after snagging Trouble from upstairs, join them she did. She glanced back once and gave me a mock look of horror before taking Mason's arm. Raymond shot me a glare, his face turning an angry shade of red, before he said something harsh to the couple.

"Jerk," I muttered, before I turned away and headed to the back room to find Beth.

She was leaning against the sink, head bowed. She wasn't crying, which I took as a good sign, but she was clearly upset.

"Hey, Beth," I said. "Are you okay?"

She nodded. "I'm fine." She didn't sound it.

I approached slowly, as I might a scared animal. "Did Raymond say something to you?"

"No." She looked up and managed a smile. "I didn't give him the chance." She took a deep breath, and seemed to relax as she let it out. "Seeing him shook me up a little, but I should be okay to work."

I searched her face, worried I'd see something that would tell me different. Beth appeared okay, if not a little rattled, but who wouldn't be with a man like Raymond stalking after them?

"Let me check to make sure he's gone," I said. "I can clock you in and you can start on the dishes." There weren't many sitting in the sink, but it would keep her busy for ten or fifteen minutes.

Beth relaxed even further. "Thanks, Krissy. I appreciate it."

I turned and headed for the door just as Jeff poked his head inside. "Someone is waiting for you out here, Ms. Hancock."

By the expression on his face, I knew I wasn't going to like it.

"Coming."

Jeff vanished back out front. I took a deep, calming breath, and strode out to see who wanted to talk to me.

My heart sank when I saw Raymond Lawyer on the other side of the counter.

"Mr. Lawyer," I said, as pleasantly as I could manage. "Is there something I can get you?" I glanced behind him, but Vicki, Mason, and Regina were gone.

"I don't appreciate you poaching my employees," he

said. "You've avoided it thus far, but we need to have a discussion."

"Do we?" I asked. "I didn't poach anyone. Beth came on her own, willingly. You should accept that." I turned away from him so I could clock her in. When I turned back to the counter, he was still glaring.

Deep down, I knew I should hold my tongue, smile, and wait for him to give up and leave. Unfortunately, his insistence that Beth and I had somehow wronged him grated on my nerves. And that's not to mention how he'd treated Vicki and Mason ever since the two of them had gotten together. The man thought he could control everyone's life, and I, for one, wasn't about to let him get away with it.

I stepped closer to the counter and lowered my voice.

"You really should try to be nicer to people," I said. "Maybe then, you'd be able to keep your employees and they wouldn't need to go looking for new jobs."

Raymond didn't respond. He just stood there, anger boiling off him, as if he thought he could intimidate me into giving him what he wanted—whatever that might be.

I softened my voice, hoping that somehow, I'd reach him. "Please, Mr. Lawyer, leave Beth alone. Let her work. Maybe someday, she'll decide to come back to you. I won't stop her if that's what she wants. You should do the same; let her make her own choices."

The door opened and Mason poked his head into the store. "Dad?"

Raymond straightened his back, puffed out his chest, and then turned and walked away. Mason gave me a questioning look, but I didn't know what to tell him, so I merely smiled and waved good-bye.

The moment they were gone, Beth appeared from the back. She thanked me and then went about wiping down tables, shooting occasional glances toward the door, as if afraid Raymond might return.

Now that trouble was gone—both Raymond's attitude and the cat—I turned my focus to work. Death by Coffee wouldn't be busy for the rest of the day, outside a small rush once most people's workday ended. Since it was warmer out, the rush would be smaller than in the winter when everyone wanted something hot to chase the chill away.

We still had guests, of course. There weren't many places you could get coffee in Pine Hills. We had no fast-food restaurants, and other than Death by Coffee, the only place you could sit down and relax with a fresh pot of coffee was the Banyon Tree. It ensured we'd always have customers.

It also rubbed some people—Judith Banyon, namely— the wrong way.

A little while later, I was humming along to a song playing over the speakers, wiping down a recently vacated table, when the doors opened and Officer Paul Dalton walked in. He was smiling, which showed off his dimples, which immediately made my knees go all weak and wobbly. He took off his hat and ran his fingers through his sandy brown hair, which was just a few shades from blond, before he made his way over to me.

"Hi, Krissy," he said.

"Paul." Irrationally, my heart was thumping in my chest. To say I had a thing for the local police officer would be an understatement. We'd even gone on a date once, though it had ended in disaster. I'd recently told myself

I'd stop holding back and would see if there was truly anything between us, but every time we came face-to-face, I chickened out.

"Can I get a coffee?" He asked it in a way that told me there was something else he wanted to say but was stalling for time.

"Of course." I went behind the counter and ignored the grin Jeff shot my way.

Paul leaned on the counter while I filled his order. "How was it this morning? Are you doing okay?"

"I'm okay. It was a nice service." I handed him his coffee. "This one's on me."

His smile widened as he took a sip. "I wish I could have come with you."

"You had to work," I said. "And you didn't really know her. I ended up helping out Eleanor's daughter, Jane, with cleaning up a little afterward anyway." And then, because I couldn't help myself. "Did you know Eleanor's brother was murdered?"

Paul lowered his coffee to the counter. "No. When?"

"It was a long time ago," I said, causing him to relax. Apparently, he'd feared I was going to tell him I'd gotten myself mixed up in yet another murder investigation. "Jane says it happened around thirty years ago."

"Oh. I wouldn't remember it even if I'd known," he said. "I'd have been just a kid."

"Yeah, I figured." Though I was a tad disappointed. I don't know why, but I'd hoped he'd remember the case and would be able to tell me something about what happened. "His name was Wade. . . ." I trailed off. Jane hadn't told me his last name—I was pretty sure it wasn't Winthrow since

Eleanor had once been married, and I don't think she'd changed her name after her husband's death.

"Sorry," Paul said. "Doesn't ring a bell."

"That's all right. It's just sad. The murder was never solved, and Eleanor lived her entire life wondering who killed him." I almost brought up Rita, but decided to hold off until I talked to her about it. I didn't need Paul getting interested until I was sure Rita wouldn't be upset if I looked into her boyfriend's murder.

We stood awkwardly at the counter for a few moments, with Paul sipping at his coffee, and me just staring at him like a dope. There were only two customers in Death by Coffee, and neither of them was paying us any mind. Thankfully, Jeff had wandered off to give us some semblance of privacy, and Beth was upstairs working with the books.

Paul cleared his throat. "I was thinking," he said, but he didn't immediately tell me what it was he was thinking about. Instead, he took a long drink of his coffee.

"And?" I prodded. My heart was racing again. I could almost *feel* the question before he asked it.

"I'm done here in about an hour," he said. "I was thinking that after you close, you might want to get something to eat."

My racing heart decided it was time to hang out in my throat. "Eat?" I croaked.

Paul's smile turned amused. "Yeah. You know, you put food in your mouth and chew."

"I know what 'eat' means," I said, blushing to my roots. "I was just . . . I thought . . ." I closed my eyes and mentally berated myself for stumbling over my words. "I would love to."

Paul's entire face lit up. "Great!"

"But I can't tonight."

And then his face fell. "You can't?"

"Tonight's the writers group meeting. I was hoping to go and talk to Rita and some of her friends there. It's been a while, and well . . ." I wanted to talk to them about Wade's murder, but he didn't need to know that yet.

"I didn't realize you were getting back into writing," Paul said.

"I'm not. But I do miss getting together with everyone, and thought tonight would be a good night to do it. I could always change my plans." Though, honestly, I really wanted to see what Rita and her friends had to say about Wade's death.

Paul shook his head and then put on his hat. "No, don't do that on my account." He shot me a dazzling smile. "We can always plan for another night."

"Tomorrow night?" I asked, rushing my words like I was afraid he might walk out and never ask me out again.

"I can't tomorrow night," he said. "But the night after would be good for me."

"Let's do it then." I nearly shouted the words. "If you still want to."

"Of course I do." He hesitated a moment and then reached across the counter to briefly touch my hand. "I'll pick you up at your place at eight?" He made it a question.

"Eight sounds great."

"Good. I'll see you then."

"Yep."

He turned and walked out of Death by Coffee. I held my breath until I saw him get into his car and drive off. Only then did I squeal in glee.

One of the two customers clapped, while Jeff appeared from the back to shoot me a wink and a thumbs-up. Beth, who'd apparently been secretly watching from the counter upstairs, grinned and shook her head as she turned away.

Needless to say, I went back to work in such a good mood, I felt as if I was floating on clouds. I'm not sure my feet touched the ground again until it was time to close up and confront my friend about a murder.

3

The Pine Hills writers group held their meetings in one of the upstairs rooms of the church in downtown Pine Hills. From the outside, the building looked splendid with its stained-glass windows, well-tended hedges, and ruby red stonework. The inside, however, showed the age of the huge building. The stairs, which had worn verses painted on them, creaked loudly as I headed up to where the meetings were held.

I was still wearing my work clothes since I'd come straight from closing to the church. There was a stain on my shirt, which I absently rubbed at as I made my way to the top of the stairs. I would have liked to have changed, but I'd hoped to catch Rita alone before the meeting started. Thankfully, when I'd parked, her car was the only one in the lot.

Rita was setting up chairs as I entered. Her back was to me, so she didn't see me right away. I took a moment to regard her, to see if I could see some sort of, I don't know, residue from what had happened all those years ago. If it was there, I sure didn't see it. All I could see was a highly energetic, somewhat plump, middle-aged woman.

"Oh!" she said when she turned and saw me standing there. "I didn't hear you come in, dear. I swear my mind wanders sometimes. Would you mind helping me finish up? I got a late start and would like everything in place before anyone else arrives."

"Sure." I snagged a chair from where it sat against the wall and placed it in the center of the room, next to the others Rita had set up.

"I'm glad to see you here, Krissy. James Hancock's blood runs through those veins of yours, so I know you've got something to contribute to our little chats."

James Hancock was my dad. He was also a mystery writer. Rita claimed to be his number-one fan, and honestly, I couldn't say that she was wrong. She also had a gigantic crush on him that made me a little queasy every time I thought about it.

It was a good thing Dad lived in California, or else I'd probably have to keep an eye on her to make sure she didn't try to drag him off somewhere.

"I'm not here for the group," I said, carefully not meeting her eye. "Well, I am, but not for writing."

"Oh?" She turned to face me. "Then why are you here?"

I set up two more chairs—which was probably two too many considering the size of the group the last time I was there—before I answered.

"I'm sure you've heard Eleanor Winthrow passed away."

Rita went still. "Yes, I heard. It's a real shame. She was the lonely sort, never really got out much, if you know what I mean. I can't say she had the best choice in friends, but who am I to judge?" When she laughed, it came out strained.

"I went to the services," I said. I was struggling to get to the point, but knew I needed to get there soon. Once the others started arriving, I might miss my chance. "I talked to her daughter, Jane."

"Did you now?" Rita said. She moved to the front of the room where a recliner sat, facing the rest of the chairs. She sat down slowly. I had a feeling she knew where I was going with this.

"I did. We talked about Eleanor's past." I paused, and then, because there was nothing else I could do but say it, I added, "We talked about her brother."

There was a moment of silence where Rita didn't so much as breathe and I couldn't bring myself to look at her. Would she be mad I'd brought him up? Would she cry? This was a subject Rita had never talked to me about since I'd known her, which meant it wasn't something she was comfortable talking about, because Rita talked about *everything*.

"I see." Her voice was strong, controlled. When I chanced a look at her, Rita's expression was thoughtful, rather than angry or sad. "And what did she tell you about him?"

"That his name was Wade. That he was murdered." I swallowed a lump that had grown in my throat. "That you dated him."

"I did." Rita took a deep breath and let it out in a huff. "I suppose our relationship is no big secret. Wade Fink and I were an item right up until the moment some no-good villain killed him."

"Do you know who did it?" I asked.

"Of course not, dear. If I did, I would have done something about it long before now."

"What about suspects?" I asked. "Was there someone who had a reason to kill him? An enemy or a rival, perhaps?"

"Well, let me think . . ." Rita trailed off, as if in deep

thought, and then her eyes went suddenly wide. "Wait. Are you going to investigate Wade's murder?"

Feeling self-conscious, I nodded. "I was thinking about it."

Rita bound to her feet and clapped her hands together. The resulting sound made me jump.

"I should have considered it myself!" she said. "I mean, the famous Krissy Hancock, living right here in Pine Hills, and I never once thought of asking you to look into our own little unsolved mystery." She rushed forward and took both my hands. "Whatever I can do to help, just tell me. I'll do anything you ask."

I squeezed her hands. "I don't know what to do yet, Rita. I just learned about it earlier today, and honestly, I'm not so sure where to start. That's why I'm here."

Rita released my hands so she could pace back and forth in front of me. "Well, coming here was an obvious first step. If you need to ask me whether or not I had anything to do with his death, you best get it out now."

"It never crossed my mind," I said, shocked she'd even think I'd consider her a suspect.

"It should have," Rita said. "You know how it is. You investigate those closest to the deceased first. I was definitely the closest person to Wade at the time." She tapped her chin. "So, where do we go from here?"

The door opened downstairs and voices drifted to us before I could so much as think of a suggestion.

"Let me take care of things, dear," Rita said. "You sit right down and once the meeting starts, I'll make sure you get exactly what you need."

I wasn't sure what that would involve—and was kind of worried about what she might do—but I did as she said, dragging a chair to the side of the room so I could see the entire group, including Rita, at the same time.

The voices belonged to two women I didn't know. They looked to be about college-aged, and of an energy I only wished I possessed. They greeted Rita warmly before taking their seats. One of them glanced my way and waved. I returned the gesture just as another group member—this one I knew; Adam—arrived.

It didn't take long for others to show. Rita's gossip buddies, Georgina McCully and Andi Caldwell sat next to one another, while the Pine Hills police chief, Patricia Dalton, took a seat directly across from me. She nodded to me once in a way that wasn't quite friendly, but wasn't outright hostile. To say we had a complicated relationship would be an understatement.

The last to arrive was one of Death by Coffee's employees, Lena Allison, with a man I hadn't met before. His hair was the same purple as hers, and his arms were covered in tattoos. When Lena saw me, her face brightened.

"Ms. Hancock!" she said. "I haven't seen you here in forever."

"Please, call me Krissy, Lena. You know that."

She reddened. "Yeah, I know. I was just surprised." She slapped the guy she was with hard on the back. "This is Zay. He's a friend."

Zay gave a lazy wave. "Hey."

I returned the wave, just as Rita cleared her throat. Lena shot me a grin, and then the two of them took their seats.

"All right," Rita said. "I think that's going to be everyone for tonight." She settled into her recliner, though she looked antsy to be up and about. She rocked back and forth, causing the chair to squeak with every movement. "We're going to start a little differently tonight. I know, Haley, I promised you'd get to lead the group, but something has come up. We'll make it up to you."

One of the young women—Haley, I presumed—gave an exaggerated sigh, smiled, and then settled back and rested her hands on a paper-thin laptop that was sitting on her lap.

"As many of you know, we lost one of our longtime residents recently. Eleanor Winthrow never came to group, but she touched many of our lives in some way." A crack appeared in Rita's calm expression. For the first time, I could see the immense sadness she was hiding.

Murmurs went up around the room. Across the room, Chief Dalton narrowed her eyes at me.

"What some of you didn't realize, Eleanor and I shared a connection. You see, I used to date her brother, Wade. I was young, and maybe a little naïve at the time, but we did love one another. Unfortunately, he was murdered before that love could truly be realized."

Someone gasped. I was shocked to realize it wasn't Andi, who had a tendency to gasp at just about every declaration.

"It happened thirty-three years ago," Rita said. "The crime remains unsolved to this day." Her gaze swept across the room, finally landing on me. "But that's going to change. Our resident detective, Krissy Hancock, is going to look into Wade's murder, and finally put his killer behind bars."

All eyes turned to me. I wanted to shrink into my chair, but there was nowhere for me to go. "That's me," I said. "But I'm not a detective."

Rita waved a dismissive hand at me. "Of course you are, dear." She turned her attention back to the group at large. "What I'd like to do is have everyone tell Krissy what they know about Wade and his death. Maybe we'll be lucky and your statements will cause something to click and she can solve this thing before we leave tonight."

I doubted that would happen, but I wasn't about to dissuade anyone from talking. I sat up straighter and put on my best "listener" face.

The woman who'd come with Haley raised a hand.

"Yes, Wendy?" Rita asked.

"I wasn't born yet, so . . ."

"Of course you weren't, dear," Rita said. "But it might be good for you to listen in. The details might help you with your own mystery."

Wendy considered that a moment before she opened a thin laptop that was the twin of Haley's own, apparently to take notes.

"I'm not sure what you expect," Patricia said, focusing on me. She was still in her uniform, though she was wearing it loosely— the top button unbuttoned, shirt untucked. "The case has remained unsolved for a reason."

"Were you in charge of the investigation?" I asked.

Patricia laughed. "Not quite. Thirty years ago, I wasn't in charge of anything. Albie Bruce was the police chief back then."

I knew the name Albie Bruce, but couldn't place where I'd heard it before. Working at a bookstore café, a lot of names and faces passed through, so there was a chance he'd come in a time or two.

"What do you remember of it?" I asked Patricia. "I imagine a murder investigation was as big of a deal in a small town as it is today."

She nodded. "It was. This was what? '85? Maybe '86?

Things were different back then, of course. We didn't have the same sort of technology or know as much about DNA as we do now, so it wasn't like we could just pop something into a computer and get the answers we needed. There were no fancy cell phones like today, so there were no recordings or texts that we could go look at."

"I can't imagine living like that," Haley said with a shake of her head.

"I never got to see the scene," Patricia went on. "In fact, some of the guys thought that me being a woman made me too sensitive and I couldn't handle a murder." If we hadn't been inside, I had a feeling she would have spat on the ground to emphasize what she thought of that. "Unfortunately, it means I don't have much I can provide when it comes to firsthand information."

The idea that anyone could think Patricia Dalton too sensitive for anything was as much of a shock to me as it was disgusting. I was glad most of the world had moved on from such primitive thinking.

"Wasn't Wade part of the Coffee Drinkers?" Georgina asked. Her glasses hung from a chain around her neck today as she rocked slowly in the only rocking chair in the room.

"I do believe he was," Andi said next to her. Her steel gray hair was thinning up top, and the lines around her eyes had deepened so much, they looked like canyons in her face.

"Coffee Drinkers?" I asked, interest piqued even more.

It was Patricia who answered. "It was a group of men who used to drink coffee together at the Banyon Tree years ago. They were all suspects at one time, but were cleared."

Rita's posture stiffened. "Cleared only because no evidence was found against them."

"I think they still go there," Andi said.

"They do." Georgina nodded sagely. "I saw Arthur Cantrell there just last week."

"Wait." I sat forward. "Arthur Cantrell? Gray hair, loud voice?" I wasn't sure how else to describe the man I'd seen earlier that day at Eleanor's services.

Georgina scratched at her chin as she considered it. "Sounds like him, I suppose. He tends to be in a bad mood often, doesn't he?"

"He does," Andi agreed.

"He argued with a group of guys earlier today," I said. "He said Eleanor wouldn't have come to their funerals. He made it sound like she didn't like Wade's friends all that much."

Andi snorted. "There was definitely no love between her and those men," she said. "If I recall, she never thought Wade should have ever hung around them. Called them a bad influence."

"That they were," Georgina said. "It's why we had a name for them, though I always thought we should have called them something a little more descriptive."

"Why?" I asked. Could one of those men have killed Wade?

"We won't devolve into rumor and speculation," Patricia cut in before anyone else could speak. "The case is dead. I'm not sure dredging it up again is in anyone's best interest." She looked to Rita, who was just barely holding on.

"Maybe we should move on to writing," Lena said. "At least for a little bit."

I wanted to press Georgina and Andi further, but held off on asking anything more. Rita might have wanted me to investigate, but the moment we'd started talking about her deceased boyfriend, she'd grown tense. She seemed all too happy to hand the floor over to Haley, who popped open her laptop and started reading.

While I wasn't interested in writing myself any longer, I did my best to enjoy the meeting. I noted there was a marked improvement in everyone's writing since the last time I was there. Even Rita read a little from her latest work, though her voice broke twice in the reading.

Once everyone finished, and after a brief discussion on the best way to attack editing, the meeting ended. I rose, intent on asking Rita a few questions, but she vanished out the door without so much as a good-bye.

"Best give her some time," Patricia said, joining me. "She'll be back to close up, but I think she needs her space for now."

"I was afraid this might be hard on her."

"It is." Patricia began moving chairs back to where they belonged. I noted Lena and Zay were helping as well, though they kept their distance from us. "It was a trying time then, and it still weighs on her today."

"She never once mentioned it." I felt like I'd failed her as a friend because of it. I should have seen something; a hint of her sadness, perhaps.

"I'm not surprised. You have to understand what it was like back then. There was an age difference between Rita and Wade Fink, one most people weren't too keen to let slide."

"They were harassed." I made it a statement, but she answered like it was a question.

"All the time. I remember responding to a call once from Wade's parents. Someone painted some pretty obscene things across the Fink house. Never caught who did that, either."

"It sounds horrible."

"It was no peach, that's for sure."

We finished replacing the chairs. Lena and Zay headed off with a pair of waves, leaving Patricia and me alone. We walked slowly down the stairs and out into the parking lot, lost in our own thoughts. I noticed Rita's car was still there, but she wasn't in it. I supposed that meant she'd gone to one of the other rooms in the church to be alone for a little while. I hoped she'd be okay, because I wouldn't be able to forgive myself if I'd upset her to the point where she withdrew into herself.

"Be careful with this one," Patricia said as she opened the driver's-side door to her car. "The murder hit Rita hard then, and she's still struggling with it now, though she doesn't like to show it."

"I don't want to upset her," I said, wondering if it was too late for that.

"I'm not going to stop you from poking around on this," she said. "But know that you're going to make quite a few people unhappy. This town doesn't like controversy, and Rita's relationship with Wade was as controversial as you could get back then. I imagine there's still some resentment floating around and I wouldn't want it to come back on you."

"I'll be careful," I promised her.

Chief Dalton started to get into her car, but paused. "I should probably warn you: Rita wasn't looked at as just the girlfriend of the victim." She ran a hand over her mouth, seemed to consider whether or not to add more, and then hit me with it. "There are some out there who still believe Rita Jablonski killed her boyfriend in a jealous rage, and I'm afraid that bringing it up again might end up proving them right."

4

"Thanks for stopping by, Cindy. Tell Jimmy I said hi."

The short librarian lifted her box in salute before making her way out of Death by Coffee to deliver the books I'd donated to the library where both she and her husband worked.

I sagged against a bookshelf the moment she was through the door. The rush was done and Vicki was due to replace me within the next hour. My legs felt like rubber, and my hands were red from a wayward cup of coffee that I'd tried to catch before it had hit the floor.

"Busy day," Lena said as she joined me upstairs in the books. After my mishap with the coffee, I'd decided to let Lena and Jeff handle the downstairs rush to see how they did. The results were more than I could have hoped for.

"Abnormally so." I couldn't say I was unhappy about it, but the morning and afternoon rushes had just about run me ragged, despite the fact I'd handled the bookstore portion of the store. I wasn't used to it, and had struggled to keep up with the demand of reshelving books *and* checking people out at the same time.

"It's nice what you're doing for Rita," Lena said,

drawing my attention back to her. "Zay thinks it's pretty cool, too."

"Is Zay your boyfriend?" I asked.

Lena's face reddened. "No. He's just a friend."

"You sure about that?"

She rolled her eyes but couldn't stop the grin from stretching across her face. "He's pretty cool, but we just like to hang out. He's just starting to write, so I thought it might be good for him to check out the writers group, see what it's all about."

"It lets you spend some time together without the pressure of a date, huh?"

"Stop, please." Lena held up her hands. "Or else the next time you make googly eyes at someone, I'm never going to let you hear the end of it."

"I don't make googly eyes!"

"Uh-huh. Keep telling yourself that." Lena winked and then headed back downstairs to wipe down the tables.

"I don't," I muttered.

Now that the rush was done, and I'd caught my breath, I turned my attention to the shelves themselves. While I liked the layout of the bookstore, I felt it could use some updates. Moving between the shelves was sometimes a tight fit when we were busy, which made browsing difficult for our customers.

I spent the next twenty minutes trying to come up with a way to reorganize the shelves, or better yet, figure out how we could budget for a new set. Taller shelves meant more books could fit in a smaller, more vertical space. I didn't want to have to remove the couch and chairs we reserved for our readers, but if it came down to that, or leaving things as they were, I thought we might have to consider it.

Vicki showed up just as I finished pricing a new set of high-quality bookshelves, Trouble in tow. She released the cat upstairs, and joined me at the counter. "What are you up to?" she asked, glancing over my shoulder.

"Something for you to consider." I handed her my handwritten notes, which included the often excessive prices I'd found. While she perused that, I headed downstairs, grabbed my things, and then left Death by Coffee. Despite my exhaustive day, there was still something I wanted to do before bedtime.

The former Pine Hills police chief, Albie Bruce, was easy enough to find online. He lived just outside of Pine Hills, in a house that had seen better days. I knew he was an older man, but when he opened the door to my knock and I saw how old he really was, I started to wonder whether or not my visit would be worthwhile.

Albie's skin was the color of old parchment paper, and was so wrinkled, it was obvious he'd spent a lot of time in the sun. He wasn't all that tall, but that could be because of a crook in his back that forced him to lean forward constantly. When he saw me standing there, his fluffy white eyebrows rose.

"Krissy Hancock, on my doorstep. Will wonders never cease." He shuffled back a step. "Come on in. I haven't had a visitor in months, and I already know this here visit's going to be a doozy."

"You know me?" I asked, accepting his offer and stepping into the small farmhouse. There was a draft, but it wasn't entirely unpleasant. The curtains fluttered at the windows, which were propped open by chunks of wood.

"I do," he said. "I'd imagine just about everyone who pays attention in this town does." He shuffled over to an armchair and lowered himself slowly into it. He let out a sigh once he was settled. "Please, sit. I imagine you've got something quite interesting to say or else you wouldn't be here."

I wasn't sure about interesting, but I did want to talk to him, so I sat on the couch across from him. The furniture was old-fashioned and made me feel as if I'd been transported back to the seventies, but it was in good condition. A grandfather clock ticked the seconds, and I noted there was no TV in the room, just an old radio, which was on, but turned down so all I could hear was a faint mumble.

I could imagine Albie sitting in his armchair, listening to the news on the radio, eyes closed. He had a grandfatherly air about him, yet I could see strength in the way he held himself.

"Not everyone is keen on talking to me," I said.

"Not everyone cares to have their dirty laundry aired. The way I hear it, you like to pry. Good at it, too."

I flushed, not in embarrassment, but in delight. "I can't help myself, I guess. I want to do what's right."

"Sometimes, it's hard to see what that is, don't you think?" He didn't seem to expect an answer. "What is it I can do for you, Ms. Hancock?"

"Krissy, please."

"Krissy." He smiled, causing his eyes to nearly vanish within the wrinkles. "Feel free to call me Albie. Most people do these days, though a few still insist on calling me Chief Bruce."

"Albie." I relaxed and sat back. "I'm not sure if you've heard, but Eleanor Winthrow passed away a few days ago."

His smile faded as he nodded. "I heard. Shame, that is. She didn't deserve none of what happened to her. Sometimes people get stuck in positions that they can't pry themselves free of, and that was our Eleanor to a T."

"Are you talking about what happened to her brother, Wade?"

Albie rubbed at his chin. "I suppose in a way, I am. Eleanor never quite got over it. Guess no one ever does, really. Especially with the way it happened." He made a strange click sound with his mouth I assumed signified sympathy.

"What do you remember?" I asked, not expecting much. From what little I'd gleaned, Albie was well into his nineties. His memory might not be what it once was.

Albie picked up a pipe from a stand next to him. He regarded it a moment, and then set it aside. "Probably shouldn't with a guest."

"I don't mind."

He folded his hands in his lap. "Everyone minds to some degree. I understand the health risks, but at this point, I don't think it's going to matter to me none. You, on the other hand, have a life ahead of you. Don't want to risk that. It can wait until you are gone." He heaved a sigh and settled back into his chair. "Let me think, this would be what? Thirty some years ago?"

"About that. I keep hearing that it happened in 1985 or '86."

"Sounds about right. I was already sixty by then, if you can believe it."

I could. "You were the police chief back then."

"I was. Was near retirement, too. I was one of those men who thought they'd keep going forever, but things were starting to catch up to me. Hip was going, and I'd taken a fall and wrenched my back something good that year. Still bothers me today, not that I'll admit that to anyone else. Don't need some nurse fussing over me. I get around well enough without it."

Albie shifted in his seat with a wince, and I wondered how much longer he could put off that nurse.

"Wade Fink." He said the name as if trying to discern some meaning from it. "He was found by a jogger off one of those runners' paths in the woods that's no longer there thanks to all the development that's happened since then. She might have zipped right past him if her dog hadn't led her off the trail."

"You've got a good memory," I said, more out of surprise than anything.

Albie chuckled. "Body might be falling apart, but my mind is as sharp as ever. I'll credit all the fish I eat."

I made a mental note to have salmon for dinner. "Do you remember the name of the woman?" I asked.

"Jill Thatcher. Died in '93, I believe. Was a good sort, but had a thing for smoking and drinking to excess when she wasn't trying to burn it off with all that running."

"What killed him?" I asked. "The most anyone has said so far was that Wade was murdered. Could it have been an accident?"

"No, not an accident. Blow to the temple did him in." Albie tapped his own temple to demonstrate. "Never found the murder weapon. Might've been a rock, but if it was, it wasn't near the scene."

"Are you sure he didn't fall and hit his head?" I asked. I was pretty sure that by now that wasn't the case, but wanted to get Albie's take.

"Anything is possible, I suppose, but the doctors back then said it was unlikely. Add to that he was hastily buried, then you question it even more. If I were to guess, someone got into a fight with Mr. Fink and then, in a fit of rage, struck him upside the noggin."

I didn't like the sound of that, especially after what Patricia had said about Rita. "Did Wade have any enemies?"

Albie snorted. "Enemies? Not so much. But people were pretty unhappy with him. Was dating that Jablonski kid at the time. Flaunted it, even. Someone come tell him it wasn't right and he'd plant one right on her lips just to show 'em how right it was. They never hurt no one, but to hear people talk back then, you'd think they were both trying to bring the wrath of God down on the entire town."

"What did you think?"

"Don't really matter what I thought then, or what I think now. He should have stuck to his own age group, but who am I to say who should do what with whom? My job was to find the person who killed him, and that's that."

Albie shifted in his chair, wincing again. He rubbed briefly at his hip before settling back in.

"Honestly, I think a lot of people were happy Wade was gone, even his friends," he went on. "No one would come right out and say it, but now, I imagine quite a few would admit to being relieved that Wade was dead."

"Why's that?"

"Why do you think? He dies, then there's no more controversy. If I'd caught the killer, I bet half the town would have asked me to let 'em go. There wasn't much pressure to find whoever did it, let me tell you. Wade's family pressed the issue, of course. Eleanor and her husband were on me the most, in that regard. Had a little pressure from the inside, too."

I took a wild guess. "From Patricia Dalton?"

Albie chuckled and shook his head fondly. "She was a spitfire back then, just as I hear she is today. Couldn't go two steps without her demanding to be put on the case. She never asked, just told me I was stupid for excluding her. Can't say she was entirely wrong, but you know what they say about hindsight."

His brow furrowed and he leaned toward me. "What's all this about anyway? I doubt you're curious just because old Eleanor passed on."

"That's it. I'm interested to hear about her life, what made her the way she was."

"Why don't I believe that? Krissy Hancock on my doorstep, asking questions about a thirty-year-old murder. You thinking you might go and do what I couldn't and find the person who did Wade in?"

I shrugged one shoulder, refused to meet his eye. "I thought I'd at least ask around, see what people remembered. Rita's my friend." The last came out defensively.

"Is she now?" Albie sat back and stroked his chin as he regarded me. "You best be careful poking around in a murder that's sat silent for this long. If the killer is still out there and catches wind you're sticking your nose in their business, they might not like it too terribly much."

"They never do."

"Well, this one has simmered for a very long time. The reaction might not be what you expect."

Something in his eye told me there was something he wasn't telling me. I didn't think he knew who killed Wade Fink, but he knew *something*.

"Did you have any leads you wished you could have pried into further?" I asked. "Something that bothered you back then, or that you've reconsidered in the years since?"

Albie stared at me for a long time and didn't respond. He weighed me with those old eyes of his. They were still keen after all these years, as, apparently, was his mind. I had a feeling Albie Bruce rarely missed anything.

Which made me wonder how a killer could have eluded him for over thirty years.

"If you insist on poking the bear, you might want to start in the den."

When he didn't elaborate, I prodded him. "Where's this den?"

"You've supposedly got a good head on your shoulders, so think about it and I'm sure you'll figure it out without my help." Albie stood with a groan. "I think it's time I took a bit of a break. As I said, body ain't what it used to be and I could use a little shut-eye."

I rose with him, disappointed our conversation was over so quickly, but happy that he'd at least taken time out of his day for me. "Thank you for talking to me."

"Don't thank me yet," he said. "By the time you're done with this thing, you might not be too happy about what you discover."

He led me to the front door, but didn't open it right away.

"Some people said Wade was robbing the cradle, while others said Rita was the one who deserved to be punished for disgracing an older man."

"Disgracing?" I asked. "They were just dating."

"Be that as it may, that's not how a lot of people saw it. Wade's family, outside of Eleanor, weren't too happy about what happened to his reputation because of her. Rita Jablonski's own family took issue with the relationship, too. Both of them suffered quite a lot for their time together. Neither kept their friends by the time it was all said and done. Even Wade's buddies turned on him in the end."

This time, I couldn't miss the reference. "The Coffee Drinkers," I said.

Albie shrugged and opened the door. "I hear the Banyon Tree's got good food, if you can abide the company."

I stepped outside and bid Albie Bruce good-bye. He parted with one last, "Be careful, Ms. Hancock," before he closed the door.

5

My Ford Focus sputtered as I idled outside Rita's house. Her car was parked in the driveway, and the lights were on inside, so I knew she was home, but I wasn't so sure I was ready to face her. I'd lived in Pine Hills for a few years now, had known Rita just as long, yet she'd never once mentioned her murdered boyfriend to me. There had to be a good reason for that.

I considered backing out and driving away to give her more time to process my interest in the case, but shut off the engine instead. The murder might have happened over thirty years ago, but it was obvious it still affected Rita greatly. I didn't want my friend to continue to suffer when there might be something I could do to help.

When I knocked at the door, Rita opened it with an, "Oh! Krissy" Despite the exclamation, she didn't seem all that surprised to see me. She was already dressed for bed, despite it still being relatively early in the evening. "You should come on in." She turned and walked into the house, leaving the door hanging open for me.

I crossed the threshold, gently closing the door behind me. Rita's house was small, but was more than big enough for a single woman. It was also rather sedate for such a loud, boisterous person as Rita. I'd expected to find colorful prints or wild rugs, but none of that was evident. Instead, the place looked like every other home. The only odd thing I noticed was Rita's cardboard cutout of my dad peering out at me from her bedroom.

I found Rita sitting on the couch in her living room. She had an open box on the coffee table in front of her. Photographs were spread out on the table, and many more were tossed next to her on the couch. I sat down in a rocking chair by the window so I wouldn't disturb her spread. Glancing outside, I could see much of the neighborhood. It forcibly reminded me of Eleanor Winthrow and how she used to keep such a diligent watch on my neighborhood from her own chair.

"I might seem morose, but I'm not," Rita said, drawing my attention away from the window.

"This has to be hard on you."

"It is, dear." She smiled at me, then turned her attention back to the photographs. "But it's been difficult to live with as well. I think that if you can somehow bring Wade's killer to justice, I might finally move past it."

"I shouldn't have sprung it on you like that," I said, truly regretting how heavy-handed I'd been at the writers' meeting. "I should have come to you and talked to you first before bringing it to the group."

"Oh, pah." She waved a dismissive hand my way. "You did what you thought was right. And we *did* talk before anyone else arrived, so put that right out of your mind. I don't hold it against you for wanting to talk to me when you did. I'd have done the same."

"Well, I regret it nonetheless." I looked down at my

hands, ashamed. "I didn't realize how hard it would hit you. When you left so quickly after the meeting—"

"Don't for one second blame yourself, Krissy Hancock."

I looked up, surprised. I'm not sure she'd ever talked to me that way before. She sounded an awful lot like my dad did back when I was a kid who thought she could talk back to him when I was rightfully in the wrong.

"I admit, I needed a few minutes alone to compose myself, but it's not because I was upset. Yes, thinking of Wade and what happened to him still makes me sad, but you had nothing to do with that. I was *happy* you're going to look into it. I still am. I want his killer found, even if they are long dead." Her voice hardened by the end. I had a feeling she'd feel cheated if his killer escaped justice through death.

Unsure where to go from there, I leaned forward and tried to get a good look at the photographs on the coffee table. They were upside down, and I was too far away to make much out.

Rita noticed my interest and picked up one of the photographs. She stood long enough to pass it to me, before sitting back down. "That one's of Wade and me. It was always my favorite, but I could never bring myself to frame it or hang it up. I probably should before it deteriorates any more than it already has."

The photo was well-worn from constant handling, and depicted the man I'd seen in Eleanor's photograph—dressed much like Don Johnson in *Miami Vice*—but this time, instead of standing with a young Eleanor Winthrow, he had his arm around a thin, beaming beauty with big hair.

"This is you?" I asked, unable to hide the awe in my voice.

"Don't act so surprised, dear. It was a long time ago."

"I . . . I'm not." Though, honestly, I was. I could see Rita in the eyes, in the way she held herself, yet I'd never imagined her in this way. A part of me had always thought of her as she was now—a bit on the plump side, almost jolly in stature as she was in nature. The Rita in the photograph could easily have been a model if she'd so chosen.

"That was taken a month before his death," she said. "I marvel now that we didn't look as miserable as we felt. The pressure was getting to the both of us by then, but our relationship was as strong as ever. We refused to let ignorance and intolerance get in the way of how we felt about one another."

The age difference between the two was obvious, but looking at the photograph, the fit *felt* right. They didn't look like father and daughter; they didn't look out of place at all. In my eyes, the photograph showed two people who loved each other and belonged together.

"You were a cute couple," I said, handing the photo back to Rita. She looked at it for a long couple of moments before setting it aside.

"Back then, we were the only ones to think so. The town was so against us, you'd have thought we'd gone back in time to the early forties or something. You know how Pine Hills is." She shook her head. "Everyone wants to know everyone else's business." Her eyes narrowed. "Don't give me that look! I can't help it if I happen to hear things."

I held up my hands placatingly. "I wasn't judging."

"Good." Rita began boxing up the photos, careful not to bend a single one. "What people didn't understand back then was that Wade and I didn't just up and decide we loved each other one day. It was a slow process. We started as friends, and the relationship grew out of that. This wasn't a fling for either of us."

"Why do you think the town was so against the two of you dating? Was it only the age? Or was there more to it?"

She stared at a photo, eyes slightly glazed, as if remembering, before she placed it in the box. "Wade and his family were prominent citizens of Pine Hills back then. His parents were both wealthy, influential people. They squandered their wealth, of course, but when we were dating, there was no shortage of money in that family, let me tell you."

I thought of Eleanor and her small house. How hard must it have been for her to drop so far in status. No wonder she'd grown so bitter over time. Between that and her brother's death, I was surprised she hadn't made a bigger nuisance out of herself.

"Much of Wade's family thought I was dating him merely for his wealth. He bought me nice things and I know many of my friends were jealous. I saw them looking at my new dresses and jewelry, how they talked about me when they thought I wasn't listening."

She replaced the lid to the box and then sat back. She wasn't looking at me as she spoke. A part of me realized she was speaking more for herself than she was me. It was a side of Rita I never knew existed.

"Both his parents tried to make him break it off with me many times, as if they could still boss him around, despite his age. His father once even threatened to disown him, but Wade stood strong. It got so bad that I even told him I'd understand if he wanted to leave me. That night was one of the best I'd ever had." A gleam came into her eye and she fell silent.

I gave her a few minutes before asking, "Do you think someone in his family could have killed him?"

"I've considered it," she said. "But I don't think so. Despite their threats, Wade's parents weren't malicious people. They were concerned about their image, of course, but they wouldn't have ever hurt their son."

I didn't want to ask, but felt I needed to anyway. "What about Eleanor?"

Rita's face clouded over briefly before she spoke. "Eleanor didn't approve of us, but she loved her brother dearly. I think she was the only other person, other than myself, who wanted to get to the bottom of the murder. There was a time we might have been friends. If it wasn't for the fact a part of her always thought it was my fault Wade had died, I wouldn't have minded talking to her about him when times grew hard."

"She thought you killed him?" I asked, thinking back to what Patricia Dalton had said about people in town thinking Rita might have had something to do with Wade's death. I prayed she was wrong, but couldn't dismiss the idea out of hand either, no matter how much I might have wanted to.

"Of course not, dear," Rita said. "But she believed that if he hadn't been dating me, then no one would have had a reason to kill him."

"And what do you think?"

Rita considered the question before answering. "I think it's a shame someone decided a good man like Wade Fink needed to die. I think that whoever did it had their own reasons, reasons I can hardly fathom. If our relationship played into it at all, it wasn't *because* of us. The killer is entirely to blame for their own decision."

She abruptly stood and snatched the box up from the

coffee table. "Would you like coffee or something to drink?" she asked.

"No, thank you."

Rita carried the box out of the room without another word. I remained seated, knowing she'd left not because she was upset at me, but because she needed a few minutes alone to gather her thoughts.

She returned a few minutes later, looking far more composed than she had when she'd left.

"I try not to get worked up about it so much these days," she said, resuming her seat on the couch. "I can keep my mind off of it most of the time. The only time I can't avoid it is on the Anniversary, but that's to be expected."

Rita had mentioned the Anniversary—caps included—once before. I hadn't known what she'd meant then, but now, I did.

"It's not like many people from my past still talk to me," Rita went on. "After Wade's murder, everyone turned their backs on me like I was contagious. His family didn't want to have anything to do with the girl who'd started the whole mess, and his friends were just as cold-shouldered."

"It wasn't your fault," I said.

"I know that, dear. But they needed someone to blame." She heaved a sigh. "Even my own friends up and disowned me. It took me years to rebuild what was left of my reputation. I haven't dated since Wade died, if you can believe it. Haven't wanted to."

I gave her a surprised look that she caught immediately and she laughed. It was a good sound to hear.

"I know what you're thinking," she said. "But James Hancock was never a realistic goal for me. He's a famous author and I'm, well, me."

"Yeah, but . . ." I trailed off, not sure how to go on. Rita had thrown herself at Dad when he'd come to town, and I mean that literally. To think that she never believed he would reciprocate was almost too much for me to grasp.

"I'm not saying I wouldn't have ended my man-fast for James Hancock, but I always knew it would never come to anything. It's safe that way. I wouldn't be marring Wade's memory by dreaming of such heights."

"I don't think you could ever mar his memory," I said. "Rita, he'd want you to be happy."

"Oh, dear, I'm happy." She smiled as if to prove it. "I couldn't live with myself if I moved on from Wade before he got the justice he deserves. It feels . . . disrespectful."

"Who do you think might have killed Wade?" I asked her. "Living or dead. It'll give me a place to start."

Rita slid to the edge of the couch. She was practically bouncing up and down in her excitement.

"I've given it a lot of thought over the years," she said. "As I said, there's always a chance someone in Wade's family did it, but they're all gone now. The only living member of that family that I know about is Jane Winthrow."

"She claims she was away at college when it happened," I said.

"It's likely she was," Rita said. "I don't remember much of her. She left town the moment she got the chance, and rarely came back. I don't know what she thought of me, if anything, but what little I know of her makes me think she could have had nothing to do with Wade's death."

I agreed. While the Finks' reputation was being harmed, what would a girl away at college care? Jane didn't strike me as a woman who worried too much about reputations anyway.

"Okay, so if not the family, who else?"

Rita's hands clenched into fists. "Those men who once called themselves Wade's friends."

I knew who she was talking about instantly. "The Coffee Drinkers?"

"That might be what everyone calls them, but I always think of them as a bunch of backstabbers."

"Why's that? Did they do or say something that makes you think they might have killed him?"

"Not expressly," Rita said. "But they weren't happy with the time Wade was spending with me. They bullied him and claimed it was for his own good, that they were doing it for him. These men were in their thirties and forties and acted like they were teenagers more often than not."

"Was there one specifically you think could have done it?"

"Take your pick!" Rita said, the heat in her voice growing. "It wouldn't surprise me in the slightest if they were all in on it together. A tragedy like what happened to Wade would tear most groups apart, yet they still show up every morning at the Banyon Tree, just like they did when Wade was alive. It's disrespectful if you ask me."

I wasn't so sure about that—they could very well have continued on in honor of Wade—but I let it slide.

"What time do they get together?" I asked.

"Eight," she said. "It's always been at eight sharp, every morning for the last forty, fifty years!"

I made a mental note and stood. "I should probably get going," I said. It looked like I had an early morning date with a group of older men and wanted to plan for it.

Rita stood with me. "What can I do to help? I can't just sit here while you do all the hard work. It would drive me crazy!"

"You can take care of yourself," I said. When Rita opened her mouth to protest, I cut her off. "For now. If I think of something you can do to help, you'll be the first to know."

She clamped her mouth shut, and while she was unhappy about it, she nodded. "I hope you find out who killed my Wade," she said.

"I do, too, Rita." And I prayed that when I did discover who killed Wade Fink, it wouldn't cause more problems than it solved.

Rita showed me out. When I got back into my car, I noted she was still standing at the door. There was so much emotion in her parting wave, I had to wipe a tear from my eye.

6

Light from next door drew me from my car, and across
the yard to Eleanor Winthrow's house. I was tired, but not
so tired that I couldn't pay Jane a quick visit and let her
know what I was planning to do.

She answered on the second knock, eyes and shoulders
heavy. Jane looked like a woman who was trying to keep
the entire world from collapsing on her, and was failing.
She managed an exhausted smile and then stepped aside
to let me in.

"You've been hard at work, I see," I said, glancing
around the living room. Boxes were stacked against the
walls and on top of the couch. The TV was gone, as were
the few decorations Eleanor had kept. The room felt life-
less.

"They're all her papers," she said, motioning toward
the boxes. "I couldn't bring myself to throw them out
quite yet."

"Are you going to keep them?"

Jane crossed the room and then sat down on one of
the boxes. It sagged, but held. "I don't know. I might put

them in storage for a little while and then pitch the lot. Or I might go through them again and look for anything mentioning my family and save those ones. I simply don't know."

She looked around the room and then rubbed at her eyes. "I've been at it all day. I should probably get some sleep before starting it all up again tomorrow."

"How long are you in town for?" I asked. Eleanor might not have had much to her name—outside her newspaper collection, that is—but it was still a big job.

"I've got three more days to get everything together before I'm due back home." She sagged, shook her head. "Not sure I'll make it, but I'm sure going to try."

"If you need help . . ."

Jane gave me a grateful smile. "Thanks. If I start to get overwhelmed, I'll come knocking." She groaned as she pushed her way to her feet. "But not tonight. I really do think I'm going to call it an early night. Was there something I could do for you before I go?"

"Nothing you can do," I said. "But I did want to let you know that I'm going to be looking into your uncle's murder. I don't know if I'll be able to solve it, not after so much time has passed, but it can't hurt to ask around." I hoped.

Jane nodded as if she'd expected as much. "Have you talked to many people yet?" she asked.

"A few. I talked to the police chief at the time, Albie Bruce, and I talked to Rita, of course. Other than a few older ladies in town, that's it. I'm hoping to meet with Wade's coffee-drinking friends tomorrow morning."

Jane's face clouded over. "You won't get much from them."

"I have to try," I said. "I'm not sure what to make of

them. They showed up for the service, but didn't seem very happy about it. And everyone I've talked to seems to think they might have had something to do with Wade's death."

"They didn't." Jane walked into the kitchen. I followed after her and waited while she got herself a bottle of water from the fridge. She took a long drink, capped it, but didn't expand on her thought.

"Why do you say that?" I asked.

"They were my uncle's friends. They might not have gotten on with Mother all that well, but I never got the impression they wanted to hurt her or Uncle Wade. Mom might not have seen it that way, but you know what she was like."

I did. I'd been accused of doing things I most definitely hadn't been part of by Eleanor more than once. She was quick to blame, and often didn't listen to reason when presented with the actual facts. I think she preferred thinking badly of everyone around her, and I wondered if that had more to do with what had happened to Wade than any actual malice on her part.

"I never knew Uncle Wade's friends, not really," Jane went on. "I can name them, but that's because they were at his funeral and I met them then. I saw them around town when I was here, of course, and I suppose I might have talked to one of them once or twice when they came around, but honestly, I can't tell you much about any of them."

"But you don't think they killed your uncle?"

"I don't." Her brow furrowed as she thought about it. "From what I heard, there was some tension between Uncle Wade and his friends, and I guess they could have fallen out with one another, but they were still friends in many ways. Maybe I don't *want* them to be guilty because it invalidates their friendship and I really want to believe the best about Uncle Wade."

"A lot of murder victims are killed by relatives and friends," I said. "Could he have done something that upset one of them enough that they might kill him, even if it was accidental?"

Jane shrugged as she finished her water. She tossed the empty bottle in one of the multitude of trash bags scattered around the room. "Like I said, I didn't know them all that well. Anything is possible, I suppose."

I mentally debated about asking my next question, fearing I might upset Jane at a time when she was already struggling, but decided I needed to ask it. "What about family?"

If she was bothered by the question, Jane didn't show it. "There was tension there," she said. "My grandparents could be hard people when they wanted to be, and when Wade started running around with Rita, they definitely wanted to be. They tried to get Mom to talk reason into Wade, but she really didn't see the harm in the relationship, not if Uncle Wade was happy. I guess there was some disapproval, but nothing that caused friction between her and her brother. And my dad . . . well, Dad stood by Mom, even when she accused him of knowing something about Wade's murder and keeping it from her."

"Eleanor thought your father knew who killed her brother?" I asked, trying my best to hide the surprise in my voice.

"I think, for a time, she thought everyone knew something about it, and that the entire town was conspiring to hide it from her."

"Were they?"

Jane spread her hands. "Who knows? Maybe they were. Maybe it really was the great big conspiracy she thought it was. Or maybe Mom wanted to find the killer so badly, she was willing to accuse just about anyone of knowing who did it in the hopes that one day she'd be proven right."

It had to have been a hard way to live, suspecting everyone. No wonder Eleanor was unhappy for so long.

Jane yawned and I realized I was keeping her from getting some well-deserved rest.

"I'd best go," I said. "Thank you for talking to me."

"No, thank you," Jane said, touching my arm briefly. "Mom would be thrilled to know you were looking into the case. I'm sure her spirit is touched."

"I hope I do her proud."

Jane smiled. "I know you will."

I left her to get some sleep of my own. The short walk to my house felt like it was miles long, and I couldn't stop yawning. Misfit came running the moment I was through the door, but unfortunately, he wasn't greeting me. I managed to get the door closed just before he managed to sneak past my leg. He came to a stop and glared before he sauntered off toward the kitchen and his food bowl, fluffy orange tail swishing.

I took a moment to get him some fresh water and some dinner. I knew I should eat something myself, but I wasn't hungry. Thoughts of Rita and Eleanor and what both women went through had my stomach churning. I couldn't imagine what I'd do if something like that were to happen to me or my family.

Once Misfit was contentedly eating, I got changed into my PJs and then snagged my laptop. I carried it to the couch and settled in. Despite my exhaustion, I figured I could do a little snooping online before bed. Almost as soon as I was seated, Misfit jumped up and curled up beside me, purring.

"We'll figure this out," I told him, before opening my laptop and getting started.

Over the last few months, the library had been archiving old newspaper articles, scanning them in and making them available online. I figured it would be the best place to start my search.

Luckily for me, the library was up to the nineties, so I could easily browse everything from the time of the murder—or, at least, everything they had access to. There were months missing here and there, and sometimes articles were incomplete, but overall, I was pleased.

It didn't take long for me to realize how monumental of a task sifting through the articles would be. I had a year, but no month to go on, and there was no search bar for me to simply input Wade's name and find everything printed about him or his murder.

I almost gave up and went to bed right then and there, but caught myself before I closed my laptop and dragged myself to bed. The murder happened so long ago, memories would have faded, and people embarrassed by how they reacted might change their stories. If I could see what people were actually saying at the time of Wade's death, then I might be able to prod some of those hazy memories into something firmer, something more concrete.

The next twenty minutes was an exercise in frustration, but I persisted. I sorted through pages upon pages of articles, mostly about new attractions to Pine Hills and the surrounding areas, and very little on crime.

And then I saw it: MURDER IN PINE HILLS!

Excited, I scanned the article but found little I didn't already know. Wade Fink had been found by a woman, Jill Thatcher, while she was on a run with her dog. No real suspects were identified. Albie Bruce was mentioned, of course, as was another police officer, Jay Miller. The article also mentioned Wade's parents, Truman and Mary Fink. There was no mention of Eleanor or any other relatives.

I jotted down the names for future reference and continued searching.

There were more articles on the murder, but I found very little of use. It was as if the town didn't want to be reminded of the crime, so they didn't bother reporting it. One article did show an old photo of J&E's Banyon Tree, back when it was relatively new, and it mentioned the fact that Wade was last seen alive leaving his friends there, but the reporter steadfastly refused to name any of those friends.

I searched the article until I found that reporter's name: Larry Ritchie.

I skimmed a few more articles, until I came across one with a headline that gave me pause: A DESERVED END.

The article was once again written by Larry Ritchie and detailed Wade's life near the time of his death—or pretended to. It was scathing, so much so, that it made me physically ill to read it. Larry Ritchie hadn't approved of Wade's life choices, and went so far as to say his death might have been for the good of the town.

"Poor Eleanor," I muttered as I continued to read. What had she thought when she'd seen the article, printed in the local paper like it wasn't anything more than the character assassination that it truly was?

Supposedly, Wade was flaunting his relationship with Rita to the point of it becoming obscene. The article claimed they were together merely to hurt the image of the town and its residents. How he was doing that, Larry never said, but he went on to speculate that Rita had been forced to date Wade, that he'd somehow tricked her into the relationship and then used something unspecified against her to keep her there.

It read like something straight out of a tabloid, and was likely as truthful as one.

But what if there was some truth to the article? Would Rita really hide that from me?

I thought of those stories you hear about people who start siding with their kidnappers and attackers; Stockholm syndrome, I believe it was called. Could Rita possibly be suffering from it? How would I know if she was?

I added Larry's name to my list of people and then closed the laptop, my taste for research ruined by his article.

As I put the laptop away and readied myself for bed, I couldn't help but wonder if the reason no one, other than Rita and Eleanor, cared to find out the truth about Wade's murder was because Wade Fink wasn't the nice guy his friends and family made him out to be.

The thought carried me all the way to bed, and I realized I wouldn't be able to sleep unless I found out more. Within five minutes of lying down, I was up and looking up Larry Ritchie's name. I found his phone number easily enough, and without thinking what I was doing—or considering the time—I dialed.

"Ritchie." Larry sounded distracted, and not tired in the slightest, despite the late hour.

"Hi, this is Krissy Hancock. Am I speaking to Larry Ritchie, the reporter?"

"Who is this?"

"Krissy Hancock," I repeated, wondering if his hearing was going.

"Why are you calling me?"

"It's about Wade Fink. He was—"

"I know who Wade Fink was," Larry snapped. "Why are you calling me about him?"

"You wrote about him when he was murdered," I said, doing my best to keep my cool. Larry didn't sound like a very nice guy, but I didn't want to get on his bad side, not when he might be able to help me understand what had happened thirty years ago. "I was hoping we could discuss some of the particulars of the case."

"Why?"

I hesitated to consider my answer. What would make a man like Larry Ritchie willing to talk to someone like me? The answer was simple: his ego.

"I'm researching the history of Pine Hills," I said, wincing at the lie. "And I came across Wade Fink's murder—and your articles about it—and thought it would be a fantastic opportunity to talk to someone who truly knew what it was like back then, get your expert take on it."

There was a pause, before, "It happened a long time ago."

"I know. And I know it's a big ask, but if you could spare a few minutes, I'd appreciate it. You would be credited in my paper."

Larry sighed. "I can't now, but I should be able to slot you in tomorrow. How about noonish? My place." He rattled off an address.

"I'll see you then."

He hung up even before I finished the sentence.

7

I parked in the parking lot of J&E's Banyon Tree, hoping the owner, Judith Banyon, was taking the day off. The lot was rather full, despite the early hour. It made me wonder why Judith was so upset with me, considering how busy they were despite Death by Coffee's existence. She'd complained that we were pilfering her customers, yet seeing how many people were here, I doubted it was the entire truth.

J&E's looked much like any other diner. There was a quaintness to it, an old-timeyness that made me feel like I was stepping into the past as I entered through the front doors. Old-fashioned country music played low over the speakers, a change from the afternoons and evenings when they often played upbeat rockabilly instead.

It took only one look around the diner to find the Coffee Drinkers. Even if I hadn't recognized them from Eleanor's funeral, I would have known who they were. The six men sat around two square tables that had been pushed together. A waitress was filling one of the coffee mugs sitting before them, though the men ignored her like she wasn't even there.

I made straight for the group, glancing quickly behind the counter to make sure Judith wasn't there. So far, so good, but my luck might not hold out for long.

"Hi," I said, approaching the table as the waitress left. "Arthur, isn't it?"

"Yeah?" Up close, Arthur looked older than I remembered from the funeral. Deep lines surrounded his mouth, as if his teeth and jaw were slowly caving in. "Who are you?"

"My name's Krissy Hancock." I offered my hand. He just looked at it. "I saw you at Eleanor Winthrow's funeral."

The comment didn't go over as well as I'd hoped. Arthur sniffed and turned away from me, while nearly everyone else looked into their coffees, as if they could make me go away by ignoring me.

"It's a shame about Eleanor," a man wearing bifocals said. "You never think anyone is going to pass, and when they do, it's always a surprise. I wish we would have made more time for her."

Arthur muttered something under his breath I didn't catch, but knew it wasn't polite.

"I was hoping we could talk a little about Eleanor," I said. "If it's not too much bother, that is." I gave the man with bifocals a hopeful look.

"This is a private group," Arthur snapped, shooting me a quick glare. "We would rather not be disturbed."

"There's no reason to be rude," the bald man who'd approached Eleanor's casket at the funeral said. He scooted his chair to the side, making room. "Grab a chair and join us. It'll be nice to have some new blood after all this time of just us old codgers."

There were grumbles around the table, but everyone

scooted over enough so I could pull up a chair without being crowded.

"Thank you," I said, sitting. "It's been a pretty rough couple of days. Eleanor was my neighbor."

"I'm sorry you had to go through that," one of the men said. His back was slightly hunched in a way I took to be a medical condition, rather than bad posture. He winced when he glanced my way, as if it pained him.

I smiled, thinking it a joke, albeit one in bad taste, but he didn't return it. *All right, then.* I turned my focus to the rest of the table. "I overheard Arthur's name at the funeral," I said. "But I didn't catch anyone else's."

"I'm Hue Lewis," the bifocaled man said. He reached across the table to shake my hand, which I took gratefully. I then turned my attention to the man with wispy white hair next to him.

He looked slightly lost when he answered, "Roger Wills." When his eyes landed on me, I noted they didn't quite focus.

Around the table we went. The bald man was Lester Musgrave and the man with the hunched back was Zachary Ross. The last man at the table had a firm grip and looked to be in as good shape as someone half his age. When he spoke, his voice was surprisingly quiet.

"Clifford Watson, but you can call me Cliff."

"It's a pleasure to meet you, Cliff."

When he smiled, it was tight, and his gaze immediately returned to his coffee.

"So, what do we owe this pleasure, Ms. Hancock?" Hue asked. He seemed to be the friendliest of the group.

"Krissy, please," I said. Hue nodded his assent. "I was hoping you could tell me something about Eleanor's brother, Wade. He was a friend of yours, wasn't he?"

If the majority of the men had given me a frosty reception before, it was downright frigid now.

"Why do you care?" Arthur demanded.

I kept my smile in place and shrugged. "Just curious, really. As I said, Eleanor was my neighbor, but she didn't talk much about her family or her friends. It wasn't until her funeral that I learned she'd had a brother and I'm curious about what happened to him."

"He died," Roger answered. "It's been what? Thirty-three years now, give or take?" He shook his head in wonder. "I can't believe it's been so long."

"Wade should have known better than to run around with that harlot," Lester said. "She put those talons of hers in him and refused to let go."

My hackles rose, but I kept my cool. "I take it you weren't happy he was dating Rita Jablonski?"

Lester snorted, took a drink from his coffee. "Wade always had to do things the difficult way. It was bad enough that he complained about the coffee they served here. He even made them carry something special just for him."

"French roast," Zachary said. "No one else cared about roasts and flavors at the time. Coffee was coffee, and that's the way it should be, but Wade insisted on it. It had something to do with his family."

"I think he had a relative that sold the stuff," Hue said. "I imagine he had the Banyons buy their stock from that family member, but don't quote me on that."

"The coffee was one thing," Lester said. "But then he had to go and get himself some kid. Used her to spite us, I say. Thought he was a big deal because someone half his age looked at him like he was a god or something."

"He *was* peculiar," Cliff said, not without fondness.

"Peculiar?" Another spiteful laugh as Arthur slapped the

table. "He was an odd duck from the start. I don't know why we let him drink with us. Caused nothing but trouble. Just because he had more money than the rest of us combined, doesn't mean he deserved special treatment."

"Do you think someone killed him for his money?" I asked.

"The Fink family had money, but not *that* much money," Hue said. "And by the time he died, Wade didn't have access to much of it, if you catch my drift. I won't say his parents disowned him . . ."

"They darn well did, and rightfully so," Arthur said. "He brought shame on this town, and on the rest of us. We should have nipped it in the bud long before he started parading that kid around town like she was anything more than a brat looking to hook up with an older man."

"She enjoyed it." Lester grimaced as he drank from his mug. "I don't think that girl cared one bit about him, not really. She only cared about the status she earned by dating someone like Wade Fink. It probably turned her into a celebrity at school."

"I don't think it was like that," Hue said.

"Sure it was." Lester set his mug down harder than was warranted. "She hung onto him like she was afraid that if she let go, he'd find someone else. Probably would have. I mean, what could a grown man like Wade see in a kid like that?"

"You know what he saw," Arthur muttered.

I was gritting my teeth by then. Rita was my friend, and listening to them talk about her that way had me close to screaming.

"Can you tell me what happened the day Wade died?" I asked in an effort to get the conversation back on track. "He was here, with you, before it happened, wasn't he?"

The waitress chose that moment to return. "Can I get you something?" she asked me.

"I'm okay," I said. "But thank you."

She checked around the table and refilled any of the mugs that had gone low since her last visit. She did so quickly, and quietly, as if she couldn't wait to scurry off and wait on someone else.

With the prickly personalities around the table, I didn't blame her.

Once she was gone, I gave the men an expectant look. None of them appeared to want to talk about it, which instantly made me think back to what Albie Bruce had said: These men knew something.

"It was a long time ago," Roger said, breaking the silence.

"We were together, of course," Hue said. "We always were back then."

"Wade made his choice," Arthur muttered before taking a drink from his coffee. He grimaced as if it had gone sour since his last sip, though I knew it was the topic of conversation that had put the bad taste in his mouth.

"There was a fight," Hue went on, which caused Arthur to curse under his breath. "It wasn't a big one, mind you. Lester merely told Wade he should break it off with Rita, and Wade refused."

"He more than refused," Lester said. "He told me to mind my own business, in not so nice terms." He shot me a smile that was anything but friendly. "But I won't repeat it with a lady present."

"He wasn't happy when he left us, that was for sure," Hue said. "But there was no real malice to the spat. Just friends and a disagreement. That sort of thing happens all the time."

"He was the first to leave?" I asked, wanting to make sure I got the timetable right.

"He was," Hue said. "Wade grabbed his coffee and left about fifteen, twenty minutes before anyone else was ready to go. We tend to follow pretty strict schedules out of habit, normally."

"Maybe if one of us had gone with him, he'd be alive now," Roger said, head drooping.

"Who left next?" I asked. If one of these men killed Wade, or saw who did it, then it would be good to know where they were at the time of his death.

"Arthur, wasn't it you?" Zachary asked.

Arthur crossed his arms and glared across the table. "It was. I had an appointment to keep."

"Zachary and Lester left next," Hue said.

"Together?"

"We worked at the same garage," Lester said. "Always went in right after our little get-together."

Zachary nodded his affirmation.

"I left just after they did," Cliff said in his too quiet voice.

"You were sick that day, weren't you?" Zachary asked. "You looked green if I remember right. Thought you might lose your breakfast before it was all said and done."

"I was," Cliff said. "I went home and spent the rest of the day in bed."

Arthur's eyes narrowed as if he wanted to say something, but he held his tongue. I imagine whatever he said wasn't going to be friendly.

"After that, it was just Roger and me," Hue said. "Roger left before me, which was how it usually went."

"Had a hot date." Roger grinned, but it slowly faded. "Can't remember her name though."

"Wasn't it Charlotte?" Arthur asked. For the first time since I'd been there, he sounded amused. "I haven't thought about Charlotte Chambers in years. Whatever happened to her?"

"Married some foreigner if I recall," Lester said. "Shame, too. She was pretty."

I didn't see how marrying a foreigner mattered, but I supposed times were different back then, and these men likely still held some of their old prejudices. "So, you were the last to go?" I asked Hue.

He nodded, a faint smile on his lips. "I hid from the wife as much as I could. I sometimes wonder if I kept this place afloat with all the coffee and eggs I consumed long after everyone else had gone."

"You should have divorced her back then," Arthur said. "Saved yourself some trouble later."

"Amen to that," Hue said, raising his mug in salute. Something told me he wasn't as happy about his failed marriage as he was letting on, however.

"Do any of you have any idea who might have killed Wade?" I asked. "There didn't seem to be a lot of suspects."

Glances went around the table. I noted Arthur's eyes lingered on Lester's before snapping away.

"I think what's in the past should stay there," Arthur said. "And I do think we work better as a six-piece, rather than seven, so if you wouldn't mind." He jerked his head toward the door.

No one spoke up in my defense, so I stood. I had a ton more questions, but they could wait. I didn't think I'd get much out of anyone while they were together, but talking to them had given me something to think about.

"Thank you for letting me sit with you," I said. "I really do appreciate it."

"It was our pleasure." Hue sounded genuine, though I don't think the sentiment was shared with anyone else at the table.

I left them to drink their coffee. It was obvious the men knew more than they were letting on, but which one would tell me what that might be? Hue seemed the friendliest, but that didn't mean he'd be willing to spill his friends' secrets. I had a feeling Arthur and Lester would be perfectly content never seeing me again. And Roger and Zachary weren't exactly forthcoming, either.

What about Cliff? I wondered. He'd been pretty quiet, soft-spoken. Perhaps there was a reason for it.

I was out of the diner and halfway to my car when a rough hand grabbed me by the arm and spun me around. I fully expected to find Arthur, demanding to know what I was up to, but instead, it was Judith Banyon.

"What do you think you're doing?" she asked.

"I was talking to some people," I said, jerking my arm from her grip. "There's nothing wrong with that."

"You were asking about Wade. I heard you."

"I was," I admitted. "I lived beside Eleanor Winthrow. You remember her, right? Your old friend?"

Judith winced, and I instantly regretted my tone. The two women might have drifted apart recently, but that didn't mean Judith hadn't cared for Eleanor.

"I'm sorry," I said. "I didn't mean it that way. Eleanor's daughter, Jane, mentioned Wade to me and I was curious as to what happened to him. I wasn't trying to upset anyone."

"Well, you did. I don't appreciate you coming around and starting something in my place of business. You've caused me enough grief for a lifetime."

"I wasn't starting anything," I said. "I just wanted to talk, that's all."

Judith's lips pressed into a tight line. It made her look even more severe, which was saying something. Her gray hair was pulled back from her face so tightly, it was a wonder she could blink.

"Do you know anything about the murder?" I asked. "If you know who killed Wade Fink . . ."

"I don't know a thing. No one here does." Judith took a step toward me, seriously invading my personal space. "If you know what's best for you, drop it now before someone else gets hurt."

And with that, she spun on her heel and marched back into her diner.

As she vanished inside, I noticed someone was watching me from one of the windows.

Eddie.

He backed away almost the instant I saw him, but in that brief moment, I noticed he looked more than curious. He looked eager to talk.

He knows something. And I had a feeling that if given the chance, he'd be willing to talk to me about it.

But for now, it would have to wait.

I slid into my car, started the engine, and with one last speculative look toward the Banyon Tree, I drove away.

8

It wasn't yet time to meet Larry Ritchie, so after my visit with the Coffee Drinkers, I headed downtown to Phantastic Candies. I was craving chocolate—apparently, I'm a nervous chocoholic—and what better place than the candy store owned by my friend and neighbor Jules Phan?

I parked out front and made my way to the front door, mouth already watering. I stepped inside to the sound of a giant piece of candy being unwrapped, and just about walked right into a group of people heading out.

"I'm sorry." The apology came automatically to my lips. I didn't realize who it was I was apologizing to until one of them spoke.

"Krissy?"

I jerked back in surprise. "Maire?" A quick look told me that it wasn't just my ex-boyfriend's mother, Maire Foster, I'd run into, but nearly the entire family.

Maire's bright green eyes lit up. "It's been too long," she said. "Far, far too long."

Before I could react, she wrapped me in a hug.

Behind Maire, her husband, Keneche, watched on. They were physically polar opposites, but somehow worked well together. Maire was five foot nothing, and not only sounded Irish, but looked it. Keneche was dark-skinned and tall. Where she was exuberant and overly talkative, he was reserved and quiet. Both were some of the nicest people I knew.

"Hi, Krissy." Jade, Will's sister, stood beside her parents, looking as beautiful as ever. Her daughter, Gemma, was in front of her, giving me a look that was part pleasure, part curiosity. She probably didn't even understand how or why her uncle Will and I had broken up.

"What are you all doing here?" I asked, even though it was obvious. Gemma had a bag of candy in hand and was happily chewing away.

"Family outing," Ken said. "We just stopped in to get a treat for our little Gemma."

The girl in question beamed. "Hi, Krissy! When are you coming over again?"

"Hi, Gemma." Tears came unbidden to my eyes. I blinked them rapidly away. "I don't know. It might be a while longer." I looked to the adults, hoping I could hold it together better with them. "I'm glad to see you're doing well."

"How are you doing, honey?" Maire asked. "I can't believe Will would up and leave you like he did. I tried to talk him out of it, but do you think he'd listen to his mother? What job is worth the loss of love?" She shook her head angrily. "He had a good thing and threw it away."

Ken rested a hand on his wife's shoulders. "I'm sure they've both made peace with it."

"I have," I said. "There's no hard feelings between us." Without needing them to say it, I could tell they all felt the same about me.

I truly did like Will's family, but hadn't seen them

since he'd left Pine Hills for Arizona. The job was a big promotion for him, and I didn't begrudge him for wanting to go.

Still, I missed him; probably always would. But a big part of me had always known we wouldn't work out.

"Have you talked to Will lately?" Jade asked.

"I haven't." He'd said he'd keep in touch, but with his new job, and my own life to keep up with, neither of us was making good on that promise. "But it's okay. Life happens."

While Ken and Jade smiled, Maire wasn't about to let her son off that easily. "He should do better," she said.

"We should get moving," Ken said. "The movie starts in twenty minutes."

"It was good seeing you," I said, accepting another hug from Maire, and surprisingly, one from Jade.

"You stop by sometime," Maire said as she allowed herself to be guided through the door. "I'll make you a shepherd's pie."

"I'll do that," I called after her. Ken and Gemma waved, and then, they were gone.

I stared after them and a piece of my heart I didn't know was wounded healed. They'd touched my life so briefly, yet they were once—and still were—an important part of it. I realized I should get ahold of Will to let him know I was doing okay and that I was happy.

I hoped he was feeling the same way.

"You look like you could use this."

I turned to find Jules offering me a chocolate. He was wearing an outlandish peppermint costume, all red and white stripes. When he worked, he often dressed up for the kids who frequented his store. He was a little less extravagant at home, at least in how he dressed. His personality was always a joy.

"Thanks, Jules," I said, taking the candy and popping it into my mouth. "It's good."

He beamed. "I'm glad to see you're on good terms with the Fosters. Breakups can be hard for everyone, not just the couple involved."

"It happened a long time ago." Though, sometimes, it felt just like yesterday that Will and I'd broken up. Had it really been over a year now?

"Well, still, it's hard. Some people never get over losing someone they love, even if it is a mutually agreed upon parting."

I briefly wondered if he was talking about Rita, but realized he was still talking about me. I decided it was time to change the subject before he started inquiring about my current lack of a love life. He knew how I felt about Paul Dalton, even if I often pretended those feelings didn't exist.

"I was happy to see you at Eleanor's funeral," I said, picking up a bag of chocolates and laying it on the counter. "She would have liked that."

"I doubt that," Jules said, but with good humor. "It's sad she passed, but I have a feeling she wouldn't have minded if I'd left town and never came back."

"I'm sure it wasn't like that." I paused, considered, and then asked, "Did you know what happened to her brother, Wade?"

Jules looked surprised by the question. "Eleanor had a brother? I never knew that."

"I did." Lance Darby walked into the room from the back, looking like an extremely fit professional swimmer with his blond hair and slightly too tight shirt. "Hello, Krissy."

"Lance."

He moved to stand behind the counter with Jules. "He was murdered, right?"

"He was. It happened in the mid-eighties."

"That's why I didn't know about it," Jules said. "I didn't live in Pine Hills back then. I didn't move here until what? 1999?"

"About then," Lance said, grinning. Something passed between the two of them, and I knew it was something personal.

"I was talking to Jane Winthrow about it, and it turns out Wade was dating Rita Jablonski at the time."

"Really?" Jules asked, eyes going wide. "I didn't know she'd ever dated anyone."

"They did date, didn't they?" Lance said. "I forgot about that. I was just a kid back then, but I vaguely remember hearing about the relationship. Everyone was talking about it, not that I understood what the fuss was about at my age. Still, it was a big enough deal, it stuck with me."

"People thought she was too young for him," I said.

"Or he was too old," Lance added. "It's a shame, that's what it is. Who has the right to involve themselves in someone else's life? Their relationship was between the two of them and their families. No one else should have cared."

Jules put an arm around Lance's waist and squeezed. Lance returned the gesture, and some of the tension that had built up over the last few seconds seeped away.

"Why the interest?" Jules asked. "If it happened so long ago, I mean."

"They never found who did it, did they?" Lance asked.

"They didn't. I figured I could look into it as a favor to Rita and Eleanor."

Lance reached across the counter and rested a hand on my wrist. "That's kind of you."

"Maybe," I said. "I'm not sure if I'll be able to do anything. It did happen over thirty years ago and no one really wants to talk about it."

"Do you think the killer still lives in Pine Hills?" Jules asked. He seemed to remember my bag of candy, scanned it in, and then took my money when I paid.

"I don't know," I said. "They might. Or they might be dead. Even if I come up with a suspect, it's not like I'll find proof of the murder just lying around. The police think he was killed with a rock, but it wasn't found at the scene. As far as I'm aware, nothing was stolen from him, but I suppose it's possible."

"It wasn't considered a big deal, was it?" Lance asked. "When it happened, there was a brief surge of interest, then nothing."

"That seems odd," Jules said.

Boy, did it. "There were a few stories about it in the paper, but little else. I was told that there wasn't much of a push to solve the case."

"Do you think the police knew who did it?" Jules asked.

It was a good question. While Albie Bruce hadn't given me much to go on, he *had* pushed me in the direction of the Banyon Tree Coffee Drinkers. Did that mean he knew who killed Wade? Or did he only suspect?

"I'm not sure," I said. "I have some leads I'm going to follow up on. Hopefully, someone can tell me something useful. You'd think someone would have to know something, right?"

Lance suddenly stood straighter. "Have you talked to the Bunfords?"

"Ted and Bett? No, why?"

He didn't answer right away. His eyes were staring off into space and he was biting his lip, as if he were in deep thought.

"I think . . ." he said, before trailing off. It took him another couple of good lip-chews before he continued. "I think they used to work with Wade."

"He worked at the bed-and-breakfast?" I asked.

"No, this was before they opened Ted and Bettfast," Lance said. "There used to be an arcade downtown where all the kids used to hang out. I used to go there all the time with my friends. It's probably why I remember some of what went on. I knew Wade by sight."

I had a hard time imagining Ted or Bett Bunford working at an arcade. "You saw Wade with them there?" I asked.

Lance shook his head. "It wasn't there, but next door to it. What was it called?" He rubbed at his temples as if he could force the memory to come. "I can't remember." He dropped his hands. "I only remember because Wade worked there, so a lot of attention was focused that way for a time after his death."

"I'll ask Ted and Bett about it," I said, already dreading *that* encounter. If there was a competition about who disliked me the most, it would likely be a dead heat between Bett Bunford and Judith Banyon.

"If I think of the name of the place, I'll let you know,"

Lance said. "I'm sure it's not important. I'm not even sure if it will help you."

"I'm sure it will," I said, picking up my bag of candy. "Thanks."

I left Phantastic Candies, thoughts racing. Could Wade's murder have had anything to do with his job? Since I didn't know what he did for a living, I couldn't make that call. I definitely needed to pay the Bunfords a visit, but it would have to wait until after I'd talked to Larry Ritchie.

Still, I had a little more time to kill, so when I got into my car, I dug into my candy and removed my phone. I considered briefly who to call, and then dialed.

I didn't expect an answer, not in the middle of the day, but was surprised when Patricia Dalton's voice came over the line.

"Ms. Hancock? Do I want to know why you're calling me on my personal cell?"

I cringed, already regretting making the call. "I'm sorry, Chief. I have a quick question for you and then I'll let you get back to work."

She sighed, and in the background, I heard something squeak; likely her chair as she sat back. "Okay. I have a moment, but *only* a moment."

"This might seem strange, but do you happen to know where Wade Fink worked at the time of his death?" I knew I could get that information from Ted and Bett Bunford, but there was a chance neither would talk to me. The more I knew going in, the more likely they'd be not to throw me out on my ear the moment they saw me.

Well, that was the idea, anyway.

"Where he worked?" Chief Dalton asked. "Why?"

"I'm not sure," I admitted. "It could be nothing."

"I don't know offhand," she said. "But I could look into it for you."

I almost told her to do so, but changed my mind. I planned on visiting Ted and Bett as soon as I was done with Larry Ritchie. Even if she came up with it while I was talking to Larry, it wouldn't give me much time to look into the place before talking to the Bunfords. I wasn't even sure why I'd bothered to call.

"No," I said. "That's okay."

There was a moment of silence on the other end of the line. "Was that really all you called to talk to me about?"

It was then I realized that no, it wasn't. There was one other name I'd come across in my research she might be able to tell me about. "Do you remember a cop by the name of Jay Miller?"

Silence.

"Chief Dalton?"

"I'm here," she said. "You just took me by surprise. I haven't heard the name Jay Miller for a very long time."

Thirty years ago, perhaps? I wondered. "He was mentioned in an article about Wade Fink's murder," I said. "Was he involved with the investigation?"

More silence; so much so, I was beginning to get worried. If Patricia Dalton knew more than she was letting on about Wade's murder, and it turned out to be some sort of cover-up, it would make my relationship with Paul that much more difficult.

"I think you'd better come see me," she finally said. "We can talk then."

"I've got a few stops to make, but I can come in afterward," I said, worry growing. She *did* know something, but I wasn't sure it was about Wade directly. Did the police know more about the case than they let the public in on?

Or was there something else going on, something that would hamper my investigation?

"I'll be here all day," she said. "And Krissy . . ."

"Yeah?"

"Be careful, all right?"

"I will."

She hung up and I lowered my phone to my lap. What was going on here? Patricia Dalton hadn't seemed too concerned by me looking into the murder when I'd brought it up at the writers group meeting, yet now, she was warning me to be careful. What had changed?

Jay Miller, that's what.

But why? Albie Bruce hadn't mentioned him. No one had, as far I could remember. Just the one article in the paper, and that was merely a casual mention of him, not a scathing report.

Chief Dalton was going to tell me something, I was sure, but would it be the absolute truth? Or would she protect a colleague, one who might have done something they shouldn't have?

And if that was the case, would the local journalist who'd covered the case at the time know anything about it?

It was a good thing I was about to meet with him.

With that thought in mind, I put my car in gear and headed for my meeting with Larry Ritchie.

9

Larry Ritchie's log cabin sat in a quiet part of Pine Hills, where the town lights wouldn't reach. There was a large pond out back that looked entirely natural, not one of those man-made ponds that were too symmetrical, too clean. I could hear the frogs even before I shut off my car's engine.

I sat in his gravel driveway a long moment, taking in the scenery. Pine Hills was a beautiful place. The trees, the gently sloping hills. Even downtown felt peaceful, a place apart from the rest of the world.

But Larry's house was truly an isolationist's paradise. I couldn't see a hint of a neighbor from his property, not unless you counted the hawk resting in a tree nearby.

His house sat close enough to the pond so that he could sit on the back deck and look out over the water, but not so close that it would become problematic if we were to get a heavy rain and the water overflowed its banks. A ramp rose next to the stairwell, which consisted of a total of three steps. If it wasn't for the slope of the property, he wouldn't have needed stairs at all.

I got out of my car and made for the front door to his cabin. Before I was halfway there, the door opened and a man who appeared to be in his early sixties wheeled himself out. His hair was a solid white, face clean-shaven. Even though he was confined to a wheelchair, he held himself with an assurance a lot of people who could walk didn't have.

"You Krissy Hancock?" he asked.

"I am. Larry Ritchie?"

He grunted in response and then wheeled back into his house. "Close the door after you." The shout came from over his shoulder.

Okay then.

I hurried to catch up to him, choosing the stairs over the ramp. I stepped across the threshold, and then closed the door behind me as requested.

Larry was seated at his dining room table. A stack of legal pads sat on a stand next to him. As I entered, he tossed a newspaper atop them. I couldn't tell if he was hiding them from me, or if he was merely setting the paper aside to keep the table clear.

"Thank you for inviting me to your home," I said, joining him in the dining room. The house had a cozy feel to it, so much so, it was a surprise when I realized the fireplace in the next room hadn't been lit.

"Wasn't like I had much of a choice." He patted the arm of his wheelchair. "People in town look at me with a pity I can't abide, so I stay here when I can."

"Do you have a nurse?" I glanced into the living room, half expecting to find someone standing there, but the room was empty.

"I do. She's not here. Only comes when I need something."

By the way he said it, I could tell he didn't like having someone wait on him. I had a feeling Larry Ritchie spent a lot of time alone, doing things for himself. He was smartly dressed, as if he was ready for a night on the town.

"Sit." He waved a hand at the chair in front of me. "It'll put a kink in my neck if I have to stare up at you."

I abruptly sat, feeling like a kid back in school.

"Want anything?" he asked. "Tea? Kettle's still hot." He touched a mug in front of him. I could smell the mint coming off the steam.

"Tea would be great, thank you." I warred with myself before saying, "I can get it if you want."

Larry's jaw tightened and he gave me a look that said, "Just try it," as clearly as if he'd spoken.

I folded my hands on the table and let him get my tea for me. A bowl of sugar cubes sat beside a pitcher of cream in the center of the table. While I didn't take either in my coffee, I decided I'd try it in my tea.

While Larry poured, I took in his home. From where I sat, I couldn't see down the short hallway where I imagined his bedroom and the bathroom were located. From the outside, I got the impression the house was only big enough for one bedroom. From the inside, I was almost positive that was the case—the living room took up much of the available space.

Despite it being a log home, there were no animal heads on the wall like there always was on TV. A plaque hung near the television, as did a few other framed items, which I took to be awards, though I'd have to get closer to be sure. I didn't see any photographs.

"Here you are." Larry set a mug down in front of me. It depicted a nature scene, which told me a little about the man I was about to talk to.

There was one of those tiny little spoons sitting on the saucer. I used a set of tongs to grab two sugar cubes, added a little cream, and then used the spoon to stir my tea. I took a polite sip.

"Thank you," I said. "It's good."

Larry grunted and resumed his place at the table. "Now, you were here to talk about Wade Fink's murder, is that correct?"

"It is." I took another sip, and then set my mug on the saucer to let my tea cool. "I saw your articles online and they piqued my interest."

"You were doing research on Pine Hills?" he asked.

"Sort of." I might have told him I was interested in the history of the town before, but sitting face-to-face with him, I found it hard to lie. "Eleanor Winthrow was my neighbor. She died recently and, well . . ."

He took a sip of tea as he studied me. Larry had hard, critical eyes that likely served him well when he was asking tough questions of someone for a story. I endured it as calmly as I could, but my insides were doing jumping jacks. The man made me nervous and he didn't even have to say anything.

Finally, he set his mug aside. "What happened to Wade Fink put a stain on this town. *He* put a stain on it, one that took a long time to fade."

"You're talking about his relationship with Rita Ja-blonski."

He nodded. "Wade flaunted it to the point where it became obscene. He was already doing something most of us didn't approve of, and having him do everything in his power to make sure we saw it day in and day out, only made it worse."

"You disapproved of the relationship."

"Of course I did!" He smacked the table, causing the little spoons to rattle on their saucers. "She was too young. It was a scandal then, as it would be today. There were other, more age-appropriate women for him, and I know for a fact there were a lot of young men interested in the Jablonski kid, boys her own age."

"Were you one of them?" I asked, before realizing he fit the "age-appropriate" portion just about as well as Wade had.

Larry's nostrils flared. "I take offense at the mere suggestion that I could have wanted to have anything to do with her. She was a child, barely old enough to understand what was happening to her, let alone the town."

"I'm sorry," I said. "I didn't mean to offend you, but I saw pictures of her. She was pretty. You can't blame someone for being interested in her."

"Yes, you can." He snatched up his tea and took a large gulp that had to have scalded his throat, but he didn't complain. "Wade knew he was walking a fine line. If her parents had wanted to, I'm sure they could have found a way to press charges against him. She might have been of legal age, but that doesn't mean Wade hadn't courted her before then." He paused. "Turns out, it wasn't necessary for them to take that step." Was that a smile I saw behind his mug?

"You can't truly think Wade's murder was a good thing?" I asked, appalled. I can see being angry about the relationship, I supposed, but to be happy about a man's death? *That* was obscene.

"If you understood what it was like then, you wouldn't say that," Larry said. "Imagine if you were standing in a room filled with gunpowder and the guy next to you insists on smoking. What do you think will happen? It might not go up right away, but the more he smokes, the more he tosses ash, the closer you come to having the whole thing blow up on you."

As vivid as the imagery might be, I still didn't believe a man's death could be a good thing. If Wade had been out killing women like one of those serial killers they make documentaries about, then maybe. Even then, I had a hard time justifying someone's death, even a bad person's. That's what prisons were for.

"You look at me like I'm a horrible person," Larry said, sitting back in his wheelchair. "I can't say you're the first. It's human nature to think the best of people, especially people you know. But trust me, there was little good in Wade Fink. If he could find a way to ruin the entire town, he'd do it."

"And you think his decision to date Rita was his way to hurt Pine Hills?"

Larry shrugged. "Could be. Or maybe he did care about her. Who knows for sure? I will say that once he was gone, things got better around here. Relationships grew stronger. There was more than one wife around town who'd accused her husband of looking at those younger girls, all because of Wade. Once that relationship ended, so did the accusations."

I wondered if he was one of those accused, but didn't ask the question. If Larry Ritchie was once married, he wasn't now. He wore no ring on his finger, and there was no indication a woman lived with him.

"What can you tell me about the police officers who'd worked the case?" I asked, deciding I wasn't going to get anywhere talking about Wade and Rita. Larry had his opinion and it was obviously marring his view on the couple.

Larry considered it a moment before answering. "They did what they could, and that's that." It wasn't much of an answer.

"Do you think they tried very hard to solve the murder?"

"As hard as they could. Like everyone else, they were relieved the relationship was over. Tensions were high, even among Wade and his friends. I remember there was a brawl once, and while I can't swear to what it was about, I'm pretty sure Ms. Jablonski was the reason."

"Wade fought with his friends?" I asked. "As in, a throwing punches kind of fight?"

Larry nodded. "Not sure who all was involved. Wasn't much of a story, so I had no real interest in it. They got into it, the cops showed up, and it was over. No one got arrested. I only know about it because I had a friend on the force and he gave me a call whenever something happened in town, just in case I needed a story."

"Was that officer Jay Miller?"

The name threw him off because he hesitated before he answered. "Yeah, that's him. Once the paper folded, we lost touch. That was, I don't know, fifteen years ago now? Can hardly believe it's been that long. Technology was a problem, even in the early two thousands. Nowadays, what chance does print have? Everyone can go online to find out whatever they want in real time, so what purpose do we serve?"

I had my own opinion on the decline of print media, but once again, I held my tongue. I didn't want to go down that rabbit hole with someone whose career was affected by the growth of social media. Needless to say, I mostly agreed with him.

"Do you know where Jay Miller is now?" I asked. "Is he still on the force?"

Larry's laugh was harsh, almost condescending. "He left not long after I was out of a job, if I remember right. Don't know why, and at that point, I didn't care."

"Why?" I asked, not quite sure what I was asking, or if it even mattered.

"People change," Larry said. "Stuff happens. I'm not going to get into it with you."

There was something there, and I wanted to press him, but I knew I'd be wasting my time. Larry Ritchie was someone who spoke when he wanted, about what he wanted, and nothing would change that.

"What about Albie Bruce?" I asked. "He was in charge of the investigation at the time, right?"

"He was," Larry said. "He was a good cop. Could be strict when he needed to be, but kind when necessary. Had a good head on his shoulders, though he didn't like me lurking around his crime scenes, as few as they might have been."

I considered going down the list of people I knew were involved with the murder, but realized he'd grow impatient with me if I tried. Still, there was one other question I wanted to ask him, just to see what he'd say.

"Who do you think killed Wade Fink?" I asked, picking up my now cooled tea and taking a sip.

Larry leaned forward and rested both his hands on the table. They were strong hands, the kind I could imagine reaching across the table and choking the life out of me if he wanted to. Something about him intimidated me, frightened me even. Could he have been involved with the murder somehow? Or was I letting my imagination run a little too wild?

"Whoever killed him was a hero," Larry said. "If you truly want to know who killed that man, I'd look for someone who cared about Pine Hills, and about the pain Wade caused. I only hope you realize that what that person did was the right thing to do because no one else had the guts to do it."

Our eyes met. There was a challenge there, a dare to press him. There was so much bitterness and hatred toward Wade in that look, I wondered if anything he'd told me was worth anything.

"Thank you for your time," I said, rising. "And thank you for the tea. It was very good."

Larry leaned back in his chair and regarded me. "There's a lot you don't know about the world, young lady. I get that you have your own views, your own beliefs, but that doesn't make them right."

The same could be said about you, I thought, but didn't say it. No sense in taking the bait; and I knew that's exactly what it was. "I'll contact you if I have any more questions," I said, knowing I wouldn't call unless something came up tying Larry to the crime. "Thanks again."

His smile was about as warm as an ice cream sundae. "I'll show myself out."

I hurried away from the table and left Larry Ritchie's log cabin, which no longer felt cozy, but the sort of place where an unhinged man might hide away to make bombs. Larry didn't follow me out, yet I could still feel him watching me, daring me to say something that would give him permission to do . . . what? I'm not sure. Whatever it was, it gave me the willies.

10

What once used to be a leafy lion sagged sideways, as did an elephant, which looked more like a melting block of green ice than an animal. I took each turn slowly as I worked my way up the winding driveway that led to Ted and Bettfast, the bed-and-breakfast where Ted and Bett Bunford lived and worked.

The next bend used to have a hedge trimmed to look like a dog. It was completely gone now. A gaping hole sat in its place.

It was a sad sight to see. The hedge animals were overgrown now when they weren't outright dead. One entire patch looked as if someone had lit it on fire; only the branches remained. I didn't think it was entirely from lack of care, but the Bunfords were getting up there in years. They'd once hoped to restore the entire property to its former glory, but it was obvious they didn't have the funds, or the energy, to do so.

I turned at the last bend and found an empty spot in the parking lot. In fact, most of the spaces were empty. There were three cars there, which I assumed belonged to Ted and Bett, and one other employee who worked for them since the Bunfords couldn't do it all on their own. The emptiness didn't bode well for the future of their business.

The mansion turned bed-and-breakfast was only partially painted. Two of the windows had recently been replaced—they still had stickers on them—and the front door was different from the last time I was there, though I couldn't tell if it was a fresh paint job or a new door entirely.

So, the repairs were still ongoing, but slowly. If I had the money to donate, I'd happily throw a little toward the restoration of the mansion. It was a beautiful place, despite its less than stellar state, and I'd love to see how it would look once the repairs were complete.

I paused at the front door. The last time I was here, I managed to get myself banned, though, honestly, I'd only been trying to solve a murder, so it wasn't like there'd been any malicious intent when I'd broken into one of the rooms. I didn't think there was anything official, like a restraining order or anything like that, but that didn't mean Bett wouldn't call the cops the moment she saw me. I only hoped she'd give me a chance to explain myself before throwing me out.

Instead of walking in, I chose to knock on the door. Maybe if I was polite, I'd be given the benefit of the doubt.

It took two knocks and one loud throat clearing before the door swung open and a confused Jo looked out at me. She was one of the first people I'd ever met here, and since that first meeting, she'd soured on me, much like her bosses had.

"Oh. You."

"Hi, Jo," I said as friendly as I could. "Nice day out, isn't it?"

"Ms. Hancock." She kept her voice low. "You know you shouldn't be here."

"I know," I said, dropping my own voice to similar levels. "But I really need to talk to the Bunfords."

She raised one eyebrow at me. "They're not going to change their minds about you. Bett gave us specific instructions as to what to do if you were to ever show again."

Since Jo wasn't running off to call the cops or screaming for Bett, I hoped that meant I had a chance to talk her into at least letting the Bunfords know I came in peace. "I promise, I wouldn't be here if it wasn't important," I said.

Jo glanced over her shoulder, to the empty room behind her. "Justin spoke up for you, you know?" she said, dropping her voice even further as she turned back to me. She was practically whispering now. "He says you aren't as bad as Bett thinks."

Justin was another employee at the bed-and-breakfast, one who'd stuck his neck out for me on more than one occasion. If he was speaking up for me now, I needed to find the time to thank him. "I'd like to prove he's right," I said. "I'm not trying to bring trouble to Bett or her business. And you've got to know I had nothing to do with the murders that have happened around Pine Hills over the last few years. I'm only interested in finding the truth."

Jo drummed her fingers on the door as she studied me. No sounds came from the bed-and-breakfast, further solidifying the idea that the place was empty of guests. I hoped that I was wrong and someone had booked one of the rooms but were currently out enjoying the sights.

After a good minute, Jo heaved a sigh. "All right. Stay out here. If Bett wants to talk to you, she can let you in. I'm not going to risk getting fired for you."

"That's fine," I said. "I wouldn't want to get you into trouble on my account."

Jo didn't look as if she believed me before she closed the door.

I paced out front, mentally rehearsing what I was going to say. While Lance believed the Bunfords had worked with Wade Fink, that didn't mean they'd *liked* him. As far as I knew, they were just as happy as everyone else seemed to be about his demise.

It did make me wonder if Rita and Jane had it wrong and Wade really was a bad man. He *had* decided to date a woman much younger than him, who was likely just out of school, if not still in it at the time. That didn't make him a bad person outright, but what if Rita wasn't the only young woman he'd had eyes for?

I refused to make assumptions, though it was a question I'd likely have to ask if I wanted to get a real idea of who the real Wade Fink might have been. As far as I knew, he'd had a string of teenage girls following after him, with none of them aware of the others.

If that was the case, I wasn't sure what it would do to Rita. I'm not sure I *wanted* to know.

The door opened again and Bett Bunford glared out at me. She was leaning heavily on a cane—something she hadn't needed before. When I'd first met her, she'd had strong hands and had looked capable of crawling around the property, weeding every inch of it.

Now, her hand trembled on the cane. I couldn't tell if it was from anger, or weakness. I was kind of hoping for the former.

"Mrs. Bunford—"

"What are you doing here?" she asked, voice wavering.

Age was quickly catching up with her, and my heart broke a little hearing and seeing it.

"I was hoping we could talk about something," I said. "A friend told me you might have some insights for me and that I should stop by to see what you could tell me."

"Why?"

"It's about Wade Fink."

Bett went completely still. Even the tremble in her hand ceased.

"Wade? Why would you want to talk to me about Wade?"

"I was told you worked with him. Since I never got the chance to meet him, I thought that you might be able to tell me what kind of man he was, and maybe a little something about his friends."

She blinked at me slowly. And was that a tear in her eye?

"Both Ted and I knew him," she said. "And, yes, he worked with us for a time. Are you . . . ?"

Even though she never finished the question, I knew what she was asking. "I hope so," I said. "His sister was my neighbor. She died recently and I was hoping to solve Wade's murder in her honor."

"I heard about that," Bett said, lowering her head. "Eleanor's death, I mean. I couldn't make the funeral, but wanted to." She coughed and cleared her throat. "You'd better come in. Ted will want to hear this."

Bett turned and walked away. Despite the cane, she moved pretty well. By the time I stepped inside and closed the door, she was halfway to the back where they kept their offices. I was forced to jog to catch up.

Jo appeared surprised as we hurried past her. I shot her a thumbs-up and a mouthed, "Thank you," before following Bett into the office.

Well, *office* wasn't quite the right word. I'd expected to

find filing cabinets and desks where they could keep track of their guests and finances. The desk was there, as was a computer, but the rest of the room looked—and felt—like a comfy den. There were bookshelves packed two rows deep with books. Ted was sitting in a rocker by the window, a hardback in hand. When we entered, he closed it and then set his hands atop it.

Bett walked across the room and sat in the rocking chair across from him. A book sat on an end table next to the chair, as did a teacup. I could imagine the two of them sitting there in companionable silence, reading and enjoying each other's presence without a word.

The only other place to sit in the room was the computer chair behind the desk. I decided not to presume and instead stood just inside the door with my hands folded behind my back.

"Thank you for talking to me," I said, taking the lead. "I know you haven't been thrilled with me lately."

Ted flashed a smile, while Bett merely nodded.

"As I told Bett, I was informed you both knew a man by the name of Wade Fink, that you worked with him."

Ted's head snapped back as if I'd struck him. "You're looking into Wade?"

"I am," I said. "I'd like to figure out who killed him and was hoping one of you could tell me something that might help."

"Wade Fink," Ted said with a sad shake of his head. "He was good people. Might have been a little too cocky at times, but he never hurt no one."

"Broke a few hearts," Bett said with a smile.

Their eyes met and something silent passed between them. With the sparkle in Bett's old eyes, I thought I knew what it was, but wasn't going to say it out loud.

"We worked with him," Ted admitted. "It was a long time ago. He did his job, and did it well. It was meaningless work, not like the bed-and-breakfast where we're actually trying to do something good. It was just a little stop and shop that closed up not long after Wade died. As I said, he was a good worker."

"But he sometimes got distracted," Bett added. "All the women loved him."

Even you? I wondered silently. "Did he favor any one woman over another?" I asked.

"Rita Jablonski," Bett said. "She had her hooks in him and he didn't even try to shake her off. He was beyond smitten. It was kind of nauseating to watch them together." She chuckled, telling me the last was in good humor.

"Other women tried to get his attention," Ted said with a sidelong look at his wife. "He wanted nothing to do with any of them. He never even let them flirt without telling them he was already attached. I think if he hadn't been murdered, those two would have gotten married."

My heart broke for Rita. She was alone now, all because someone came along and killed what very well might be the only man she'd truly loved.

"Were there jealous boyfriends?" I asked. "Did anyone confront him because their girlfriends were interested in him?"

"Some," Ted said. He rocked slowly in his rocker. "But it never got violent. Wade always made sure those men understood he had no interest in their girlfriends and wives. I'm not sure Wade ever raised a hand to anyone."

"Well, there was that one time . . ." Bett said.

"What one time?"

It was Ted who answered. "It had nothing to do with jealousy as far as I'm aware. It was a spat between friends."

"The fistfight?" I asked. "Someone told me Wade got into a fight with some of his friends."

"It wasn't some, just one," Ted said. "The others were there, of course—they were always hanging around—but they didn't step in. I'm the one who called the police. I was afraid that if it went on too long, someone might do something they'd later regret."

"It happened right in front of where we worked." Bett continued the story. "Wade was done for the evening and stepped outside to wait for Rita, who was supposed to meet him there. She was running a tad late, and while he waited, his friends showed up."

"There were words," Ted said.

"A lot of them," Bett agreed.

"Do you know what the fight was about?"

Ted shook his head. "We were inside when it started. I didn't realize anything was happening until the shouting alerted me to it."

"I saw who threw the first punch," Bett said. "It happened so fast, I wasn't sure if it was a real fight, or if they were just messing around like men sometimes did with their friends."

"Who threw the punch?" I asked.

Bett frowned, eyes going hazy. Ted's answer was slow, uncertain. "I think his name was Arnold. I didn't know them all that well."

"Arthur?" I asked. "Arthur Cantrell?"

"That might be it," Ted said. "The memory is a bit fuzzy, but I do recall his name starting with an *A*."

"He was arrested a few years later," Bett said. "I do re- member that."

"Arrested?" I asked, interest growing. "For attacking Wade?"

She shook her head. "No, it was something else. I can't remember the details, but do remember it being news for a few days. I think he went to prison, didn't he?"

"I believe so," Ted said. "It was for a violent crime of some sort. Probably another fight that went too far. Some men can't handle their tempers, especially if they had a little too much to drink."

"Was Arthur a drinker?"

Ted shrugged. "You'd have to ask him."

"I always wondered if that friend of Wade's was the one who killed him," Bett said. "It was a shame. Wade Fink didn't deserve to die, and if it was one of his friends who did it, it only makes it that much worse. If you can't trust your friends, who else is there?"

Ted murmured an agreement and lowered his head.

"How long before Wade was killed did this happen?" I asked.

"Oh, I'd say a week, maybe two."

I'd taken up enough of the Bunfords' time, so I thanked them and said my farewells. When I left, there were no warnings not to come back again, no threats that they'd call the police on me. I hoped that meant my ban was over. Maybe I'd stop by when this was all over and see if there was anything I could do to help them around the property. I didn't know anything about hedges, let alone how to trim them into the shape of animals, but I could always help with the painting.

I got into my car, mind turning over what I'd learned. Wade had stirred the pot by dating Rita and his friends weren't happy about it. Was that what got Arthur so fired up and caused the fight? If so, did Arthur take it a step further and then kill Wade for it a week later?

Checking the time, I decided there was one place where I could find out more about Arthur and his crimes, and see if somehow it could all be traced back to Wade Fink's murder. Besides, Patricia Dalton already wanted to talk to me about Jay Miller anyway. It would allow me to ask about both men at the same time.

11

The Pine Hills police station sat smack-dab in the middle of the downtown area. As it was on most days, the parking lot was mostly empty, with only a few cars in the lot that didn't belong to officers on the force.

As I parked, I noticed Paul Dalton's personal car sitting in the corner of the lot, next to one I knew to belong to John Buchannan. I didn't know which patrol car Paul used, however, so I couldn't be sure he was there until I went inside. I kind of hoped he was out so I could talk to his mom without my thoughts—and eyes—drifting to him.

It felt good to pass through the front doors of the station without it being because I was in some sort of trouble. I practically skipped across the threshold, to the front desk, where no one currently sat. In fact, there were no police officers evident at all.

"Huh," I said, glancing around the empty police station. I knew crime in Pine Hills was low, but this was ridiculous.

Before I could get myself into trouble and go wandering the halls to look for someone, the door to the police chief's office opened and four officers poured out, laughing and smiling, each carrying a small piece of cake on paper plates.

One of the officers stopped dead in his tracks when he saw me standing at the front desk.

"What did you do now?" John Buchannan asked. His customary scowl shot to his face the moment he realized it was me. It might have been intimidating if it wasn't for the small bit of icing stuck to the corner of his mouth.

"Nothing," I said. "I'm here to see Chief Dalton. She's expecting me."

His eyes narrowed and he said something to the woman next to him. I knew her too: Officer Becca Garrison. She nodded at whatever Buchannan said and then wandered over to her desk, where she proceeded to finish off her cake in two large bites. The other two cops paid me no mind, choosing to chat amongst themselves as they moved deeper into the station, leaving me to face off with Buchannan alone.

"What do you want to see her about?" he asked, walking over to the desk. He took a bite of cake before setting it aside and crossing his arms.

"She asked me to come," I said, eyeing the remains of his cake. I'd hardly eaten anything at all today and my stomach was starting to complain. "Was there a party?"

Buchannan actually moved his plate farther away from me, as if he thought I might try to steal it out from under him. "Why did she ask you here?" he asked, ignoring the second question. "Do I need to take you to the interrogation room?"

"Just let her know I'm here," I said. "We have something to discuss." And then, just so he knew, "There's no need for an interrogation room."

I expected him to argue that, too, but Buchannan

picked up his cake, and with a warning for me to stay put, he returned to Chief Dalton's office.

"Jerk," I muttered, and then corrected myself. Buchannan wasn't a bad guy. He just didn't like me always poking my nose into murder investigations. I couldn't fault him for that. I mean, solving crimes was *his* job, not mine.

Well, I did seem to be involved in the cases one way or the other, but that didn't mean I actually *enjoyed* it.

Who was I kidding? A part of me loved putting bad guys behind bars. The only difference between me and John Buchannan was he got paid for it.

While I waited for Buchannan to verify my story, I noted Officer Garrison was watching me. I waved, hoping she was back to liking me again. We had an on-again, off-again relationship, although we seemed to land on the off side of things more often than I'd like.

Garrison nodded her head once, acknowledging me, and then she looked away. It was as best as I could hope for, I supposed.

Buchannan returned a moment later, looking put out and was, unfortunately, sans cake.

"Fine," he said, sounding almost like a petulant child. I think he really was hoping to throw me out on my car. "You can go back."

"To her office?" I was actually surprised. The only places I ever found myself in the police station were the interrogation room and the cells. I'd expected Chief Dalton to come out and meet me, or maybe tell me to wait outside. This was definitely a big upgrade.

"It's what she said." Buchannan turned to Garrison. "Let's go."

I waited until both officers were gone before rounding the desk and heading to Chief Dalton's office. One of the other cops raised his eyebrows at me, but he didn't comment or try to stop me. At this point, everyone on the force knew me, so he probably figured I'd landed myself in hot water again and was going in for my quarterly reprimand.

"Ah, there you are," Patricia Dalton said when I entered her office. "Close the door behind you, would you?"

I did as she asked and then turned to face her, not quite sure what to do next.

"Take a seat." She motioned to a chair on the other side of the desk at which she sat. There were files stacked all over the place and about two dozen Post-its stuck to her monitor.

I eased slowly down into the chair, still half expecting her to yell at me, though I hadn't done anything wrong. Habit, I supposed.

My eyes immediately found the half-eaten sheet cake sitting on the desk amid the file folders. I could read the words *Hap* and *Birth* written in blue icing.

"It's your birthday?" I asked, shocked I hadn't known before now.

"Don't remind me," she said. "Take some if you want it. I don't need all the sugar."

She didn't need to tell me twice. The cake was already sliced into squares, so I snatched up a small paper plate and slid a corner piece onto it. Chief Dalton offered me a box of plastic forks and I took one of those, too.

I inhaled half my slice before taking a moment to breathe. The cake was really good and I was far hungrier than I'd realized. And, well, I had a notorious sweet tooth, so even if I was stuffed to the gills, I'd have eaten the cake without complaint.

"Thank you," I said, as soon as my mouth wasn't full. "And happy birthday."

She flashed me a smile that faded almost the second it appeared. "Have you made any progress on Wade's murder?"

With some regret, I set the cake aside. I'd finish it before I left, but I didn't want it to distract me during the conversation.

"Some," I said, feeling strangely like a real cop at that moment. "I'm hoping you'll be able to fill in a few blanks for me."

She nodded, as if she expected as much. "Shoot."

I decided to start with the most recent revelation first. "Do you remember anything about one of Wade Fink's friends getting arrested?"

"Which one?"

"Arthur Cantrell. All I was told was that it was a violent crime of some sort and that it didn't have anything to do with Wade."

Patricia nodded as I spoke. "It happened a few years after Wade's death," she said. "I can't tell you the details without looking it up, but I do remember it being a big deal. He nearly killed a man, if I'm remembering correctly. There was more to it than that, but I'd have to check the records to know what it was."

"I doubt it's important to Wade's murder," I said, though I *was* curious. If Arthur almost killed someone, that meant he was most definitely capable of murdering his friend.

"I agree," she said. "Arthur Cantrell isn't anyone's idea of a model citizen. He's had a few more brushes with the law over the years, but nothing like what happened when he'd gotten arrested. He has a temper. I'm sure if you've talked to him, you've noticed."

An image of Arthur's scowls flashed through my mind. "I have. It wasn't a pleasant experience."

"I wouldn't recommend talking to him alone if you can help it. Avoid him entirely if you can. You won't get anything from him."

"Do you think he knows who killed Wade?"

Chief Dalton shrugged. "Hard to say. I do know that if he does, and if it was one of his friends who did the deed, he'd never speak of it. He's protective of his friends, and even if that wasn't the case, he's downright contrary. He'd keep it to himself just to spite us."

I wondered if Wade had still been Arthur's friend at the time of his death. Could Arthur have attacked Wade, thinking he was doing it for his own good? Or had their fight ended their friendship, meaning Wade no longer belonged within Arthur's protections, which in turn, led to Wade's murder somehow?

"I was told Arthur and Wade got into a fight a week or two before Wade's death. Do you remember anything about that?"

Patricia's face clouded over. "Like when Arthur was arrested, I don't have the details, but I remember the fight. I could have answered that call, was on my way to do so when I got told to leave it to one of the men. It didn't seem right, but I did as I was commanded and backed off."

"Did Albie Bruce make the call to pull you off it?" I asked.

She surprised me by shaking her head. "He wouldn't have liked me going anywhere near an act of violence since I was a woman, but he would have allowed it since I was on duty and only a few blocks away at the time."

"Who took the call then?"

"Jay Miller."

I stared at her. There was that name again.

"That's the officer I asked you about earlier," I said.

"He was." She sat back in her chair. "Back then, he was pompous, egotistical, and as arrogant as you can imagine. That might sound like I'm reiterating the same description of the man, but he honestly encompassed all three."

"You speak of him in the past tense," I said. "Is he dead?"

"No, he's not dead. He still lives in Pine Hills and occasionally stops by here to make a nuisance of himself, but he's no longer on the force. He was in his late thirties when Wade was killed, and quit the force soon after, well before retirement. He hasn't been involved with police work since, yet he insists he knows how to handle things better than I do. He always believed he should have become police chief after Chief Bruce retired."

"But you got it instead."

Her smile was savage. "Damn right, I did."

I could only imagine the hurdles she'd have had to leap to earn the job. It probably cost her some friendships within the force, and likely in her personal life.

Come to think of it, almost everyone in the Pine Hills police force was my age or younger. There might be a few older police officers around, but no one near Chief Dalton's age. Did that mean everyone she'd worked with back then had quit? Could it have been because of Wade's murder? Or was I looking too much into it?

"Jay Miller is a dangerous man, Krissy," Patricia said. "He's not a killer, so don't get that idea, but if he puts his mind to ruining you, he'll find a way to do it. He'd ended a few promising careers in his time."

"He was the cop who answered the call when Wade Fink was murdered," I said, thinking it through.

"He was. He was also friends with those men—Wade's friends."

"Wait," I said, sitting up. "He was *friends* with them? Was he friends with Wade, too? And if so, wasn't having him on the scene a conflict of interest or something?"

Chief Dalton spread her hands. "This is a small town. It was even smaller back then. Everyone knew everyone else, so it wasn't like we had someone we could call that could go in with fresh eyes and a clear head."

"But if he was friends with them . . ."

"I know what you're thinking," she said. "Honestly, I've considered it, too. Jay was vocal about what he thought about Wade Fink. I always suspected him of giving inside information to the press whenever it suited him. There was a reporter who always knew more than he should, who would use that information to attack Wade and anyone else he didn't like."

My head was spinning. "A reporter?" I asked. "Do you know his name?"

Imagine my total lack of surprise when she said, "Larry Ritchie."

Larry had said Jay used to give him a call whenever something happened in Pine Hills worth reporting, but hadn't mentioned Jay slipping him inside information.

He also hadn't mentioned Jay and the Coffee Drinkers were friends.

Could Arthur and his friends have gone to Jay to tell him something unflattering about Wade, something that might have even been a lie? Could Jay have taken that information, embellished it, and passed it on to Larry Ritchie? And if so, could whatever was said have led to Wade's murder?

That was a lot of assumptions, but I found it plausible. Some people were perfectly content believing whatever they are told, even if it is a pack of lies, just as long as it coincides with their worldview.

I was so lost in thought, it took me a moment to realize Chief Dalton was still speaking.

"I want you to be careful," she said. "Jay Miller didn't want anyone looking into Wade Fink's murder but himself when it happened. He claimed it was because he was far more determined to find the killer because they were closer than the rest of us. I imagine he wouldn't want anyone looking into it today, even though he's not involved in the force anymore. I don't want you talking to him, do you hear? He will find a way to make your life miserable if you try."

There was more to it than that, I could hear it in her voice. I wasn't sure if it was guilt, or if she was afraid that Jay had covered up the murder to protect one of his friends. The only way to find out was to ask.

"Do you think he had something to do with Wade's death? Or know who killed him?"

"Keep clear of Jay Miller, Ms. Hancock," she said. "You know the way out."

I rose slowly. I wanted to press her, to force her to tell me every last suspicion she had, but knew I'd be wasting my time if I tried. She wasn't hiding anything that she thought was important to my little side investigation. If she suspected Jay Miller had anything to do with Wade's death, she would have done something about it.

Then again, had she tried, and failed? It was entirely possible she'd brought her concerns up with Albie Bruce when the murder originally happened. Could he have shot her down?

Or was there indeed a cover-up here, one that originated from the Pine Hills police station?

I left Chief Dalton's office without finishing off the cake like I'd promised myself I would; I'd lost the taste for it. I waited until I was outside the station before I took out my phone and dialed.

I got voicemail, which I'd expected.

"Paul, it's Krissy. Can you meet me at Death by Coffee as soon as you get this? Or call me if you can't so I'm not waiting forever. There's someone I want to talk to, and I don't want to do it alone. It might help solve an old, unsolved murder case. Thanks. Bye."

I clicked off and took a deep breath. When I'd first set out to solve Wade's murder, I hadn't expected to find much after all this time.

But now, it appeared as if I was uncovering a dark underbelly to the town I loved. I was afraid that if I dug too deep, I might never be able to look at Pine Hills—or the people who lived here—the same ever again.

12

The afternoon rush at Death by Coffee was over by the time I walked through the door. Vicki was behind the counter, busily cleaning, while both Lena and Beth were upstairs, rearranging some books. The dining room was clean, with only a couple of regulars sitting in their usual spots. They waved to me as I entered, before going back to their conversations.

"You're not working today, are you?" Vicki asked, when she saw me. "I thought today was your day off."

"It is," I said. "I'm meeting Paul here." Hopefully. He had yet to text or call, so as far as I knew, he hadn't gotten my voicemail.

"Really?" Vicki leaned against the counter with a smirk. "Big plans?"

"It's about the murder," I said. And then, because I couldn't resist, "The big plans are for tonight."

"Oh?" The smirk widened to a full-on grin. "And what plans might that be?"

"We're going out." I might be in my forties, yet I could feel my face flush like I was a teenager talking about her first date. "Paul asked if I wanted to go to dinner and I said yes."

"Finally!" Vicki said loud enough that everyone in the store looked our way. She lowered her voice. "Really, Krissy, it's about time you two stopped pretending."

"We weren't pretending."

"Uh-huh. You've been mooning after him ever since you two met, and he's been the same way about you. It sometimes felt like you two were the only ones who didn't realize you had it bad for one another."

I almost argued that I didn't have it all that bad, but realized I'd be lying to not just Vicki, but to myself. Every time I even talked to a good-looking guy, Paul would drift through my head and I'd immediately feel guilty, like I was betraying him somehow. Even when I was dating Will Foster, I couldn't help but think of Paul every now and again.

"I'm sure you're exaggerating," I said. "Paul's not *that* interested in me. He would have made a move by now if he was."

She gave me a flat look.

"What?"

"Do you really think you'd get away with as much as you do if Paul didn't have the hots for you?"

"I have no idea what you mean."

"Right. You just bully your way in on murder investigations without much more than a slap on the wrist when you do something wrong, but, no, you don't get special treatment." Vicki shook her head and turned away with a grin. "I've got to get some more coffee on. You think about it for a little bit, and I'm sure you'll see that I'm right."

I stood there, not sure if I should be offended, or if I should feel like an idiot. Okay, maybe I did notice how

Paul looked at me, and how we both tiptoed around each other, as if we were afraid that if one of us did or said the wrong thing, we'd be tearing each other's clothes off.

Or does that make it the right thing?

Either way, Vicki was right; without Paul bailing me out of trouble every time I made a mistake, or him letting me in on things I shouldn't be party to, I'd never have helped solve so many crimes. Heck, I'd probably be in jail by now. If John Buchannan had his way, I *would* be sitting in a cell with my name on it. He'd locked me up a few times already, albeit temporarily.

I slid behind the counter, snatched a cookie from the display, and dropped it into a cup, which I then filled with coffee. I carried my prize to a table near the door to sit and wait for Paul.

As much as I wanted to focus on where my relationship with Paul Dalton might be headed, I forced myself to shift gears and focus on Wade Fink's murder instead. I could worry about my feelings—and emotions—later.

While I waited, I searched for Arthur Cantrell's address on my phone, and was surprised by how easily I found it. I typed a note into my phone so I wouldn't lose it and then sat back to wait.

I was halfway through my coffee when the door opened and Paul walked through. He was dressed in his uniform, complete with his wide-brimmed police hat. He paused just inside the door and glanced around until he saw me sitting right there. A smile immediately lit up his face.

"There you are," he said, sliding into the seat across from me. He removed his hat and set it on the table between us. "I got your message." The smile slipped somewhat. "What murder are you talking about?"

I spent the next ten minutes telling Paul about Wade

Fink's life and death. I'd already mentioned it to him once, but it had been in passing. He listened attentively, though his smile had faded completely by the time I was finished.

"Should you be looking into this?" he asked.

"It's for Rita and Eleanor," I said. "Rita deserves to know the truth, and I think it would be a good way to honor Eleanor's memory. Besides, Chief Dalton signed off on it."

Paul winced at mention of his mother's name, but nodded. "I suppose you realize how dangerous it can be poking around in people's lives?"

"I know." Boy, did I ever. "But this is an old case. The killer might already be dead or have moved out of Pine Hills long ago. If someone knows something, I have to ask." And then, because I really wanted him to help me willingly, "Your mom really does think it's a good idea. I've gotten quite a bit of information from her." I left out the bit about her warning me to be careful and to avoid a certain former police officer. No sense causing him undue worry.

Paul ran his fingers through his hair and sat back with a sigh. "Okay, tell me about this guy you want to talk to who you think can help solve a murder that the professionals couldn't crack." I might have been offended if his eyes weren't sparkling in mild amusement.

"His name is Arthur Cantrell. He's a member of that group, the Coffee Drinkers, I told you about. He was one of Wade's friends."

"I see. And you think he had something to do with the murder?"

"I'm not sure. He and Wade got into a big fight a week or so before Wade's death, and I wonder if it led to either Arthur killing him directly, or being a part of it somehow.

Arthur got into trouble a few years later for a violent crime of some kind, but I don't have the details on that yet."

"And you think talking to this guy is a good idea?"

"I do," I said. "I've talked to him before, but he was with his friends at the time and didn't do much more than grouch at me the entire conversation. I'm hoping if we catch him alone, he'd be more willing to talk. And with you at my side, I figure it might cause him to worry or let something slip if he *did* have something to do with the murder. If he did kill Wade, you'd be there to keep me from getting myself into too much trouble."

The smile finally returned. "It's about time you started thinking about your safety."

I returned his smile. "I have my moments."

We grinned at each other for a long couple of seconds. My heart fluttered in my chest and something in the pit of my stomach started churning. I wasn't sure if I was going to be sick, or if I was going to faint dead away.

Paul broke the moment by looking away. "Let me hit the bathroom real quick and I'll drive you over. I have some time, so we can visit this Arthur guy now if you want?"

"Great!" I said, surprised at how easy it was to convince him to help, though, I supposed after Vicki's comments, I shouldn't have been. "I'll be here."

Paul rose and headed to the restrooms on the other side of Death by Coffee. The moment he was gone, Vicki appeared, a question in her eye, as well as on her lips.

"Well?"

"Well what?" I asked. "He's going to help me with an interview."

"Just like that?" I could tell by her smile, what she really meant was, "I told you so."

"Yeah, yeah," I said, finishing off my coffee. I didn't

have time to scoop out the soggy cookie, which was a shame. It was often the best part. I settled on tipping back the cup and sliding what little I could into my mouth before rising and tossing the remains away.

"Mason and I are going to be going on a double date with Charlie Yow and his wife next weekend," Vicki said, following me over. "You should come and bring Paul. We'd love to have you."

"We'd be imposing," I said. Charlie was Mason's best friend and had been his best man at the wedding. He'd walked me down the aisle, but otherwise, I didn't know much about the man.

"You know that's not true. Mason told me to invite you, even if you had to come alone. He said he could always hook you up with one of his friends if need be, but now that you're actually going out with Paul, there'll be no need."

"I'm not going *out* with him," I said. "We're going on a date."

Vicki rolled her eyes. "Ask him. Next weekend. It starts at seven."

"I'll ask," I said. "But I can't promise he'll want to come."

"He will." And with that, she spun and headed back behind the counter.

Paul returned then and scooped up his hat. "Ready?"

I regarded Vicki a moment before answering with a distracted, "Yeah."

We left Death by Coffee and got into Paul's cruiser. It felt strange riding in the front of a police car rather than the back, but it *would* make our visit to Arthur Cantrell feel a little more official. I pulled up Arthur's address on my phone, showed it to Paul, and then sat back for the ride.

"I was thinking about Geraldo's for tonight," Paul said after a few minutes on the road.

"Geraldo's?" I asked, surprised. I kind of thought he'd take me to one of his favorite places to eat: J&E's Banyon Tree. It wasn't fancy, but he found it comforting. Then again, with my history there, it was no wonder he'd found an alternative.

"Is that okay? I haven't been there yet and have heard good things."

"Yeah, it's great. I really like the food."

"Good." He smiled. "A part of me was afraid you might not like it."

Not like it? I was through the roof he was taking me to the nicest place in town. Of course, now, I was going to have to plan on something a little more elegant to wear.

I spent the rest of the ride planning my outfit, mentally dismissing every single one that came to mind. I wasn't a dress-up kind of woman, which only made it harder. Give me jeans and a T-shirt and I'm good. Ask me to wear a dress, and I suddenly feel awkward and a little like a fraud.

Paul pulled to a stop in front of a small house just outside of town. A stack of firewood leaned dangerously near the steps. It looked like a stiff breeze could blow it over. It appeared as if the wood had sat there for years; it was almost gray in hue.

"This is it," Paul said, getting out of the car. "You ready for this?"

I nodded, nervous. Paul had yet to meet Arthur Cantrell, but I had, and none of those interactions had been pleasant. Now that I was here, I was questioning the wisdom of asking him about Wade's murder, even with a cop in tow.

Paul led the way to the front door and knocked. I was happy to let him take the lead. I stood behind him, hoping I'd be invisible if and when Arthur answered.

It took a few long seconds before the door banged open and Arthur Cantrell peered out at us. His gaze slid right over Paul and landed on me, as if it had been drawn there. When he saw me meekly hiding behind Paul, he scowled.

"What do *you* want?"

I'd hoped Paul would speak up and draw Arthur's ire away from me, but instead, he looked at me expectantly.

It *was* my investigation, I supposed, but still, I didn't like being thrust into the spotlight, even if it was my own doing. "I have a few more questions I'd like to ask you about Wade Fink, Mr. Cantrell. Can we come in to talk?"

"You brought a cop?" His gaze flickered to Paul, then back to me.

"He drove me over," I said, smiling for all I was worth. Maybe if I was nice enough, some of it would rub off on Arthur. "I just need a few minutes."

Arthur's eyes narrowed briefly before he sighed, shrugged, and then turned and walked away, leaving the door hanging open.

"I guess that's your answer," Paul said. He sounded mildly amused. "Seems like a nice guy."

"He's a barrel of laughs."

I followed after Paul, who led the way inside. I was immediately struck by how, I don't know, *country* the house was. I counted at least five shotguns hanging on the wall amid a smattering of animal heads. I wasn't thrilled by the heads, but was glad to note they were mostly deer and elk. Glassy eyes watched over us as we moved to sit around an unlit fireplace. The furniture was unsurprisingly done in a camouflage print.

"Speak your peace," Arthur said.

I decided to cut right to the chase. I didn't like the atmosphere in Arthur Cantrell's house. I felt like I was being watched, even though I knew the animals watching me were dead. Arthur's attitude didn't help matters.

"When we spoke earlier, you didn't mention you and Wade got into a fight a week or two before his death."

"Is that an accusation of some kind?" Arthur asked. "Because, if it is, I'll kindly ask you to get lost."

"It's not an accusation," I said, glancing at Paul, who was sitting upright, tense. The humor had left him the moment he got a good look at Arthur's house. I assumed he felt as oppressed as I did. "It was merely an observation."

Arthur ran his tongue over his teeth before he shrugged. "We fought. It happens."

"The police were called."

"And? It got out of hand. So what? Blood gets hot and the next thing you know, it gets spilled." He seemed to realize how I might take that, so he added, "I got a few good licks in on him, busted his nose."

"What was the fight about, Mr. Cantrell?" Paul asked.

Those hard eyes swiveled Paul's way. "Wade liked to rub people the wrong way on purpose. If he could get under your skin, and knew he could get a rise out of you, he'd do it. That night, he did so. I rose to the bait and we scuffled."

"Was it about Rita?" I asked.

"It was always about Rita." Arthur practically spat her name. "Everything Wade did was about her. He got on my nerves that night and I snapped. Big deal."

"You've gotten in trouble for violence before, haven't you, Mr. Cantrell?" Paul asked.

"And?"

"I'm just wondering if you 'snap' often." Paul gave all the appearances that we were having a casual conversation, but I could tell he was thinking the same thing I was: If

Arthur was quick to temper, could he have gone too far and killed his friend?

"When people ask me stupid questions, I do," Arthur said. "Why are you asking me about that? It's in the past, and quite frankly, none of your business."

"What did you get arrested for?" I asked, causing Arthur's glare to return to me.

He sat there, fuming, for a good long minute. I was almost positive he wasn't going to answer when he finally relented.

"Guy cut me off after I'd had a few too many. I rear-ended him. He called me a few choice names. I returned the favor. When that didn't feel like enough, we got into it."

"You fought?" Paul asked.

"Of course we fought! He blamed me for something that was obviously his fault."

"You don't get arrested and sent to prison for a fight," I said.

He bared his teeth at me in what I supposed was as close as he could come to a smile. "You do when the guy can no longer walk and when his own mother couldn't recognize him."

"Did you kill him?" Paul asked.

"No. And I didn't kill Wade, either. Wade and I might have been on the outs, but I wouldn't have killed him. If you must know, I'd been thinking about him the night I got arrested. I drank too much because of it, shouldn't have been behind the wheel, and things got out of hand. As I said, it happens." He stood. "But I'm not a murderer."

Both Paul and I rose. I don't think either of us were comfortable with this man towering over us, not with his guns hanging on the walls within easy reach. It made me wonder why a man convicted of a violent crime was allowed to have so many weapons lying around.

"Mr. Cantrell—" Paul started.

"No, I'm done answering questions. I'd like you to leave."

I wanted to object, but Paul nodded his head and moved for the door. I followed after him, not wanting to be left alone in the room with Arthur Cantrell, even for a few seconds. The man seemed to get angrier and angrier every time I saw him.

"Why didn't you press him?" I asked once we were back outside. Arthur slammed the door behind us, causing me to jump.

"He wasn't going to talk," Paul said. "And this isn't an official police investigation. We were guests in his home, asking uncomfortable questions. He had every right to kick us out."

I didn't like it, but Paul was right. "Do you believe him?" I asked, getting into the police cruiser.

"I don't know," Paul said. "But I don't want you coming back here. He's volatile, and he's proven he can't control his temper."

"Don't worry about me," I said. "I'm not coming back here." And if I did, I'd make sure I had an army at my back.

13

The rest of the day dragged by. I felt like I should be doing something, but was at a loss as what to do next. I could have kept poking around those who knew Wade Fink, but how long could I do that before someone poked back? I was already worried I'd gone too far with Arthur Cantrell. Did I really want to add any more names to the list of people who might want to do me harm?

Misfit was snoozing on the couch next to me as I flipped through television channels. I wasn't actually paying attention to what I was watching, and I wasn't looking for anything in particular, but it kept my hands busy, while it allowed my mind to wander.

Who killed Wade Fink?

And worse: How many people were in on it?

It seemed like every time I talked to someone, one more suspect got added to the list. A lot of people had disapproved of Wade's choice in girlfriends, and any number of them could have decided to do something about it.

"Would someone really kill over a relationship?" I asked out loud. "It wasn't like he was stealing someone else's girlfriend."

Misfit lifted his head, huffed, and then spun in a circle so his back was to me.

"Lot of help you are," I muttered before turning off the television and tossing the remote aside.

I glanced at the clock and sighed. Paul wasn't due to pick me up for another two and a half hours. That was a lot of time to wait, stewing in my own thoughts. By the time he got there, I'd be half crazy.

I'd already gotten cleaned up and dressed for the evening, which had been a mistake. Not only had Misfit tried to sleep on my lap, shedding his orange fur all over my dress, but I also was limited in what I could do with my time. I wasn't a slob or overly clumsy, but I also knew my luck. The moment I tried to do something potentially messy, I would be wearing whatever I'd touched.

Needing a distraction, I picked up my phone and dialed. It rang twice before a much beloved, raspy voice came over the line.

"Krissy! It's good to hear from you."

"Hi, Dad." I moved to the dining room and sat at the table, some of the tension already bleeding away. "How are you and Laura doing?" Laura Dresden was his girlfriend.

"Good, good." He groaned as he settled down for our conversation. "She's out right now or I'd put her on. She's been itching to talk to you about coming out this way for a visit."

"It's been a long time since I've been home," I said. It's funny; I still thought of the place I grew up as home, even though I was now a permanent resident of Pine Hills. I suppose some places would always *be* home, no matter how far away I went.

"California is a long way from where you are," Dad said.

"We understand it's not easy to make time to stop by for a visit. It's not like you can just pop on over anytime you please." He laughed.

"I should do better." And I meant it. Dad wasn't getting any younger. While his relationship with Laura had rejuvenated him, it still would be a good idea for me to pay him a visit a little more often.

But, unfortunately, it seemed like every time we planned on getting together, something always got in the way.

"It's fine," Dad said. "You've got a busy life. You don't need to drop everything for me."

"I'll make time soon. I promise." And then, because the direction of the conversation was getting me down, I changed the subject. "How's your writing going?"

Dad had semi-retired from mystery writing once, but the bug had gotten to him again. He was back to writing near full time, which was probably a good thing. It kept his mind active, and it genuinely seemed to make him happier when he was working.

"Great, actually. I just finished a new project. I've shot it off to Cameron." Cameron Little was his literary agent, a man I'd met once, who seemed decent enough. He was a huge upgrade over Dad's last agent, that was for sure. "Here's hoping I've still got it."

"I'm sure you do."

There was a pause where I wasn't quite sure what to say next. Dad read far more into that little pause than anything I'd said thus far, which was one of the things that made me love him even more.

"What's on your mind, Buttercup?" he asked, shifting to my childhood nickname. He'd finally started using my name every once in a while, but I'd forever be Buttercup to him.

"Nothing." Even *I* wasn't convinced by that.

"Mmhmm. Tell me. You'll feel better."

"Nothing actually *happened,*" I said. "Well, I mean, my neighbor, Eleanor Winthrow, passed away. You remember her, right?"

"The older woman who used to spy on you?"

"Yeah." I couldn't help but smile at the memory. It used to annoy me while she was doing it, but now that she was gone, I kind of missed it. "Anyway, I was helping her daughter, Jane, clean up the house when she told me about a murder that happened over thirty years ago."

I could hear the excitement in Dad's voice when he said, "A murder? Unsolved?"

"Unsolved."

"Well, now, you're going to have to tell me all about it." I did just that.

Dad listened attentively as I went through the whole tale—what I knew of it, at least. Talking it through helped ease my mind, but I was no closer to coming up with a solid suspect. Since Dad was a mystery writer, and he would love to solve a mystery of his own, I hoped he'd use that sharp mind of his and would spot something I'd missed.

"Do you think one of his friends did it?" Dad asked when I was done.

"I'm not sure. I haven't had the chance to talk to the police officer who was on the scene, but he was friends with the Coffee Drinkers. It makes me wonder if he knows more about what happened than what he'd let on. I mean, could he really arrest a friend for a murder that all of them thought justified?"

"It's hard to say," Dad said. "Especially in a small town. People are closer together, and I don't just mean in proximity. And since everyone tends to know everyone else, things get buried just a little more often."

I thought about it. If I found out Vicki kept a body in her basement, would I be able to call the police on her? Or would I try to pretend I'd never seen it? Without actually being in that situation, I wasn't sure which way I'd lean. "Could it be a cover-up?" I asked.

"It's always possible, Buttercup, but be careful about jumping to conclusions before you have all the facts. Just because he was friends with the suspects, it doesn't mean he would help them cover up a crime. This guy was a man of the law, and some people value their work above their relationships."

"I know," I said, deflating. "I really need to find this Jay Miller and talk to him. The police chief warned me against it, and I'd like to abide by her wishes. . . ."

"I can hear the *but* in your voice."

"But if he knows what happened, I can't just let it slide," I said. "It's possible he's no longer friends with the Coffee Drinkers, so perhaps he'd be willing to talk about the murder now that some time has passed."

"As I said, be careful, Buttercup. A murder that's been unsolved for thirty years has baggage that builds up over time. If he *did* cover up the murder, then it might have weighed on him all these years. He might not like you sniffing around, threatening to bring light to something he's kept in the dark for decades."

"I'll be careful," I said, though at this point, I knew I was going to have to find Jay Miller and make him talk to me. The only question would be whether I'd take Paul along with me or go it alone. I knew which would be safest, but would a former cop talk if a current cop was there? I doubted it, especially if he'd committed a crime of his own.

Dad and I said our good-byes and I hung up feeling much better. I might not know who killed Wade Fink, but I felt I was on the right track. There was a chance he might not have been killed because of his relationship with Rita, but that didn't mean his friends didn't know why someone had it in for him.

But how to make them talk?

An idea formed. Checking the clock to make sure I still had plenty of time, I went online in search of a number. It didn't take me long to find it. I memorized the number, then closed the tab, but before I could dial, there was a knock at my door.

My heart fluttered. Could Paul have shown up early? If so, why?

A new thought hit before I could make a move toward the door. *What if it's someone who doesn't like me looking into Wade's murder?*

Misfit was standing in the living room, his fur standing on end, eyes wide. The knock had spooked him, just as much as it had me.

All the talk of murder had me paranoid, so I slipped into the kitchen and grabbed a knife before I made my way to the door. The knock came again, this time louder. It was followed by a voice calling my name.

The tension bled from me and was replaced by annoy-ance as I opened the door to Robert Dunhill, my ex from California who'd followed me all the way to Ohio in an ill-fated attempt to win me back. He'd failed in that regard, but had decided he liked it in Pine Hills well enough that he'd stayed.

Robert was grinning from ear to ear and dancing from foot to foot. His gaze flickered to the knife in my hand, but it didn't faze him. The guy not only thought he was

God's gift to women, but he also believed he was near invincible.

"Hey, Kris," he said. "Mind if I come in? I have something I'd like to ask you."

I cringed at the shortened name, but stepped aside. "Make it quick," I said. "I've got somewhere to be." I hoped. Time was quickly ticking away, and I didn't plan on being late for my date with Paul.

Robert slid past me and into my house. The last time he was there, he'd come begging me to help him beat a murder charge. He'd been half frozen from the snow and miserable, and despite how unhappy I was with him—he'd cheated on me before I'd moved to Pine Hills—I'd decided to help.

He waltzed into the living room and was nosing around when I joined him. Misfit was long gone, likely hiding in my bedroom.

"Robert," I said, hand finding my hips. "Why are you here?" It was then I realized he was alone. "Where's Trisha?"

"She's at work," he said. Trisha was his latest girlfriend, and somehow, against all odds, she'd stuck with him. Even though it was hard for me to believe, it appeared as if Robert had changed and his cheating ways were over.

"So, why are you here?"

Robert turned to face me. He had a small black box in his hand.

"What is that?" I asked in a squeak. I knew exactly what was in the velvety little black box and my throat constricted, fear of what he might say making me near panic.

He opened the box to reveal a diamond ring. It wasn't big by anyone's standards, but it was still beautiful.

I stared at it, openmouthed, completely at a loss as to what to say. He couldn't be thinking what I thought he was thinking. I mean, we were over, had been for a long time. And I was almost positive he'd come to terms with that fact.

"Well?" he asked, holding the box, and the ring inside it, out to me.

"Well what?" I asked, making no move to take it.

"What do you think?"

"It's a lovely ring." I met his eye. "Why are you showing me a ring?"

"Because I want to marry Trisha."

I practically sagged to the floor in relief. I wouldn't have put it past Robert to come begging me to take him back, despite how our lives had diverged. He'd stopped asking me to give him another chance a long time ago, but it was hard to reconcile the new Robert with the old in my mind.

"I haven't asked her yet," he said. "I've been saving up for like a year now, and decided it was time to take the plunge. I know it's not much . . ."

"It's perfect," I said, and I meant it.

He grinned. "Well, I wanted to come here and ask you if it was okay with you if I ask her."

My brow furrowed. "Ask me? Why?"

He snapped the box shut and shoved the ring into his pocket. "We've got a history, right? I mean, we can't just ignore that."

"Our history *is* history," I said. "You don't need my permission for anything."

He shrugged. "I know that, I guess. But it didn't feel right. If it wasn't for you, I wouldn't be here to ask her now. I thought it best if I stopped by to check to make sure you'd be okay with me marrying Trisha."

"It's okay, Robert," I said. And then I did something

I thought I'd never do again; I reached out and rested a hand on his shoulder. "It's more than okay—it's a fantastic idea. Ask her."

He met my eye for a heartbeat and then rushed forward to wrap me in a hug. "Thank you, Krissy. You don't know how much your acceptance means to me."

I hugged him back, genuinely happy for him. Robert had made mistakes. A *lot* of mistakes. But he was working to make himself a better person. I had to respect that.

We parted and I hurriedly wiped away a tear that had somehow gotten into my eye.

"When are you going to ask her?" I asked.

"Tonight, after she's off. I'm taking her out, going big, you know?"

My heart did a hiccup. "Taking her out? Where?" *Please don't say Geraldo's.*

"Place in Levington called Le Petit. It's French."

I breathed a sigh of relief. "It sounds lovely." I took him by the arm and guided him to the door. I still had one more thing I wanted to do before Paul arrived, and the minutes were quickly draining away. "Good luck tonight, Robert. You'll have to let me know what she says."

"You'll be the first to know," he said.

Robert practically skipped to his car. He waved at me, and then grinned when I gave him two thumbs-up. As soon as he backed out of my driveway, I had my phone in hand and was dialing. I still had two hours and I planned on using them to the fullest.

"Hi," I said as soon as the call was answered. "It's Krissy Hancock. I was hoping we could talk about Wade Fink and his murder."

There was a pause before a timid, "When?"

"Tonight," I said. "Now?"

Another long pause. I waited it out, knowing that if I pressed, he very well might balk.

"Okay," came the reply. "Meet me in the parking lot of the Banyon Tree in fifteen minutes." The line went dead.

As I snatched up my purse and keys, Misfit sauntered back into the room, head on a swivel.

"He's gone," I told him. "And I've got to go."

He swished his tail, headed into the kitchen to check to make sure I was leaving him some food. He turned to face me once he verified I wasn't going to try to starve him.

"I'll be back in an hour. If Paul shows up, let him in."

Misfit did what any cat would do when confronted with an ounce of responsibility: He sat down to wash his back end.

"Thanks for the help," I muttered. I left my cat to his bath and then was on my way to talk to a man about a murder.

14

Only a few cars sat in J&E's parking lot. There was still quite a bit of light, so my clandestine meeting wasn't quite as thrilling as it might have been deeper into the evening. I was parked in the shadiest corner of the lot, beneath an old tree that was slowly drooping toward the pavement. Within the next year or so, no one would be able to park in that space, not unless someone removed the tree or cut it back.

The door to the diner opened and I sat up straighter, expecting Eddie Banyon, but it was only an older couple, walking arm and arm after their meal. They looked content, happy. It made me think of Paul and our dinner in a little over an hour, and I hoped that when we left, we looked as happy as the two of them.

I sank back down in my seat and tried to look inconspicuous while I continued to wait for Eddie. With every second that passed, Judith Banyon could happen upon me. I doubted she'd take kindly to me lurking in her parking lot, even if I had a good reason to be there.

Another five minutes passed and I started to wonder if something had come up and Eddie wasn't going to be able to meet with me. It took fifteen minutes to get here, and it would take another fifteen to get home. That gave me an hour for Eddie to join me, for us to have our conversation, and then to finish readying myself for my date with Paul.

Normally, that was more than enough time, but tonight, I wanted the date to go perfectly, and didn't want to look—or feel—rushed.

Staring at the door to the diner was getting me nowhere, so I pulled out my phone and did a quick search for Jay Miller.

Unfortunately, there were about a million Jay Millers on Facebook, and while there were tons of articles mentioning the name, none of them were what I was looking for. And then, when I added Pine Hills to the search criteria, all I got back were the articles I'd already read.

"Who are you?" I muttered, flipping through pages of useless information. Jay was an older man, sure, and he was a former cop, but to have zero online presence? You'd think there'd be something more about him, even if it was a retirement announcement, but as far as I could tell, there was nothing.

The passenger door opened, startling a yelp from me, and I dropped my phone. It hit my thigh, and then somehow managed to turn sideways so it slid right between the seat and the cupholders.

Eddie Banyon looked frazzled as he closed the door and hunkered down next to me. "Couldn't you have faced the car the other way?" he asked, eyes focused on the front of his diner as if he feared who might come out of it next.

"Sorry." I tried to slide my hand into the gap so I could reach my phone, but all I could manage was to get my fingers in. The tip of my middle finger brushed my phone, but I couldn't get hold of it, not sitting as I was. I gave up. "I wasn't sure how you'd arrive."

"I work for a living, Ms. Hancock," he said. "I should be working now. If Judith knew I was talking to you, she'd kill me."

"Well, thank you for taking the time to talk to me." Considering his wife's intense dislike of me, I was actually surprised he'd been willing to talk to me at all. Eddie had always struck me as something of a victim. He often bowed down to whatever Judith wanted, refusing to stand up for himself.

But he was here with me now, telling me there was some fight within him. Hopefully, that meant whatever he had to say was important to my investigation.

"I don't know what you expect from me," he said. "I had nothing to do with Wade's death."

"He was a customer of yours."

"So?" Eddie wrung his hands together. I couldn't tell if it was because of the topic of our conversation, or out of fear of his wife. It was probably a little of both.

"So, I know how it is. I own a café. People talk and you can't help but overhear things. You see how they are together, can determine who are friends and who might be on the outs. Their lives, in some ways, become your life. The regulars become almost like family, and Wade Fink *was* a regular, was he not?"

"He was," Eddie said. "He was peculiar, but was a good man. Don't get me wrong, he made mistakes. Some of them big ones, but that doesn't mean he deserved what happened to him. I suppose some people couldn't handle his eccentricities."

"He liked French roast coffee," I said, remembering what I'd been told by the Coffee Drinkers.

"He did." Eddie seemed to relax a little. "It was one of his oddities. I had no problem making sure we always had some in stock, though, back then, it was strange that anyone cared what kind of roast we used. It wasn't like today with all these new fancy flavors." He sighed. "He had some of my coffee on him when he died."

"Was there anything else about him that stood out?" I asked. "Anything that might have led to his death?"

Eddie shrugged, looked down at his hands. "He was flashy. He liked to show off, make himself seem more important than others around him. I don't mean it like I thought he was conceited. I honestly think it had more to do with the fact he had money and was always in the public eye. Either way, people didn't like how he held himself. They thought he was an arrogant jerk, when in reality, he just didn't know how to act around others without making himself stand out."

"Were there ever any fights at the diner involving Wade?" I asked. "With his friends or other customers?"

Eddie's lips pressed together, going almost white, while he stared toward the Banyon Tree.

I felt for him; I really did. It wasn't easy talking about something that might have happened at your place of business. I still hated it any time anyone brought up the deaths that had taken place near Death by Coffee, let alone the one that had happened inside.

But I needed to know, especially if whatever had happened led to Wade's death.

"Please, Eddie," I said. "I'm trying to help. I don't want to get innocent people into trouble, but I do want to find Wade's killer. If you know who it is, or who it might be, you should tell me. He deserves justice, even after all this time."

"That's just the thing—I don't know anything. There were arguments, sure, but that happens everywhere. Wade was involved in some, wasn't around for others. And back then, people were pretty hot about his choice in women."

"You mean Rita?"

He nodded. "She didn't come around much—still doesn't—but her presence could be felt even when she wasn't there." His soft voice flowed through the car, almost soothingly. He plucked at his old sweater, refused to meet my eye.

"It caused tension among the group, didn't it?"

"It did. There were times Wade left them steaming. Other times, he left in a huff and they laughed it up afterward. I sometimes wondered if their disapproval was all for show, that because of her age, they felt the need to pretend to be angry with him, but were only just teasing. I never got the impression there was any real malice in the fights."

There was a long stretch of silence where Eddie continued to work at his hands. Then, he turned in his seat so he could look at me in the eye when he spoke. "And then he was murdered."

I was shocked to see tears in his eyes.

I reached across the seat and took one of his old, weathered hands. He squeezed my fingers, closed his eyes briefly, and then went on.

"I overheard you talking to Wade's old friends this morning," Eddie said. "I heard what they told you." He released my hand, resumed picking at his sweater. "My memory isn't what it once was, but I'm pretty sure one of them wasn't completely honest with you."

"Who?" Arthur's name was on my lips, but I refrained from speaking it. I didn't want to lead Eddie on, or distract him.

"Cliff Watson. He left when he said he did, but he wasn't home all day like he claimed."

"You saw him afterward?" I asked.

"He came back to the diner about an hour, hour and a half later. He looked sick, just like he claimed he was, but he also appeared shaken, like something had really upset him. He drank a coffee, ate half a sandwich, and then left again. He didn't even pay until the next day. He was all apologies, yet I could tell something was still bothering him."

My mind was racing. "Did anyone else see him?"

Eddie shrugged. "Anyone else who was there, I'm sure. His friends were all gone, though. I didn't think much of it at the time. He said he wasn't feeling too good, and he didn't look it, so I left it at that."

There was something in his voice that made me ask, "But now?"

"He was upset," Eddie said. "And as the years passed and I'd think of Wade, those images of Cliff sitting there, staring at his sandwich like it was made of worms and dirt, kept coming back to me. The more I thought about it, the more I realized it was the look a man might get if he was feeling guilty about something."

"Do you think Cliff Watson killed Wade Fink?" I asked.

Eddie faced me, lower lip quivering ever so slightly. "If he didn't, then I'm almost positive he knows who did."

Eddie didn't have much else to say after that, so I left him at the diner and returned home. I couldn't quite make myself believe shy Cliff Watson was capable of murder, but what did I really know of the man? He might have lost his cool and killed Wade in a fit, or he might have become shy and reserved after killing his friend. I needed to talk to him soon to get his side of the story before I made my mind up about him.

I parked and was halfway to my front door when a small white streak made straight for me as if intent to knock me flat on my back.

I jerked back, but instead of knocking me down, the little dog put its front paws on my knees, thankfully just below the hem of my dress.

"Maestro!" Jules clapped his hands as his Maltese started to lick at my hands as if I'd dipped them in steak juice. I ruffled the little dog's ears, which only caused his tail to wag at a rate that was liable to take him airborne if he kept it up.

"I'm so sorry about that," Jules said, hurrying over and picking up his wayward pet. "He saw you coming and got excited."

"Well, I'm happy to see him too," I said. Maestro barked his affirmative.

Jules looked me up and down and a smile spread across his face. "Why, you look rather nice tonight, Krissy. Do you have something planned?"

Me being me, I blushed at the compliment. "Thank you," I said. "I'm going out tonight. It's not too much, is it?"

"Too much?" He chuckled. "Of course it isn't. Not unless you're going to a rodeo or tractor pull."

"They have those around here?"

"Probably. Though if they do, I can't say I've been to one." The thought of Jules at a tractor pull was as ridiculous as it sounded. "So, you're going out tonight? Is there a special occasion that calls for such extravagance?" It was obvious he already suspected my reasons for getting dressed up.

"I have a date," I said, unable to stop my schoolgirl grin.

"A date." His hand fluttered to his chest. "Have you finally found the one?"

"It's with Paul," I said, as if that somehow changed things.

"Really? I thought . . ." He shook his head. "No, what I thought doesn't matter. It's about time you two have finally taken the next step. Everyone's been waiting for it."

"I don't know about everyone," I said.

Jules merely rolled his eyes.

I was already nervous enough about the date, and talking about it was making me more so, so I changed the subject.

"Do you know Clifford Watson?" I asked. "He's an older man, drank coffee with Wade Fink."

"Is this about the unsolved murder?"

I nodded. "It is. I was hoping you might be able to tell me something about him."

Jules tapped his lower lip, eyes going distant. I noted his nails weren't painted and he was wearing a polo and khakis, rather than his usual work attire. He looked so, I don't know, *normal* when he wasn't at work.

"The name doesn't ring any bells," he said finally. "I knew a Madeline Watson, but she moved away a couple years back. Had a kid, but I don't recall if she ever mentioned a husband." He frowned. "Well, depending on how old this Clifford is, he might be her father. She was only in her forties, maybe early fifties, when I last saw her."

"Cliff is still in town," I said, but I filed Madeline's name away, just in case they were related somehow.

"I'm sorry I can't help." Maestro squirmed to be let down, but Jules kept a firm hold on him. "There's been a buzz going around about your investigation. I overheard a couple of ladies talking about it earlier."

"People are talking about it?" I suppose it wasn't surprising, but it still came as a shock.

"They are. Seems you have ruffled a few feathers with your inquiries. Not everyone is happy that you're looking into something that—how did they put it?—'something that didn't deserve a second thought.'"

"A man died," I said. "I can't let it go." Especially because it involved Rita.

"I know you can't," Jules said with a wide smile. "That's what we all love about you." He shifted Maestro from one arm to the next. The little dog was desperate to get down. "Well, I best let you go so you can get ready for your date. You'll have to tell me how it goes."

"I will," I promised him. "It was good to see you." I crouched so I could look the Maltese in the eye. "And you too, Maestro." I gave him one last ear scratch, before I let Jules return home.

By the time I was back in my house and cleaning off the dirty doggie prints on my knees, I had only about thirty minutes before Paul was due to arrive. I mentally forced everything that had to do with Wade and his murder from my mind and resolved to get back to it in the morning when I could think about it with a clear head.

15

"It doesn't look too busy tonight," I said as Paul pulled up in front of an unassuming brick building. A simple sign that read GERALDO'S hung out front. I knew from experience that the place was much nicer on the inside than its exterior indicated.

"That's good," Paul said, driving around to the small parking lot in the back. He slid into a spot and shut off the engine. "I'm starved."

"Me too."

We got out of his car and headed for the restaurant. Paul had chosen to dress in a pair of black slacks and a simple button-up shirt, which made me feel good about my choice of dress. We didn't look overdressed, nor did we look like we'd just come from the rodeo Jules had mentioned.

Paul opened the door for me and I stepped inside Geraldo's. Light jazz played over the speakers hidden among the dim colored lights. Though you could see other tables, the seating felt intimate, private. There was a soft murmur of voices that created just the right ambiance to the room, adding to the odd sense of public seclusion. Even before we were seated, my heart was stuttering.

We were led to a table near the windows. Paul looked as if he was going to pull the chair out for me, but I hurriedly did it myself. I'm not sure why I did it. Maybe it was an independence thing. Or maybe I was just scared that it would start to feel like a real, romantic date.

Isn't this what I wanted?

It was, but now that I was there, I was afraid I was going to screw it all up somehow.

Paul looked momentarily crestfallen, before he relaxed and took his own seat. We began to peruse the menu.

I was dying to ask him about Jay Miller or anything else he might have uncovered about Wade Fink's murder, but I held my tongue. This was a date, and I needed to remember that the investigation was mine alone, and that the cops weren't involved this time. He might have taken me to see Arthur Cantrell, but that didn't mean he needed to do anything else.

I'd just chosen the lemon herb chicken when the waitress appeared. She looked to be in her fifties and looked mildly distracted when she approached our table.

"Hi, I'm Candace. Are we ready to order?"

"I am," I said, checking with Paul, who nodded.

We both ordered, with Paul adding a bottle of wine to go with our meal. I asked for a water, just in case, but was pleased we weren't going the soft drink route. Somehow, wine made the date feel even more like, well, a date.

Candace's smile was distant, and was clearly there out of habit, as she jotted down our orders. She didn't look at us again before she hurried to the back.

"I hope the wine is okay," Paul said. "I know you don't usually drink . . ."

"It's fine," I said. "One or two won't hurt."

"Good." He cleared his throat, seemed to consider what to say next before deciding on, "I'm glad you got ahold of me earlier. I looked into Mr. Cantrell some more after we left his place, and I'm not so sure aggravating him is such a good idea."

"Did you learn something else about him?" I asked, happy he'd brought it up so I didn't slip up and do it first.

"Nothing major that we didn't already know," he said. "But there were a lot of little things that added up to a man who is no stranger to the law. Citations, complaints. I found a few instances out of town where he'd had the cops called on him. No arrests, outside the one we know about, but it's clear Arthur Cantrell is a troubled man."

Troubled enough to kill? I wondered. "I'll stay clear of him. And if something does come up and I need to talk to him again, I'll be sure to call you first."

Paul grinned. "You'd better."

The waitress returned with my water and the bottle of wine Paul had ordered. She filled each of our glasses, and then left the bottle.

"I can't believe you bought the whole thing." I said. A single glass was expensive enough.

"Why not?" he said. "If we don't finish it, I can always give it to someone else." He glanced around the room as if searching for that lucky someone.

I picked up my glass and took a sip. The wine was sweet and didn't have the normal tartness I disliked. "It's good," I said.

"I'm glad you liked it. I . . ." Paul trailed off, eyes moving over my shoulder.

I glanced back to find Shannon, Paul's former girl-friend, walking toward us. Her jaw was tight, eyes pinched, though she was trying to hide her displeasure at seeing us there. She was dressed for a night out, and I wondered if she'd abandoned a date of her own to pay us a little visit.

"Shannon," Paul said when she reached the table. "It's good to see you."

"Paul." Her eyes flickered to me. "Krissy."

"Hi, Shannon. You look lovely tonight." And she did. She might not be very happy with me since she blamed me for causing her and Paul to break up—not that I'd done any such thing—but she had the grace to smile.

"Thank you." She turned back to Paul. "Can I talk to you for a minute?"

He looked at me, and I could tell a part of him wanted to see what she had to say. I didn't get the impression that he was hoping she'd ask him to give their relationship another go, but my chest tightened anyway.

"Perhaps later," he said. "Krissy and I are having a quiet meal together."

Shannon stepped closer to him. "Please, Paul. It will take just a minute. I don't want to interfere, but . . ." She glanced at me, as if hoping I'd help her out.

Against my better judgment, I did just that. "Go on. I'll be okay for a few minutes."

"You sure?"

I gave him what I hoped was a reassuring smile. "Yeah, I'm sure."

Paul reached across the table and rested his hand on my own. "I'll be right back. Don't go anywhere."

"I wouldn't think of it."

He rose and followed Shannon back toward the bathrooms. There was a hallway back there that was likely the closest thing to privacy they could get without going outside.

It would be easy to get jealous—I mean, my date *had* just walked off with another woman—but I trusted Paul. I took another sip of wine, and then folded my cloth napkin onto my lap in preparation for the meal. Shannon could try all she wanted to get Paul back—if that was what she was actually doing—but I felt confident that Paul wouldn't abandon me so easily. We had a history.

Okay, that history was marred with murder investigations and awkward encounters, but darn it, it was still a history.

A minute passed. Then two. After five, a part of me started to get worried. What if I was wrong? What if Paul was still interested in Shannon, and seeing her dressed up now made him regret coming to dinner with me? What if they were pressed against the wall, lips locked, hands frantically roaming over one another?

I mentally slapped myself upside the head. That was old insecurities talking. As much as I'd grown since I'd come to Pine Hills, they still liked to creep up on me sometimes. I had more than enough proof that Paul and I were a fit. I wasn't going to let anything come between that; not anymore.

I nearly sagged in relief when Paul returned alone. He sat down with a smile and a shake of his head.

"Sorry about that."

"What did she want?" I asked, unable to keep the question from slipping out. I might trust *him,* but I didn't know Shannon well enough to know what she was capable of. I didn't even know her last name.

"Nothing," he said with a wave of his hand. "She wanted

to clear a few things up between us." He met my eye. "They're all clear."

I didn't like that he wasn't being more specific, but honestly, what happened between them was none of my business. Now, if Paul and I moved beyond the occasional date and she kept showing up, then we'd see.

I was about to change the subject to something lighter when my phone buzzed in my purse. I steadfastly ignored it, but it succeeded in wiping whatever I'd been about to say from my head.

Who'd be calling me now of all times?

Paul's gaze flickered to where my purse sat in the chair next to me, and then back again as it fell silent.

"How was work?" I asked.

"Same as most days. Though there was this one older lady who called in claiming someone was trying to break into her house. Turns out it was her cat. She'd somehow trapped him between the screen door and the heavy wooden front door and he couldn't claw his way out."

"Is the cat all right?"

Paul chuckled and nodded. "He was a little wild-eyed when I opened the screen door to knock. When she opened the door, the poor cat just about knocked her over as he bolted inside. I have a feeling he'll be a little more careful where he roams from now on."

"That's good." My phone started buzzing again.

Paul and I looked at each other.

"No," I said.

"It might be important."

I bit my lower lip. I had a sudden image of Dad lying on the floor, clutching at his chest, with Laura frantically trying to reach me.

Why she'd call me instead of an ambulance, I didn't

know. But it did serve to make me break down and fish my phone out of my purse.

"I don't know the number," I said, glancing at the screen. It was local, so it wasn't Laura or Dad.

The buzzing stopped.

"Maybe they'll leave a message this time."

My phone buzzed again. Same number. "Nope." With a sigh, I answered it. "Hello? Krissy Hancock speaking."

"Ms. Hancock." There was relief in the man's voice. "I wasn't sure I had the right number. I had to ask around, and even then, I wasn't positive I'd be able to reach you. You weren't at home when I tried to call."

"You tried to call my house?" I asked before shaking off the question. "Who is this?" I recognized the voice, but I couldn't quite place it.

"Sorry, sorry. It's Cliff, Clifford Watson."

"Cliff?" I just about stood in my shock. The waitress returned with our plates, just then. She hesitated before setting mine down, as if unsure if she should interrupt. "What can I do for you, Cliff?"

"I need to talk to you." His voice shook. "It's been a tough couple of days." He laughed, though there was no humor in it. "No, it's been a tough thirty years. I have some information on what happened to Wade Fink."

"You know who killed Wade?" I said it a little louder than was necessary, but he'd surprised me. Candace gave a little gasp at my outburst.

"Please, not on here. Let me give you my address. We need to talk. Tell me you can come tonight? I'm not sure I'll be capable of talking about it later, not if I have more time to think about it."

"Tonight?" I looked to Paul, who nodded; he knew

what I was asking, and was on board. "Sure. Give me your address."

Cliff repeated it twice before he said, "Please, come soon. This is tearing me up and I can't live with it any longer." He hung up.

"Well, that was interesting," I said, tucking my phone away. "He sounds scared."

"We should go now."

I looked at my full plate of food and sighed. It smelled fantastic, and I knew it would taste just as good. My stomach grumbled in protest. "Probably."

Paul spun in his chair to look for our waitress, but she was long gone. I'd probably frightened her off with talk of murder. Poor Candace. She'd already been working distracted, and now to put thoughts of dead men in her head.

"I'll take care of the bill," Paul said, pulling out his wallet and a wad of cash. It appeared he left more than what our meals cost, but I supposed that since we were abandoning the feast to be thrown away, it was the right thing to do.

"It seems a shame to leave this here." Unable to resist, I took a small bite of my chicken. It was good, but not as good as I was expecting. I imagine the roiling of my stomach had a lot to do with that.

"I'll make it up to you," Paul said, rising. "Shall we?"

We left Geraldo's and got into Paul's car. I gave him Cliff's address and we headed that way, dutifully going the speed limit, though I was anxious to get there as soon as possible. Cliff had sounded unsure about talking to me, and I feared that by the time we arrived, he would have changed his mind.

It took nearly twenty minutes to get to Cliff's place, thanks to a small fender bender a block away. Paul got out of the car briefly to check to make sure everyone was okay and that the police were on the way, and then took us down a side road, which added a little time to our trip.

"Did he give you any specifics about what he wanted to talk to you about?" Paul asked as we pulled to a stop outside a tiny house that looked barely big enough for one older man to live comfortably. The gutters hung woefully low, and a small plant was growing out of one of them.

"He just said that he had something to tell me about Wade's murder. I'm thinking he might know who killed Wade." Or that he might have done it himself.

My mind drifted back to what Eddie had told me. Cliff had looked guilty when he'd returned to the Banyon Tree. If he *had* killed Wade, it didn't appear as if he was happy about having done it. Living with it for a few hours was hard enough. Living with it for over thirty years had to take a toll.

We got out of the car and went to the front door. Paul took the lead and knocked.

There was silence from within.

He knocked again, this time with a frown. "Mr. Watson?" he called. "It's Paul Dalton. I'm here with Krissy Hancock, as per your request."

Still no answer.

"Maybe he doesn't want to talk with you here," I said. If he was about to admit to murdering his friend, I doubted he'd want to do it in front of a cop.

"He's got no choice." Paul hammered harder on the door.

It opened with an ominous creak.

Every hair on my arms and the back of my neck stood on end. Paul gave me a serious look, and then pushed the door open.

"Mr. Watson?"

When there was still no answer, Paul turned back to me. "I want you to stay here," he said. "I'm going to make sure he's okay."

I nodded, worried. Clifford Watson wasn't a young man. The stress could very well have gotten to him and he'd had a heart attack the moment he'd hung up from me. If that was the case, there was a chance I might never learn who killed Wade Fink.

Paul entered the house, calling Cliff's name. I shifted from foot to foot, just outside the door. I could make out the corner of a couch and a small box television to the right. A hallway led deeper into the small house to the left. I could see nothing else, not even a photograph on the wall.

I glanced back toward the road. There were other houses in the neighborhood, but they were spaced far apart. No one was looking out a window as far as I could tell, and no one drove by.

Paul was gone for only a minute, but in that time, I'd imagined every horrible thing that could have happened to Cliff Watson. I prayed he'd merely closed his eyes and had fallen asleep. Older people did that sort of thing all the time.

When Paul returned, the look on his face was grim. "Go ahead and go back to the car," he said.

"Why? What happened?"

"Go on," Paul said. He was pale, which combined with the tone of his voice, told me all I needed to know.

"He's dead, isn't he?"

Paul nodded. "I've got to call it in." He sucked in a breath and I noted it trembled. "I'm going to have to ask you to stop looking into Mr. Fink's murder. This is now an official police investigation."

I knew what he wanted to say, even without him saying

it, yet the mere idea made me feel both sick and faint. I wanted to do nothing more than to fall to my knees and weep, though I managed not to do either.

I was too late, I thought as I returned to the car. I'd come here to learn what Cliff knew about Wade's death, but instead, something far worse had happened.

Cliff Watson had been murdered.

16

The next couple of hours were awful.

I could only sit and watch as more cops arrived to secure the scene. Paramedics went in, and after everyone else was done, they carried poor Cliff Watson away in a body bag.

Paul asked me to call someone to get me more than once, but I ended up waiting around instead. I might not have been allowed to poke around the scene, but I felt I owed it to Cliff to watch in the hopes of spotting something that would help me figure out who killed him.

This is my fault.

The thought kept zipping through my head as the hours passed. If I'd made Paul drive faster, or if I'd answered when he'd first called, then things might have been different. Perhaps if I hadn't been looking into Wade's murder at all, then Cliff might still be alive, sleeping soundly in his own bed.

But I was, and now he was dead. And since I felt responsible for his death, I also felt the need to figure out who had killed him.

I was sitting in Paul's car, staring at the house, thinking

through all the people I'd come into contact with since I started looking into Wade's murder, when there was a knock at my window. I nearly jumped from my skin before I noticed who had come over to check on me.

I rolled down the window, letting in a blast of chilled air. "Officer Garrison," I said. "I didn't know you were here."

"You shouldn't be."

"I'm staying out of the way." I hugged myself. I hadn't thought to bring a jacket, and the night would only get colder.

Garrison walked around the car and got in beside me. I rolled up the window and turned up the heat.

"Are you okay?" she asked.

"Yeah, I guess so." Tears threatened, but I held them in check. "I feel like this is all my fault."

"You can't think that way," she said.

"I can't help it." I turned in my seat to face her. "Cliff told me he had information on why Wade Fink was murdered and he wanted to talk to me about it. And now he's dead. There has to be a connection, don't you think? I mean, why else would someone want to kill him?"

"Wade Fink?" Garrison asked, brow furrowing.

Oh, right. She didn't know I was looking into a thirty-year-old murder.

I explained it as quickly and concisely as I could. As I spoke, a frown grew on Garrison's face. By the time I was done speaking, she was shaking her head.

"I can't believe Chief Dalton was okay with this."

"It wasn't an active police investigation at the time," I said. "I talked to a few people, got an idea of what Wade was like, and that was about it. I didn't go throwing accusations around, if that's what you think."

Garrison's frown eased. "It's not that," she said. "It just seems like a dangerous thing to have a civilian doing, cold case or not. She should have assigned someone to watch over you." Her gaze traveled to the house, where Paul was still hard at work.

"I was trying to help a friend." What would Rita think now that someone else was dead? "I didn't think it would come to this."

Officer Garrison laid a hand on my shoulder. "I know. That's what you do." There was a moment of silence before she went on. "Don't let this get you down. There's a good chance that even if your investigation led to that man's death, it would have happened anyway. Emotions build up over time, as do resentments. You didn't do this. The killer did. Remember that."

"I'll try."

She squeezed my shoulder, and then started to get out of the car, before she paused. "I could always drive you home if you'd like. I'm done here."

"Thanks," I said, touched. "But I'll wait for Paul."

She nodded and then walked away.

My little chat with Garrison had helped, but I still felt as if I'd caused Cliff's death, even indirectly. There was no way to feel good about that.

Thankfully, I didn't have to stew in my guilt for much longer. Paul strode from the house, head down. When he got into the car beside me, he groaned, leaned his head back, and rubbed at his eyes. He looked beat.

"Were there any clues as to who killed him?" I asked.

"The tech guys are looking into it now, but I'm doubt- ful. Whatever happened, happened quick. There wasn't a struggle."

I felt oddly relieved. I didn't want to think of Cliff

struggling for his life. I kept seeing him sitting at the table at the Banyon Tree, looking down into his coffee like he was afraid to meet anyone's eye. Who would kill someone like that?

"Let me get you home."

Paul and I didn't talk as he drove. Both of us had far too much on our minds, and I was afraid that if I spoke, I'd break down into heaving sobs. I didn't know Cliff Watson, not really. As far as I knew, he was Wade's killer and someone else had found out about it before me and killed him for it.

But even if he was a killer, he didn't deserve to be murdered; no one did.

We pulled up in front of my house. It looked empty and cold from the outside. Paul left the engine running, but didn't speak right away or make a move to get out.

"Would you like to come in?" I asked him.

He looked at me. I must have looked a wreck, because his eyes grew worried and he turned the key. "I think I'd better."

I led the way to the front door. I was happy to see my hand didn't shake as I inserted the key in the lock and pushed my way inside. Thankfully, Misfit decided not to make a run for freedom, and both Paul and I were inside without having to fight with my cat.

I went straight for the kitchen and put on a pot of coffee. It was already past eleven, but I needed the comfort. Besides, it was decaf, so it shouldn't keep me up. My brain would do that for me.

Paul sat down at the island counter and watched as I set the coffee to percolating. "How are you holding up?" he asked.

"Not good," I admitted. "I keep thinking that this is all

my fault, that if I'd done things differently, then he'd still be alive."

"You can't think like that."

I plopped down across from him. "I can't help it. He calls me, and then he's dead. You know it's not a coincidence."

He looked grim when he said, "Yeah."

"I know you can't give me details, but can you tell me anything about how he died? It might ease my mind." How? I had no idea, but wondering wasn't any better.

Paul sighed and scrubbed at his face with his hands. "He was stabbed. As I said, there was no sign of a struggle, and as far as I can tell, there was no sign of forced entry."

"So, he knew his killer."

"That would be my guess. There's always a chance he'd left the door unlocked, but I doubt this was a random killing."

That narrowed the suspects considerably in my mind. If Cliff had let the killer in, that meant he must have known them well enough to feel comfortable alone with them. Since he'd just told me he was going to talk about Wade's murder, I couldn't help but think his own murder tied back to that original death.

"Do you think the killer was there when he called me?" I asked, thinking it through.

"I don't know. Why do you ask?"

"It took us what? Twenty, twenty-five minutes to get there after his call?"

"Something like that."

"So, Cliff calls me, tells me he's got information about Wade's death to tell me, and in that short window of time before we can get there, he's murdered. How did the killer know he was going to talk?"

"There's a chance that his death has nothing to do with Wade Fink's murder," Paul said.

"Yes, true, but it's likely it's connected. I mean, what are the chances that a guy is about to tell me something that might break the case and then die to a random killing?"

Paul nodded, though he didn't look happy about it. "They're not good. Did it sound like anyone else was with Mr. Watson when he called?"

"No," I said. "No one else spoke, but that doesn't mean they weren't there."

"Why would he make that call in front of someone else?" Paul asked. "I have a hard time believing he would, especially if that someone was tied to the original murder."

"Maybe he told Wade's killer what he was going to do," I said. "Cliff seemed like a nice guy and might have wanted to give a friend a heads-up. Maybe the killer tried to talk him out of it, and when Cliff called me, he decided to silence him before he could talk."

Paul was shaking his head, even as I spoke. "Assuming this ties back to Wade's murder at all, I don't think Mr. Watson would tell the killer what he planned on doing ahead of time. I have an even harder time believing the killer would let him call you if he had."

"What about afterward? He calls me, then calls Wade's killer to tell him what he's doing. If they were friends, then he might have needed to admit what he was doing for his own conscience."

"That sounds more reasonable, but he had to know how dangerous making that call would be."

"If we assume he called his friend within a few minutes of hanging up from me, that leaves the killer ten to fifteen minutes to get to Cliff's house, kill him, and then leave again. It's not a lot of time."

"No, it's not. But the killer didn't need long. He or she shows up, stabs him, and then leaves. That would take five minutes, maybe less if he went straight for the kill."

While all that sounded plausible enough, something still bothered me. If one of my friends were a murderer, would I tell them I was about to tell someone about it?

"What do we do now?" I asked. I felt lost, uncertain. Could I keep poking around an old murder if it ended up getting people killed? Paul had already told me to drop it, but I wasn't so sure I could do that, not with Rita counting on me.

Not to mention Eleanor's spirit. She might not have lived to see justice for her brother, but darn it, I desperately wanted to solve the case for her.

Paul gave me a stern look. "We? I think you'd better sit back and stay out of trouble."

I tried to look innocent, I really did, but something in my face must have betrayed my thoughts.

"Krissy," Paul said, placing a placating hand on my wrist. "I know you want to get to the bottom of Wade Fink's death, but it's now a police matter."

"His death isn't," I said.

"Yes, it is. At least, indirectly." Paul slipped his hand around so that he could grip my fingers and squeeze. "We'll be investigating Mr. Watson's death. If we're right and it ties back to the cold case, then I can't have you putting yourself at risk or stirring up more trouble."

"I don't stir up trouble," I said, but without force. It seemed like that's all I ever did these days.

"Not intentionally, you don't, but I do think you've got the killer scared. If we're right and the person who killed Cliff Watson also killed Wade Fink, how long do you think it will be before they come after you? The more you pry, the more frightened they'll become."

I looked down at our joined hands. Oh, how I wished for different circumstances because I could really use his company right then.

"I don't want to let Rita down." Or Eleanor.

"You won't," Paul said. "You might not be the one to catch the killer, but as long as he or she is caught, you've done your part. You got the ball rolling again. That's got to count for something."

A "Yeah, but" was on my lips but I swallowed it back. He knew what he was asking me was against my nature, but he was right. I wasn't a cop, let alone a real detective. Someone had died and I needed to let the police deal with it.

Unfortunately, knowing the right thing and actually doing it are two completely separate things.

"Come here," Paul said when I didn't speak. He stood and, without releasing my hand, he stepped around the island counter to wrap me in a warm, comforting hug.

I closed my eyes and pressed my face to his shoulder. I wanted to cry, wanted to hold him forever. Why couldn't we have a good quiet moment together like this that wasn't marred by murder?

We hugged for what felt like an eternity before he released me and stepped back. A cold chill replaced him, causing me to shiver.

"What a way to end a date," Paul said, doing his best to lighten the mood with a smile. There was still concern in his eyes, but I chose to ignore it.

"That makes two," I said. "It's starting to become a trend."

"Let's hope the third date ends on a better note."

My heart just about stopped in my chest. "You want a third date?" I asked.

Paul managed a laugh, though I wasn't sure if he was laughing at himself, or my surprise. "Yeah," he said. "We deserve to have an uninterrupted date for once, don't you think?"

"I do." And then I remembered Vicki's offer. "What are you doing next weekend?"

Paul thought about it a moment before answering. "Nothing as far as I know."

"Vicki asked if you and I might like to go on a triple date with her and Mason. Charlie Yow and his wife will be there, too."

"Sounds great." This time, when he smiled, it was all warmth.

"Then you'll come?" I asked, surprised how easy that was. "I mean, if you don't want to tag along, I totally understand. I know you're busy, and now with this new murder . . ."

"I'll be there," Paul said. "Better yet, I'll pick you up. Just let me know when and where."

"I'll tell you as soon as I know."

The coffeepot beeped, but it was a distant distraction. I'd already forgotten I'd even put any on. My entire focus was on Paul and the prospects of actually seeing him again outside of his job.

"I'd best go," Paul said, glancing at his watch. "I still have to write up a report and get some sleep before tomorrow's shift."

I hated to admit it, but he was right. "I open tomorrow morning," I said, thinking back to my original plan of looking into Jay Miller and Wade's death some more. It was going to be tough to squeeze it all in. "I should get some sleep, too."

We stood awkwardly staring at one another. We'd just been on a date, but we'd also just come from a murder scene. How in the world did you end a night like that?

Finally, Paul stepped forward and leaned toward me. I had a moment of panic where I didn't know if I should turn my cheek to him or go in for the kiss.

Our lips met briefly. It was chaste. It was bliss.

When he stepped back, he looked just as shocked as I felt.

"I'll talk to you tomorrow, Krissy," he said.

I think I managed a "Yeah," but I was too busy memorizing the tingle of my lips to really hear what he was saying. I wish I could say I blamed it on the exhaustion, but darn it, I'd waited so dang long for this moment, I deserved a few minutes to savor it, however brief it might have been.

Still, I had enough wits about me to walk with Paul to the door and hold it open for him. As he got into his car, I considered asking him to stay. A killer was on the loose, one who might have their targets set on me, so it wouldn't be too strange of an ask.

Paul closed the car door and waved from behind the wheel. I returned the wave. Now wasn't the night to ask him to stay. I wanted *that* to happen when circumstances were better.

He backed out of my driveway and vanished down the road. I watched him until his car was gone, and then, unable to stop myself, I looked toward Eleanor Winthrow's old house. The lights were off, the house quiet. Jane was likely asleep inside.

I won't let you down.

I closed my front door, and not willing to let good coffee go to waste, I filled a mug part of the way full. I drank it slowly, mind turning over the murders and what to do about them, because one thing was for sure, there was no way I could back off now that someone else had died, especially since it might have happened because of me.

17

"You look beat."

I stood up straighter as if to prove I wasn't as tired as I appeared, but quickly sagged back against the counter. "It was a long night."

Lena grinned and joined me where I stood. The lunch rush was over and we'd just finished cleaning up, so there wasn't much else to do but chat.

"I heard you had a date with Officer Dalton."

"I did." I looked toward the books, where Jeff was helping a pair of teens. He was laughing at something they were saying. Even when there was a murder, life went on for those still living it. "But it wasn't Paul that kept me up most of the night."

"Oh?" Then her eyes widened. "Wait. Someone died last night, didn't they? I heard something about it on the radio this morning, but wasn't paying much attention. Was it someone you knew?"

I shook my head. "Not really. But Paul and I found him."

"Man, that sucks." Lena tugged on an earlobe that was adorned with so many earrings, I could hardly see any skin. "Seems like no matter what you do, dead people find you."

"Yeah." I turned to face her, determined to change the subject. "So, how about you and Zay? Anything new there?"

Lena rolled her eyes and pushed away from the counter. "You wish. I'm going to get a few dishes done." She hurried to the back, but not before I noted the pleased smile on her face.

I was tempted to follow her to the back room and grill her about Zay some more, but decided to let her be for now. It was good Lena had found someone, even if nothing long-term came from it. Her punk rock skater girl image put a lot of people off before they even got to know her. She deserved to be happy, and if Zay could give that to her, even for a few months, I approved.

The door opened and Rita walked in with both Andi Caldwell and Georgina McCully in her wake. There was a spring in all three of their steps, which was good to see.

"Hi, Rita," I said, greeting them in turn. "Georgina. Andi."

"Ah, Krissy, I'm so glad you're here." Rita hurriedly moved to the counter. "I was hoping we could talk a little about the you-know-what."

Oh, I knew. "I could always take a break," I said. "But if it gets busy again, I'll have to go."

"That's fine." Her gaze flickered to the menu board behind my head. "Can I get a vanilla latte?"

I looked at her in surprise. "I thought you didn't like flavored coffees?"

She waved a dismissive hand my way. "That was ages ago. After that con we went to, I decided to expand my horizons a little. You can't truly live without trying something new, or at least, that's what I've heard."

Rita, along with Vicki and I, had attended JavaCon a

few months back. While the event had been plagued with a murder of its own, it *had* helped both Vicki and me run a better coffee shop. Apparently, it had done wonders for Rita as well.

"One vanilla latte coming up. What about Georgina and Andi?" The two older women were already seated, talking animatedly to one another.

"They'll have the usual," Rita said. "They aren't nearly as adventurous as I am."

I filled the order, adding two iced lattes to Rita's hot vanilla latte. Rita carried her cup, while I took Andi and Georgina theirs. They thanked me and then fell silent, like they didn't want me to overhear whatever they'd been gossiping about.

Rita took her seat and I sat in the last remaining chair, angling myself so I could keep an eye on the counter. Lena was still in the back, and while Jeff could run the front, he was upstairs with the books, which was busy today.

"Did you hear about Clifford Watson?" Rita asked the moment I was seated.

"I was there." I felt myself pale at the memory.

"Really?" Rita's eyes widened. I could see her file the information away for later gossip. "Now why on earth would you be at Cliff Watson's home in the middle of the night?" Her eyes widened. "You weren't—"

"No, I wasn't," I said, cutting her off. "He called me and said he needed to talk to me about Wade's murder."

Rita flinched ever so subtly. Georgina reached across the table and rested a hand on her wrist.

"Such a shame," Andi muttered with a sad shake of her head.

"What did he say?" Rita asked.

"I never got a chance to talk to him," I said. "Paul and

I rushed straight to his place, but when we got there, he was already dead."

Normally, Rita would have reacted to my mention of Paul Dalton, especially since my comment could be interpreted that we were together at the time, but she didn't so much as twitch, let alone question me about the date. It said a lot about how this whole mess was affecting her.

"Cliff was a good man," Georgina said. "He was prone to drinking, but he never got mean."

"He only drank when he thought of his wife," Andi said. "And even then, never to excess."

"He's married?" I asked. There'd been no indication that he lived with anyone, though I hadn't actually seen the inside of his house.

"She died, what? Seven years back?" Georgina asked, looking to Andi.

"Eight, I think it was," Andi replied. "Remember, that was when she was pushing to implement a smoking ban for the entirety of Pine Hills."

"Would have had it, too, if she hadn't died." Georgina took a drink from her iced latte. "That woman could convince anyone of just about anything."

"Might explain why Clifford married her instead of that other woman," Andi said.

Georgina gave a knowing nod, but didn't comment further.

"I can't imagine why anyone would want to kill Cliff," Rita said. "He and his wife were good people. I might not have known them as well as I should have, but I do know that."

"How did she die?" I asked. If the circumstances of her death were suspicious, it could very well connect back to Cliff's own murder.

"Heart attack," Georgina answered. "Was marching in front of that old smoker's place, screaming how the products they sold were killing everyone in town, and she just up and collapsed."

There was no "smoker's place" in Pine Hills now, which made me wonder if her protests hadn't been entirely in vain.

"It had nothing to do with Cliff or Wade," Rita said. "And I refuse to believe anyone we know could be responsible for their deaths, either. There has to be another explanation."

"What about Hue Lewis?" Andi asked.

To my absolute shock, Rita's face reddened. "Hue had nothing to do with Cliff's death. Nor did he have an ill thing to say about Wade before or after his death and I won't hear otherwise."

Georgina's mouth pressed into a fine line. She wanted to say something, but was keeping herself in check. Why?

Rita refused to look at me, choosing instead to stare into her vanilla latte. There was something she didn't want to tell me, which made me *need* to know, especially since there was a good chance that whatever it was might connect to one, or both, of the murders.

"Rita?" I asked. "What does Hue have to do with anything?"

"It's nothing, dear," she said. "You can just forget you heard anything and focus on something else." She shot an angry glare Andi's way before taking a drink from her coffee.

"Nothing?" Andi asked. "We all know what happened between the two of you. Don't pretend otherwise."

"I don't know," I said. "What happened?"

Rita closed her eyes and sighed. "Well, you might as

well tell her, Andi. But I'll tell you now, Hue had nothing to do with Wade's death. I'd swear my life on it."

Andi glanced at Georgina, who nodded, as if telling her it was okay to take the lead, before she started speaking. She didn't dally in getting to the point.

"Hue Lewis asked Rita out."

"Out?" I asked. "As in, on a date?"

Andi nodded. "He was smitten. Those of us who saw them together could see it every time he looked her way. There was a gleam that came into his eye, a sparkle that lit up his entire face."

"It was just a mild crush," Rita said. "He wasn't serious about me."

"He was," Andi corrected her. "But he was respectful to her wishes. When she turned him down, he let it drop right then and there."

"That's not what I heard," Georgina said. "Way I heard it, Hue tried more than once to win Rita's favor. Rumor says he even went to Wade and tried to get him to leave Rita. I bet he was hoping that if Wade was out of the picture, then Rita would give him a chance."

"So, he asked you out while you were still dating Wade?" I couldn't wrap my mind around it. She'd dated one older man, so did Hue think that she'd be willing to go out with another?

Rita heaved a sigh. "As I said, there was nothing to it. I told him I was taken and that was that."

"How long before Wade was killed did this happen?" I asked.

Andi and Georgina looked to Rita for an answer, though I could tell both of them knew. They were going to make her say it, and I think they were doing it for her own good.

"Two weeks, give or take," Rita said. She was clearly unhappy with the way the conversation had shifted. She might like to gossip about others, but she wasn't a fan of being the target of it herself.

"Wasn't that right around the time when Arthur Cantrell and Wade got into a fight?" I asked.

"It was," Rita said. "But the events aren't related. Hue was jealous that Wade found someone younger than him. He wanted the same thing, but couldn't find anyone who interested him. So, he came on to me because I was convenient. It was flattering at the time, but I was faithful to Wade, so nothing came of it."

A memory surfaced. "Wait. Wasn't Hue married at the time? I remember him saying something about hiding from his wife."

Andi clucked her tongue. It was Georgina who answered.

"They didn't have a very good relationship," she said. "Everyone in town knew it. They fought often, and I heard they didn't sleep in the same bed. It was no wonder he was looking for a way out."

"Even if all of that was true, it had nothing to do with Wade's death," Rita said. "Hue doesn't have it in him to hurt anyone." She met my eye. "If you met him, then you know that."

My first impression of Hue jibed with how Rita viewed him, but people did stupid things all of the time.

"Did Wade know about Hue asking you out?" I asked, thinking that if he had, there was a chance he'd instigated a fight that ended up costing him his life.

Rita shook her head. "Of course not, dear. It would have ruined their friendship, and I wasn't about to do that over a silly lapse in judgment."

"What about the others?" I asked. "If Georgina and Andi knew, could one of the Coffee Drinkers have known and told Wade?" If that was the case, and Arthur was the one who'd brought it up, it would explain why they'd fought.

"Oh, we didn't know for certain that was how it happened," Andi said. "We heard rumors and kept it to ourselves, didn't we, Georgina?"

"We did," Georgina said with a nod.

"Rita filled in the details years later."

"I wish I wouldn't have," Rita muttered.

"Oh, we suspected much of it already," Georgina said. "And we did manage to put a lot of it together long before Rita became our friend. Back then, we were nobody to her."

My mind was racing, trying to connect the pieces. Just because Rita thought no one knew about Hue's proposition, didn't make it true. If what Georgina said was true, and Hue had gone to Wade to get him to leave Rita, then perhaps he'd also told him *why* he wanted them to break up. Could Wade have confronted him about it later? Or did Hue become jealous enough that he decided to remove Wade from the picture permanently?

I needed to talk to Hue again and ask him where he was last night. I was almost positive the person who killed Wade over thirty years ago was the same person who'd killed Cliff. I could be wrong, of course, but I didn't think so.

"I'd better get back to work," I said, rising. "Was there anything else you wanted to talk about before I go?"

Rita shook her head. When she looked up at me, she looked worn out, as if the conversation had drained her. "No, dear, I think that's about it."

"But—" Andi started, but the words died on her lips when both Georgina and Rita gave her warning looks.

I was tempted to pry. If there was something else they could tell me, something that would help me find the murderer, then I wanted to hear it.

But Rita had been through enough already. If it was important, I was sure she would tell me eventually.

I was headed back toward the counter when the door opened and Robert slunk in, head hanging. He dropped into the nearest chair and put his head in his hands.

Oh, no. I veered off and went to him, despite my instincts screaming at me to run the other way.

"Are you okay, Robert?" I asked, dreading the answer. Robert was a changed man from when I'd dated him, but I didn't doubt that if he and Trisha were on the outs, he would try to worm himself back into my life.

"Krissy," he said. He leaned back and took a deep breath. "I talked to Trisha like you said I should."

I had to clamp down on the urge to yell at him—I didn't tell him to do anything. "And?"

"She said maybe."

"Maybe?" I asked. "That's not a no."

"No, but it's close." He lunged out of his chair and grabbed my hands. "What am I going to do if she says no?"

I pulled free of his grip and took a step back. Out of the corner of my eye, I saw all three of the women I'd just left leaning forward to listen, eager for something new to gossip about.

"If she says no, you move on with your life," I said. "It might not even be the end of the relationship. She might not be ready. These things take time, Robert."

"But how could we ever come back from a failed proposal?" Robert wailed, completely oblivious to the onlookers.

I took him by the arm and walked him across the room,

up the three stairs, into the bookstore portion of Death by Coffee. Rita gave me a disapproving look, while both Andi and Georgina looked disappointed.

"Robert, you can't force her into anything," I said. "Your proposal might have caught her by surprise. She might say yes as early as tonight. Or she might need months to think about it. The only thing you can, and should, do now is wait and see what she decides."

"But if she—"

"No buts. Treat her like you've been treating her. If she decides she doesn't want to marry you, honor her wishes and let her go. If she decides she wants to wait for a few months before she makes up her mind, then let her do that. You won't help by pressing her."

Robert's shoulders slumped and his head drooped. "I guess you're right."

"I am," I said. "If you act like she's ruined your life by telling you maybe, you'll either make her say yes because she feels bad for you, or she'll break it off completely. You don't want either of those things to happen, right? You want her to marry you because she *wants* to, not because you guilt tripped her into it."

"She's all I've got," Robert said.

"Trust that it'll work out the way it's supposed to," I told him. I refused to let the cynical part of me surface, and to tell him it served him right for how he'd treated me. Robert was trying to be a good person and I had to respect that, even though my own memories of him weren't so rosy.

"All right. I'll try."

"Good." I patted him on the shoulder.

The door banged open downstairs and a voice rang out loud in the mostly quiet shop.

"I'm looking for Krissy Hancock! Where are you? We need to talk."

I peered down, past the books, to find Lester Musgrave stalking near the counter, face red and angry. He turned away from the counter and, as if he had some sort of built-in radar, he looked directly at me. Our eyes met. His fists bunched.

And then he started my way.

18

Everyone in Death by Coffee was watching. Lena had come from the back, and Jeff had moved toward me, a hardback book in hand. If I asked him to, I was sure he'd happily use it as a weapon. Even Robert appeared ready to throw down if it came to a fight, though I had a feeling his bravado would fade the moment fists started flying.

It won't come to that. I'd make sure of it.

"It's all right," I said, loud enough for everyone in the café to hear. "Go back to your coffees. We're just going to talk."

"Are you sure?" Robert spoke under his breath, his eyes never leaving Lester, who was nearing the stairs.

"I'll be fine," I said. "Go find Trisha. Try to have a normal day without worrying about whether or not she'll say yes." I gave him a reassuring smile and then turned my focus to the approaching older man.

Robert hesitated. He bit his lower lip and he looked between me and Lester, as if unsure he should leave me alone with the clearly irate man.

"Go," I said, nudging him. "There's nothing you can do here."

Finally, he went.

Robert passed slowly by Lester, giving him the stink-eye the entire way. Lester didn't notice. He kept his eyes on me, nostrils flaring. He was angry, obviously, but there was something else behind his gaze: hurt.

Lena raised her phone, a question on her face. I subtly shook my head, but was glad she was prepared. If Lester decided to do more than talk, not only would I have Jeff nearby to help fight him off, but Lena could have the cops here in no time.

"Lester," I said as he climbed the stairs and walked right up to me.

"You." He leveled a trembling finger at me, shoving it within an inch of my nose. "This is your fault."

I was pretty sure I knew what he was talking about, but wanted to hear it from him, just in case I was wrong and something else had happened. "What is?"

"You know what you did." He took a step forward so that our noses nearly touched. When he spoke, I could feel his breath on my cheek, and noted a faint whiff of alcohol. "You just had to bring up old, painful wounds. And look what happened. Cliff's dead because of you."

I flinched, but didn't back down. "I'm sorry. I wasn't trying to get anyone hurt. And I most definitely didn't do anything to Cliff."

"Bah!" Lester stepped back from me and ran a hand over his bald head as he turned his back to me. Down below, Rita and her crew were watching with interest, as was Lena, who had yet to set down her phone. I felt oddly exposed standing there.

"Please, Lester, let's talk about this. I didn't kill Cliff. I might have had a hand in his death by bringing up Wade's murder, but that doesn't mean I'm responsible for it. The killer needs to face justice, and I plan on making sure that happens."

With his back to me, I couldn't see how Lester was taking my words. He kept rubbing his head, shoulders hunched as if against a blow. As far as I knew, he was revving himself up to strike a woman in the middle of her own store.

Taking a chance, I stepped forward and rested a hand on his shoulder. He tensed, but didn't jerk away. "I'm sorry about Cliff. I know he was your friend. He seemed like a good man."

"He was." It came out choked, almost whispered.

"Please, let's sit and talk."

Lester let me guide him away from the stairs, toward the couch and chairs we kept upstairs for readers. No one was there now, for which I was thankful. It put us out of easy view of the onlookers downstairs, but not so far out of the way that they wouldn't notice something amiss if Lester decided to choke me out. I motioned for Jeff to leave us be, and he did so with one last worried look.

Downstairs, a handful of customers came in, which would hopefully distract the looky-loos further. Lester collapsed onto the couch with a heavy sigh. The tension seemed to rush straight out of him—and the room—as he did.

"I'm sorry if I gave you a fright," he said. "I was just so angry and there was no one else I could yell at. You made a convenient target."

"It's okay." I sat down across from him. "Trust me, I feel guilty for what happened to Cliff. But believe me when I say I never wanted it to happen, and I plan on making it right somehow."

"I know." He looked up and smiled. Most of the anger

was gone. The pain had taken over. "It's been a rough couple of days, and once I heard what happened, well, I guess I kind of snapped."

"You were close?"

Lester nodded. "Cliff and I didn't always get along, or see eye to eye on most matters, but what friends do?" His laugh was hollow. "He was never the same, you know? After Wade died, Cliff pulled within himself, became semi-isolated from everyone. He rarely left his house. He even started missing our morning meetings until I forced him to come back."

"Do you know why he changed?"

"I wish I did. I asked him about it at least twice a week for the last thirty years. I always figured he blamed himself for what happened to Wade. I don't mean I think he killed him, but that he thought he should have been there for him. I think we all felt the same way, but Cliff took it the hardest."

"He called me the night of his death," I said. "He claimed he had information on Wade's murder."

Lester stared at me. I couldn't read his face, whether he was afraid or angry or in disbelief. His eyes were rimmed in red, his ears the same.

After a moment, he made a slashing motion with his hand. "Cliff had nothing to do with Wade's death and I won't listen to anyone who says differently."

"But he might have known who did."

"Cliff Watson never hurt a soul." This time, there was some heat in his voice. "If I ever even suspect you plan on smearing his name, I will . . ." He trailed off and looked away.

"If he's innocent, then you have nothing to worry

about." I leaned forward, forced him to look at me. "Do you know what Cliff might have wanted to tell me?"

Lester shook his head, but his eyes strayed from mine. *He's lying.* "Lester, please. If you know something . . ."

"I don't. Not really." He closed his eyes and knuckled them with the back of his hands hard enough it had to hurt. "It doesn't make sense."

"What doesn't?" I kept my voice soft, friendly. He knew something, as, I was starting to believe, did the rest of the Coffee Drinkers. I wasn't sure if it was a big conspiracy or if they'd made deductions over the years. Either way, I needed to know what it was they knew.

"I wasn't entirely honest with you when we talked at the Banyon Tree," he said, dropping his hands into his lap. "I didn't know you—still don't—and I never liked that harlot Wade was seeing, so I saw no reason to go spreading rumors."

My gaze flickered downstairs to where Rita sat to make sure she hadn't heard. She was deep in conversation with Georgina and Andi, though I noted she'd look my way every now and again. She knew what the conversation was about, and I was positive she was dying to know what Lester was saying.

I prayed she'd stay downstairs, out of Lester's line of sight. He'd been too intent on me to notice Rita sitting there when he'd first come in, but I doubted he'd fail to notice her if she came storming upstairs, demanding to be filled in.

"What rumors?" I asked, turning my attention back to him.

"You know how we said Zachary and I left together the day Wade died?"

I nodded.

"Well, while it was true enough, we didn't stick together after we walked out the door."

"You went separate ways?"

"We did." Lester's fists clenched. "I headed to work, but Zachary begged off. Asked me to cover for him, and like a fool, I did just that."

"Do you know where Zachary went?" I tried to keep the excitement out of my voice, but I couldn't help it. Finally, it felt like I was getting somewhere.

"How should I know." Lester's anger flared, then died. "All I know is, I watched him walk away, and a few minutes later, Cliff came strolling out of the Banyon Tree, heading the same way."

"Didn't he say he was sick that day?"

"I'm sure he was," Lester said. "And he did appear to be heading home, but I had no idea what Zachary was doing."

"You don't think the two of them had plans, do you?"

Lester lowered his head. He was muttering something, but I couldn't make out the words.

"Lester?"

He glanced up, scowled, and then looked back down.

"Lester? Do you believe Zachary and Cliff had plans to do something together?" What I really wanted to ask was if they had gone after Wade, but figured that would only set off the volatile man.

"I don't know what they did," he snapped, head jerking upward. His eyes were blazing. "And I never pried. I will tell you that neither man had it in him to kill Wade back then, and I'm damn sure Zachary wouldn't have killed Cliff now."

"What about Arthur?" I asked.

"What about him?"

"When we last talked, I noticed how he looked at you, like he thought you knew something." Or they were sharing a secret.

Lester snorted. "Arthur thinks he knows everything. I probably told him about Zachary and Cliff wandering off together once. Might have implied I thought something happened between them. Luckily, they married women, and it came to nothing."

I ground my teeth together to keep from calling him out on his prejudices. I still found it hard to believe people still thought that way, even today.

"Do you think Arthur came to believe they might have killed Wade?" I asked.

"Who knows?" Lester shrugged. "Probably does. Probably thinks it was justified."

"And you?"

"Wade got what he had coming to him. None of us disputes that. Even the law was on our side. The cops know when it's a rightful, just killing. And the guy who investigated Wade's death was no different."

"Jay Miller," I said.

"He knew what kind of mess Wade was causing with his antics. He should have locked that Rita woman up long before Wade was killed. It would have changed things, I'm sure."

"Do you think Jay Miller knew who killed Wade and covered it up?" I asked, refusing to get into it with him about Rita. It would help nothing, and would only make me angry.

"If he did, who cares?" Lester leaned forward. "What matters now is that Cliff is dead. If you know what's good for you, you'll stop asking questions, stop prying into things that you have no business involving yourself in. I don't want no one else to die, you hear me?"

"Is that a threat?"

His smile looked more like a wolf's grin. "If that's how you want to take it, then be my guest." He stood. "Stay out of it. Stay away from us. I don't want to lose any more friends because of you, or any other woman."

He made as if he might walk away, but I had one more question for him.

"Who's Madeline Watson?"

Lester stopped in his tracks. "You leave Madeline alone."

"Just tell me who she is. Her name was mentioned to me and I'm curious to know how she fits in." If at all.

Lester turned slowly to face me. His expression was stone. Cold. "Madeline has nothing to do with any of this."

"I never said she did," I said. "I just want to know who she is in relation to Cliff."

"She's his sister." Lester's face broke. Behind his anger, he truly was hurting. A man like Lester didn't like to show it, but it was there. "*Was* his sister. She's a good woman. She doesn't need any of this coming back on her."

"She'll be told of Cliff's death," I said. "No one can protect her from that."

"She doesn't need to know why he died," he said. "I don't want you telling her. She doesn't need that falling on her shoulders. She's already been through enough."

It was obvious by the tone of his voice, how he spoke of Madeline, that Lester cared deeply for her. I had a feeling it went beyond mere friendship.

"You love her," I said, not meaning to speak, but it slipped out anyway.

Lester blinked twice rapidly before turning away. "Leave her alone."

He walked away without looking at anyone in the room. Rita watched him go, curiosity written all over her face. The moment he was through the doors, her gaze swept to me, but I wasn't ready to discuss my conversation with her, or anyone else.

I returned to work and busied myself the best I could, but my mind was on anything but my job.

Lester might not think Cliff had anything to do with Wade's death, but I wasn't so sure. He didn't know Cliff had returned to the Banyon Tree later that day, looking shaken. Maybe Cliff and Zachary hadn't made plans to get together. Maybe Cliff had been completely honest with everyone and had intended to go home, just like he'd said.

But instead of making it there, he ended up watching one of his friends murder another.

19

The rest of the workday was thankfully uneventful. Lena was replaced by Beth, and I went ahead and sent Jeff home since business had died down to a crawl with no sign of it picking back up before close. Vicki was coming in for a few hours with Mason, who was now a full-time partner at Death by Coffee, to relieve me.

"Well?" Vicki asked as soon as she was through the door.

"Well what?"

"How was your date?"

"Good, right up until we found a dead guy."

"You were there?" Mason asked. He pulled on an apron and then spun in a circle, as if looking for something.

"Yeah." I told them what happened as quickly as I could. "But Paul did agree to come to the triple date with the Yows if you still want us there?"

"Why wouldn't we?" Vicki asked.

"Because every time I spend any time with Paul at all, someone seems to die?"

"She's right," Mason said. "We should probably leave the country, just to be safe."

"We *could* ship *her* to Russia instead," Vicki said, barely hiding her grin. "No sense in us leaving because *she's* bad luck."

"Ha, ha," I deadpanned. "You'd miss me if I was gone."

"Of course we would." Vicki put an arm around my shoulders and squeezed. "Who else could we tease like this?"

"We'll see both you and Paul next weekend," Mason said.

"I'll let him know, but it's your heads."

Vicki laughed. "I think we'll be okay, but we'll be sure to warn Charlie and Sadie just the same."

I finished up stocking a fresh batch of cookies, and then took off my apron. "If you don't need me, I think I'm going to head home."

"We have this," Mason said. "Go home and relax. You look like you need it."

Boy, did I ever. "Thanks." I gathered my things, but before I left, I headed upstairs to where Beth was straightening the books. "How are you holding up?" I asked her.

"I'm good." She flashed me a smile. "Thanks."

"If you need anything, you know where to find me."

She nodded, and then went back to work.

I watched her a moment, concerned. When I'd first met her, I'd pegged her as something of a fake. Working for Raymond Lawyer, I guess she had no choice but to pretend to be happy since he was always so hard on everyone. If she'd pouted around the office, I was sure he would have screamed at her loud enough for the entire town to hear.

But now that I'd spent more time with her, I realized Beth was just as insecure as the rest of us. She wanted to fit in, wanted to be normal, but wasn't quite sure how to go about doing so. Coming to work for me had helped. She acted far more natural now than she ever did when working for Raymond.

But with him badgering her about leaving his employ, I was afraid she'd pull into herself, or revert to the shallow woman he'd made her out to be.

I left her without pressing her about it and got in my car to drive home. I figured I could have an early dinner and then see if I could get hold of Zachary Ross and Hue Lewis to get their takes on what I'd learned about the both of them. The only other Coffee Drinker I had yet to talk to one-on-one was Roger Wills. His name had yet to come up in any of my conversations, which I hoped was a good sign. I was tired of suspecting everyone around me every time someone died.

Still, I planned on finding time to talk to him anyway. Roger might not be involved in the murder, but that didn't mean he didn't know someone who was.

I passed a car parked at the side of the road near my house. No one was in the car, or else I would have stopped to see if the driver needed help. You didn't find abandoned cars out my way all that often, but it did happen on occasion.

Jane Winthrow was just leaving her mom's house when I pulled up in front of my own place. I waved to her before fumbling with my keys. She honked once as she drove off. I wondered how she was doing with packing up her mom's things, and made a mental note to pay her a visit soon to check. As I moved to insert my key into the lock, I noticed the door wasn't completely closed.

My heart skipped a beat and then started racing. I knew for a fact I'd locked the door this morning. I always double-checked before I left.

I removed my phone from my purse and readied Paul's number, just in case. I eased the door open and peered inside, but couldn't see anyone from where I stood. Misfit wasn't sitting in the entryway waiting to make his grand escape, either.

"Hello?" I called. "Anyone in there?"

"Come on in, Ms. Hancock. No need to call the police."

A scream tried to rip from my throat. I managed to keep it to a startled yelp, but just barely. "Why shouldn't I?" I asked, staying right where I was. There was no way I was going to go inside. "Who are you? And why are you in my house?"

There was a groan as my unwelcome visitor stood from my couch. He strode into view. The sight of him caused me to take an abrupt step back.

He was a tall man, eyes dark as flint. His hair was shaved close to his scalp, and despite his age—I'd put him in his late fifties—he was lean with muscle.

"My name is Jay Miller. You've been asking around about me."

"The cop?" My mouth ran before my mind could catch up with it. *Of course he's the cop.*

Jay merely smiled. I wasn't comforted by it in the slightest.

"What are you doing in my house?" I demanded, anger slowly replacing my fear. "You have no right to break in."

He moved forward so suddenly, I scuttled back off my front stoop before I could catch myself. He stepped outside and closed the door behind him.

"Better?"

"Not really, no," I said. "I should call the police right now." My thumb was still poised over the CALL button. I made sure he could see it there, just in case he had foul intent.

"For what? I was merely waiting for you."

"You *broke into my house!*"

"A minor infraction at best. Nothing was stolen or damaged. I waited for you, you arrived, and now I'll say my piece." He moved closer. This time, I held my ground. "Keep out of it. Wade Fink is better off dead. The whole town improved once he was gone, and no one wants someone like you digging up old graves."

"Afraid I might find something among the dirt?" I asked.

That sinister smile returned. "Watch yourself, Ms. Hancock. I wouldn't want something to happen to you."

He pushed past me and strode down my driveway, toward the abandoned car I'd seen parked at the side of the road. I watched him go, my entire body quivering with both outrage and fear. How dare he threaten me in my own house!

As soon as he was gone, I hit CALL. Paul picked up after the second ring.

"Paul," I practically gasped his name, "I just got home and when I tried to unlock the door, I found it was already open. Someone broke into my house. In fact, he was still there."

"What?" He sounded so startled, I almost laughed. "I'm on the way."

"No, he's gone." I took a deep breath, which I was proud to note, only trembled slightly. "He showed up to warn me off of looking into Wade's death."

"Do you know who it was?"

"Yeah. He even introduced himself. Said he was Jay Miller."

"The former cop?"

"The same." A new thought hit me and I rushed through the front door. "Oh, no, Misfit."

"Did he—" The rest was lost as I lowered the phone and started searching for my cat.

A meow from down the hall had me racing toward the laundry room. The door was closed, which it never was since Misfit's litter box was in there. I jerked open the door to find him sitting just inside, glaring at me like he blamed me for his current predicament.

"He's okay," I said, sagging against the wall. "Paul, he's okay."

"That's good. Tell me what happened."

"There's not much to tell," I said. "I came home and Jay was sitting in my living room like he owned the place. He told me to back off and then left."

"Nothing is missing?"

"I haven't had a chance to check, but I don't think he came in here to steal anything. At least, he said he didn't."

Paul was silent a long time before he asked, "Do you want to press charges? You caught him in the act, and while we can't hit him for much, maybe we can scare him a little. Besides, I wouldn't mind paying him a little visit." There was genuine anger in his voice.

I thought about it for a moment before I said, "No, that won't be necessary."

"You sure?"

"Yeah."

Paul didn't sound happy about it when he said, "If you change your mind, let me know. You don't want guys like this to think they can do whatever they want and get away with it."

"I will." I leaned down and petted my cat, who was winding around my legs. "It just startled me. I'll be okay."

"Be careful, Krissy. No more investigating, all right? Leave it to the police. With Cliff Watson's murder, it's up to us to find the killer now, not you."

"I know." I closed my eyes and hoped Paul didn't hear the intent in my voice. There was no way I could drop it now, not with people showing up to my place of business and my home, threatening me. I had a feeling that even if I stopped looking into Wade's death, it was already too late to stop the ball from rolling. I might as well see it through.

"I mean it, Krissy. Leave it to us."

"I'd better go take care of Misfit," I said. "I'll talk to you later, okay?"

Paul sighed. "All right. Let me know if Miller comes back."

We hung up and I sank to the floor. Misfit leaned against me, purring. He looked okay, but I knew he was probably just as rattled by Jay Miller's presence as I was.

"He won't come back," I promised him, stroking his fur. "You're safe now."

Misfit rubbed against me and then sauntered down the hall, toward the kitchen and his food dish.

I remained seated, forcing myself to calm down before I did something stupid. I was getting close to something; I was sure of it. Cliff died, likely because he was going to tell me who killed Wade, or at least, who he suspected of the crime. The killer found out and then silenced Cliff for it. And then, after my confrontation with an angry Lester Musgrave, the cop on the case, Jay Miller, shows up and warns me off.

So how did it all connect?

I rose on shaky legs and looked up a number. Paul might want me to drop it, but that simply wasn't happening.

I found the name I was looking for and then, after a handful of calming breaths, I dialed.

"Hello?" It was a female voice.

"Hi, can I speak to Zachary Ross please?"

"Who's calling?"

"Krissy Hancock. He and I met at the Banyon Tree."

"One moment."

I waited, forcing myself not to pace. It took nearly five minutes before he picked up.

"Yes?"

"Hi, Zachary, it's Krissy. Do you remember me?"

"Of course I do." Not exactly said kindly, but I was undeterred.

"I was hoping I could ask you a quick question about your statement. You said you left the Banyon Tree at the same time as Lester on the day Wade Fink died, correct?"

"I did."

"Why didn't you tell me you parted ways almost immediately?"

There was a moment of silence. "Why should that matter?"

"The way you two talked, it sounded like you both left for work." No response, so I pushed on. "But that day, you didn't. You went the opposite direction, and were soon followed by Cliff Watson."

This time, I waited him out.

"And?" Zachary said. "There's no crime in taking a day off."

"No, there isn't, but a man died that day. And now, Cliff's dead. It all connects somehow, and I have a feeling you know what that connection might be."

"Cliff was my friend." There was genuine pain in his

voice. "I don't like the implication that I might have had anything to do with his death."

"I'm just trying to figure out what happened, and I can't do that if I don't have the whole story. Where did you go after you left the Banyon Tree that day? Did you and Cliff meet up?"

"I'm tired, Ms. Hancock. Good-bye."

The line went dead.

My first instinct was to dial him again and demand he answer the question, but I held off. If I called him back right away, I'd just anger him. I could let him stew on it for a little while, and hopefully, he'd decide to come clean on his own.

I called Roger next, but his line was busy. I gave it five minutes and tried again to the same result.

"Well, fine," I muttered, looking up Hue Lewis next. I found his number and dialed. This time, there was an answer.

"Hue speaking."

"Hi, Hue, it's Krissy Hancock from the Banyon Tree. We talked the other day."

"Ah, yes, Krissy. How are you?"

"I'm good," I said, keeping my voice chipper and friendly. I was still shaken by my unwanted visit, but it was fading fast.

"Good, good. It's funny you should call—I was just thinking about you."

Really? I thought, none too kindly. Could he have sent Jay Miller after me? "Good thoughts?"

He laughed. "Shall we call them neutral thoughts? You brought up some old wounds the last time we spoke. And now that Cliff has died, those wounds have been ripped right open." He sounded genuinely sad about the loss of his friend.

"I'm sorry about Cliff," I said. "But I do want to talk to you more about what happened to Wade."

"Okay, but I'm not sure what else I can tell you. It was a long time ago and while I would like the culprit to be caught, I'm beginning to wonder if that will ever happen in my lifetime."

"If the same person who killed Wade, killed Cliff, then I'm sure they will be."

"I hope so." There didn't appear to be deceit in his voice, but it was hard to tell over the phone.

I debated on how best to hit him with what I was going to ask him, and then decided it best to come right out and ask it. "Why didn't you tell me you were interested in Rita Jablonski?"

Hue erupted into a coughing fit on the other end of the line. It was so violent, I had a sudden fear that I'd shocked him so badly, he was choking on his tongue.

Before I could fully panic and break down and call 911, the fit abated and Hue was able to speak. "Where did you hear this?"

"It doesn't matter. Did you ask her out while she was still dating Wade?"

There was a hesitation before he spoke. "We should talk about this, but not over the phone. Can you meet me at the Banyon Tree in twenty minutes?"

I was sure my appearance at the diner wouldn't go over well, but I didn't want to miss this chance to hear Hue's side of the story.

"I can."

"See you there, Ms. Hancock. I want to make it clear that I had nothing to do with either of my friends' deaths."

He hung up.

"Well, that's interesting," I told Misfit as I put my phone away. The deeper I got into this, the more convoluted everything became.

I took a moment to replace Misfit's water with fresh, and gave him a handful of treats to make up for his fright and unlawful incarceration, before I left my house. I triple-checked to make sure the door was locked, and then I got into my car, determined to finally get to the bottom of Wade Fink's murder before someone else ended up dead.

20

Hue was sitting alone at a corner table, hands wrapped around a mug of steaming coffee. When he saw me enter the Banyon Tree, he stood and motioned me over. While he was smiling, I could tell he was nervous. His eyes darted around the room, even as he pulled out a chair for me.

"Thank you," I said, taking the proffered seat.

"I was surprised by your call," Hue said, settling back in. He spun his coffee cup slowly in front of him. "I know how it must have sounded, learning I was . . . smitten with young Rita. I admit it now, and would have done so then if you'd asked me when we'd first met. But it never came up, and honestly, it never amounted to anything, so I didn't think it was important."

The waitress headed our way, but I waved her off. "You must be able to see how it looks, right? Rita and Wade were dating and you go and ask her out. And then, after she turns you down, Wade is murdered."

"It wasn't connected," Hue said. His eyes found mine and held them. "I was stupid and yeah, I admit it, I was a little jealous. Wade had this wonderful, beautiful young woman on his arm who could light up a room with her laugh and smile. I was married to a woman who wasn't interested in me any longer, who preferred to sleep alone than next to me. It was hard on me, to say the least."

"But Wade was your friend."

"I know." Hue's expression turned somber. "If I could take it back, I would. I spent years wondering if my bad judgment caused Wade's death somehow. For a time, a fanciful part of me thought that maybe Rita killed Wade with an intent to get with me afterward, but had chickened out after the deed was done."

I didn't know if the idea was romantic or creepy, so I left it alone. "You fought with Wade over Rita, didn't you?"

"I did. A part of me hoped if I broke them up, she'd give me a chance. I could get out of my marriage and start anew. Maybe this time *I'd* be the one everyone looked at with envy."

"It didn't sound like anyone was very envious of the relationship," I said. "From what I gather, nearly the entire town was against Rita and Wade dating."

"That's true to a point," Hue said. "And quite a lot of people were indeed against their relationship because of the age difference."

"But not all?"

Hue shook his head. "Jealousy is a strong motivator. Do you know how many men wished they were in Wade's shoes? I wasn't the only person who gave it a shot with Rita. Some waited until Wade was dead, but there were quite a lot of men who tried to coax her into leaving Wade, long before his death."

I wondered how many of the Coffee Drinkers were included in that. It sounded like most, if not all of them, wanted Wade to leave Rita. If they'd succeeded, would they have fought over who earned the right to date her next?

But if that was the case, why not court her after Wade's murder? Guilt? Shame? Or had one of them come on to her and Rita had turned them down? And was it possible she might have consented, and had chosen to keep it a secret? I prayed that wasn't the case.

Hue shoved his coffee mug aside and leaned forward. "I don't want to give you the impression that Wade's relationship with Rita Jablonski defined my life. I tried some underhanded tricks to make them break up, but it never worked, and now, I'm glad of it. I never would have hurt either of them—and that includes murdering Wade."

"What about the rest of the group?" I asked. "Did Arthur or Zachary feel the same way?"

Hue shrugged. "You'd have to ask them, but I'd say neither would have harmed Wade. Arthur is very stuck in his ways. Like Lester, he believes everyone should follow strict rules, often devised to benefit him. He never would have gone after a woman as young as Rita because, quite frankly, she wouldn't have been mature enough to deal with his radical ideas. He'd want someone who would be able to handle his venom, and amplify it."

"It doesn't sound like you have a high opinion of Arthur. Why remain friends with him?"

Hue's smile was sad. "Arthur's not all bad. I don't believe in the same things he does, but when he's not on one of his rants, he's a pretty decent guy. You just sometimes have to look deep for it."

It seemed like a lot of work to remain friends with someone, but what did I know? I thought all my friends were angels.

"And what about Zachary?" I asked.

"As far as I know, he wasn't interested in Rita, either. He had his own troubles to work through, so he wouldn't have wanted to add another."

"Troubles? Such as?"

"That's for him to tell you, not me." Hue folded his hands in front of him. "I don't believe Wade's death was tied to his relationship. In fact, it wouldn't surprise me in the least if money was the cause."

"It often is," I said, though I didn't really believe it. Nothing in any of the conversations I'd had about Wade hinted that money had anything to do with his death. That didn't mean it wasn't there, though. "Do you know if Wade had any debts he refused to pay?"

"If you're asking if he was a gambler, I'd say no," Hue said. "But it's always possible he was into something the rest of us weren't aware of."

"What about Jay Miller?"

Hue's face went carefully blank. "What about him?"

"Could he have had something to do with Wade's death? Or know who did?"

"I couldn't say."

"He came to see me today," I said, watching Hue carefully for some indication he knew about my unwelcome visitor. "I found him sitting in my living room when I got home from work. He threatened me, Hue. He doesn't want me looking into Wade's death, and now that Cliff is dead too . . ." I left the rest hanging, not quite sure how best to finish the sentence.

Hue paled and rocked back in his chair like I'd gut-punched him. He opened his mouth once, closed it, and then looked out the window.

"What does Jay have to do with any of this?" I pressed.

"I know he was friends with the group. I know he was the cop who responded to the call. Now, he's threatening me."

"He's not my friend," Hue said, voice hushed. "He hasn't been for a very long time."

"Why?"

"Jay Miller is not a good person," he said. "He never was. Arthur could be trouble when he wants to be, but Jay . . . He isn't someone you want to hang around for any length of time. He's poison. It took me far too long to realize that."

"Do you think he's capable of murder?"

"Isn't everyone?" Hue asked. "Could I see Jay killing someone?" He shrugged one shoulder. "Maybe. Could I see him helping someone commit a crime? Most definitely."

"Would he have killed Cliff if Cliff was about to talk about Wade's death?"

Hue actually flinched. "I honestly can't say. I wish I could help you there, because Cliff was my friend. He didn't deserve to die."

A thump somewhere behind me caused me to jump, thinking Judith Banyon had seen me, but when I glanced back, no one was paying me any mind. A kid was sitting at a table, a smug grin on his face as he smacked the salt-shaker against the table. Neither of his parents cared enough to stop him.

"What can you tell me about Madeline Watson?" I asked, turning back to Hue.

"What about her?" He seemed surprised by the question.

"I'm just curious," I said. "She's Cliff's sister, right?"

"That's right."

"Do you think she might know why her brother was killed?"

"I don't see why she would," he said. "She hasn't lived in Pine Hills for years now."

"Did she get married?" I asked. "Find a new job? Why leave?"

"I don't know why she left," Hue said. He sounded oddly hurt by not knowing. "She never married, had no interest in dating when I knew her. When she left, Cliff was heartbroken. The two of them were close for the longest time, but right before she left, I sensed things weren't right between them."

"Do you know where she is now?" I asked. "Does she know about Cliff?"

"I'm sure someone has informed her by now." He sighed. "I suppose I should call her and send her my condolences."

"You have her number?"

He nodded, a frown slowly creeping across his features. "I do, but I haven't called her in years."

"Would you mind giving it to me?" When he looked like he might object, I talked over him. "I won't harass her. Cliff called me and told me he knew something about Wade's death. He didn't specify what that might be, and was murdered before we could meet. If Madeline knows or even suspects what he knew, it might help solve both murders."

I keep my gaze level with Hue's own. If he wavered, or outright refused, did that mean he knew something too? Or worse, that he was the killer?

After a long moment, he nodded and sighed. "All right," he said. "I'll give it to you."

I fished a pen from my purse and grabbed a napkin.

I slid them both across the table and watched as Hue checked his phone and then scrawled Madeline's name and number down. I carefully folded the napkin and pocketed it before he could change his mind.

"Take it easy on her," Hue said. "This must be a very trying time for her. She might have drifted apart from her brother, but I know she still loved him dearly."

"I will," I said. "I only want to get to the bottom of the murders and make sure the culprit gets put behind bars."

"Me too," Hue said, lowering his head. "Me too."

I left him to play with the dregs of his coffee, thankful I'd managed to have an entire conversation in the Banyon Tree without Judith chasing me out. I wasn't sure if my chat with Hue helped anything, or if I'd only confirmed more of my suspicions.

Someone in the group knew who killed Wade, and then later, they killed, or had someone kill, Cliff. I didn't think it was Hue, but that could be wishful thinking. He was a nice man, seemed genuine, but some killers often did.

As soon as I was in my car, I pulled out my phone and Madeline's number. I didn't know what role Jay Miller played in all of this, but I wasn't about to give him a chance to intimidate Cliff's sister before she had an opportunity to talk to me.

I dialed.

"Hello?" The voice on the other end of the line was strong, feminine.

"Madeline Watson?"

"Yes?"

"Hi, my name is Krissy Hancock. I knew your brother."

"Oh." The strength slipped on that one word, but was back when she spoke again. "What is this regarding?"

I wondered how many calls she'd received about Cliff,

and decided to make my own call as quick and painless as I could.

"I'm so sorry about Cliff," I said. "He called me right before he died."

"I see."

"He wanted to talk to me. I was neighbors with Eleanor Winthrow, who also recently passed away."

"I'm sorry to hear that," Madeline said. She sounded genuine.

"I promised her daughter, Jane, I'd look into Wade Fink's death. I've solved a few murders in my time, and figured I could see if I could solve this one."

I paused, but Madeline didn't respond. I couldn't even hear her breathe.

"I know this is kind of abrupt, and I totally understand if you don't want to talk to me, but Cliff called me last night because he said he knew something about Wade's murder. I was hoping you might know what it was."

There was a long stretch of silence where I feared Madeline had set the phone down and walked away before she said, "I don't know the specifics."

"But you do know something?" Hope bloomed in my chest.

"I . . . I'm not sure. Cliff and I were close when we were younger. He looked out for me since I was his little sister. You know how it is."

I didn't have a sibling, but I said, "Yeah," anyway.

"I knew most of Cliff's friends, and while I didn't approve of some, I did like Wade. When he died, Cliff grew distant. I didn't press him on it then, though I wish I would have. Maybe things would have turned out differently."

"Do you think he had something to do with Wade's

death?" I asked. I did my best to keep my voice friendly, concerned, as not to offend her.

To her credit, Madeline seemed to understand why I asked. "I wish I could tell you for sure, but I simply don't know. I don't believe for one second he killed Wade Fink. But he might have known who did. Cliff was loyal to his friends, would have done anything for them."

"Even if it meant covering for a murder of another friend?"

"He might have, if he had reason enough to do so. Cliff was, shall we say, easy to manipulate."

My mind flashed to Arthur and his aggressive tone. "Did Cliff ever give you a hint as to what he knew?"

"I'm sorry, Ms. Hancock, but Cliff refused to talk about Wade's death with me." She paused. "Well, that's not entirely true. There was one time, just before I moved away, when he broke down in my kitchen. He kept saying he thought he deserved to be punished, that he'd done something horrible. When I pressed him about it, he swore he didn't murder Wade, but he'd done something that he felt was just as bad."

"But he never said what."

"He did not. When I told him to go to the police, he said he couldn't, that if he did, he'd be a dead man." Her voice broke. "Do you think that's what happened? After all these years did someone kill him for knowing too much?"

I wished I had an answer for her, but I didn't. Not yet, anyway. "Did he ever say who he was afraid of?" I asked, choking back my own tears. I might not have known Cliff Watson well, but his death was really hitting me hard.

"He didn't," Madeline said. She sniffed and her voice strengthened. "But I always got the impression it was someone close to the police somehow. Perhaps it *was* a cop."

I hung up after passing on my condolences once more, and then sat in my car until I was in control of my emotions. Then, I considered my options.

I needed to talk to Paul, that was for sure. Maybe I'd been too hasty to let Jay Miller off the hook, because, if I didn't miss my guess, he was the man Cliff was afraid of. Could Jay have killed Wade and Cliff caught him in the act? If so, why stay silent for so long? Because Jay was a cop?

As much as I hated to admit it, it was possible. A police officer held power over people. He could have threatened Cliff, told him that if he ever told anyone else about the murder, then he or someone in his family might be next.

There were still holes with my theory, like how Jay could possibly have known Cliff was willing to talk to me since I doubted Cliff would have called the man he was terrified of to let him know what he was doing. But I wasn't about to go looking for Jay Miller to ask him about it.

Still, there was one other avenue I could explore on my own.

When I'd looked up a phone number earlier, I'd seen the address next to it. Zachary Ross might not have wanted to talk to me over the phone, but perhaps he'd reconsider if I paid him a little visit.

21

Zachary Ross lived in a small, two-bedroom house, tucked away in between a dozen similar homes that looked as if they'd been constructed to appear identical, though that was no longer the case. Some had additions built on, while others had fallen into disrepair. A rusted basketball hoop sat in the road at the end of the lane. It leaned near half bent over, forgotten.

I parked on the street next to a Chevy that had seen better days. Its front bumper was hanging off, one battered end resting on the street. Two of its tires were flat, both on the road side, and someone had spray-painted something that looked to be a cross between a cow and chicken on the driver's-side door.

Laughter came from behind one of the houses. It sounded like an entire army of kids, but from where I stood, I couldn't see them.

I stepped around the dilapidated car, and over a crushed Pepsi can that looked as if it had been there since the nineties, and made for Zachary's front door. The curtain in the window next to it swished open briefly, revealing a woman's face, before closing again.

Before I could knock on the door, it opened.

"Yes?" the woman asked. She appeared to be Zachary's age, if not a little older. Her eyes were rheumy, and her hand trembled where it gripped the door.

"Hi, I'm sorry to bother you. I'm here to see Zachary. I called earlier." I offered my hand. "Krissy Hancock."

The woman stared at my hand a moment before tentatively taking it in her own. Her grip was weak, her hand oddly warm. "Vera Ross. I'm not sure Zachary wishes to speak to you."

"You're his wife?" I asked.

Vera nodded. "I am. Married for fifty-five years now."

"Congratulations," I said. "Sticking with someone for so long isn't easy."

"No, it's not." She didn't smile when she said it. "We've had our ups and downs. And now with his health, things have been tough."

"How bad is it?" I asked, wondering if the hunch in Zachary's back was a symptom of whatever was wrong with him.

Vera's eyes turned grim. "He was fine up until early this year. Since then . . ." She glanced over her shoulder, and then lowered her voice. "I'm scared for him. He claims he's fine, that the pain isn't too much for him, but when he thinks I'm not looking, I can see how much he hurts."

"I'm sorry to hear that," I said, and I meant it. I didn't like to see anyone in pain, even a man like Zachary Ross. Perhaps his foul mood had less to do with a frosty personality, and more with how he was suffering.

"You can see why I might be hesitant to let you in," Vera said. "After your call earlier, Zachary wouldn't even talk to me. He sulked in his chair and stared out the window until he fell asleep."

"I understand," I said. "But it's important I talk to him. His friend died recently and I'm worried it might connect back to the death of one of his other friends. Did you know Wade Fink?"

"No, we never officially met. I've heard the name, of course, but never met him myself. Never met many of them, to tell you the truth. I never got on with Zachary's friends."

"Does that mean you didn't know Cliff Watson?"

Her gaze dropped. "No, I knew *him*. He was a good man. When Zachary first fell ill, he came to see him. He was the only one who deigned to do so."

"He seemed to care for his friends," I said, thinking back to what Madeline had said about her brother.

"I don't know how Zachary can help you, Ms. Hancock. He's not been himself, and honestly, I'm beginning to wonder if the pain is starting to eat away at his mind."

"Please, call me Krissy."

Vera shot me a flash of a smile.

"I just want to talk to him," I said. "Two of his friends were murdered. There's a chance he might know something that could help prevent it from happening again."

"I don't know . . ." She glanced over her shoulder again. I imagined Zachary sitting back there, watching her end of the conversation with a glower.

"Please," I said. "I won't stay long. And I promise I'll try not to upset him. I only want answers."

"Let her in." Zachary's voice was sharp.

Vera flinched at the sound of it and then stepped aside so I could enter.

I found Zachary sitting in a chair next to a window that

looked out over the Rosses' backyard. A cane lay against the wall next to him, and he reached for it as I entered the room.

"You don't need to stand," I said, holding out a hand like I might shove him back down if he tried to rise. "I won't keep you."

Zachary huffed, but he sat back with a wince that caused his entire face to scrunch up. The hunch in his back was more pronounced, and his head tilted to one side as if he couldn't quite hold it up on his own. Both his eyes were watering from pain. A small, round table sat next to his chair. Five pill bottles were scattered atop it.

"What do you want with me?" he asked. "I thought I made it clear I wasn't interested in furthering our conversation."

It took me a moment to find my words. At the diner, Zachary had looked mostly fine. Here, he looked near crippled. Just looking at him, I couldn't imagine him going to Cliff's house and killing him. If the murder had been committed with a gun, then maybe. A knife? I doubted Zachary would have had the strength to lift it.

Unless he looks worse because he had *stabbed his friend and threw his back out in the process.*

"I'm sorry about what happened to Cliff," I said. "I know he was your friend."

Zachary bowed his head slightly "He was. And I didn't kill him if that's what you're thinking."

"Do you know who did?"

He snorted and then looked out the window. "If I did, the police would already know."

Vera stood just inside the room, wringing her hands. She was watching our conversation like she wasn't quite sure what Zachary would say. It made me wonder if she suspected her husband of being involved somehow and was worried he'd say something incriminating.

"What about Wade?" I asked.

"What about him?"

"Do you know who killed him?"

Zachary's jaw tightened. He continued to stare out the window.

"He couldn't have done it," Vera said. "Zachary doesn't have it in him to hurt anyone. And if he knew who killed his friends, he wouldn't keep it to himself."

I glanced back at her and noticed the photograph on the wall next to her head. It was framed, but unlike the television below it, it was clean and dusted.

"Your daughter?" I asked. The photo was old, black-and-white, and of a thirty-something Zachary and Vera with a young girl who could be no more than ten.

Vera looked surprised by the question. "Oh, why, yes."

I glanced around the room, but didn't see any more photographs of her. In fact, the one photograph was the only one in the room. "Does she still live in Pine Hills?"

"What does our daughter have to do with anything?" Zachary snapped, turning in his chair with a hiss of pain so he could face me better. "Are you going to start accusing her of killing people now?"

"No, I—"

"I would like you to leave." This time, when he reached for his cane, I didn't try to stop him. Zachary wobbled on his feet, but when he strode toward me, his intent was clear; he'd shove me out the door if I didn't go under my own power, even if it broke him in doing so.

Vera looked concerned, but she merely backed into the kitchen. I briefly wondered if he'd come at her in the same way during their fifty-five years together.

I raised both hands in surrender. "Okay," I said. "I'm going."

I scurried back outside and to my car. Zachary didn't follow me out the door, but he did remain standing just inside it. Anger contorted his features, and for the first time, I saw a man capable of murder.

But could Zachary Ross have killed Cliff Watson in his condition? I doubted it. I *could* see him threatening someone, and perhaps his threats were enough to get Cliff killed.

Who would he threaten? Why? *I* was the one running around asking questions. Why not go after me?

Someone had, I reminded myself. Jay Miller had appeared, uninvited, in my house. Could Zachary have sent him after me?

Wilting under Zachary's stare, I started up my car and drove down the road a ways. Once his house was out of sight, I pulled to the side of the road again and considered my next move.

What I needed was a motive for Wade's murder. It was pretty clear that it likely had something to do with his relationship with Rita. As much as I wanted it to be about money or something else, everything pointed right back to the way Wade held himself and had flaunted their relationship.

Hue wanted to date Rita, so he had motive to want to be rid of Wade. But she'd turned him down, and it was unlikely she'd go out with him after her boyfriend was murdered. Did he try again, once Wade was out of the picture? I should ask Rita, because it was unlikely Hue would admit to it if he had.

Then there was Arthur. He had gotten into a fight with Wade over his relationship with Rita. Arthur had a history of violence, and wasn't too keen on talking about it with me or the cops. Ever since I'd met him, he seemed angry. Did that make him a killer?

Lester was prejudiced, but seemed to care about his friends. I couldn't see him killing them, especially Cliff. But did he know more than he was letting on? He'd practically handed me Zachary on a silver platter.

It was then I realized I hadn't gotten the chance to ask Zachary about where he'd gone when he'd parted with Lester on the day of Wade's murder like I'd intended to do. I had a feeling he wouldn't have told me outright, but his expression, and how he responded to the question, might have told me something.

So, who did that leave? I had yet to talk to Roger Wills, not that anything pointed to him knowing anything. Cliff was dead, and whatever he knew about Wade's death very likely died with him.

I picked up my phone and checked for Roger's address. As long as I was making a nuisance of myself, I might as well do a thorough job of it.

Luckily, Roger didn't live too far away, so I put my car in gear and headed to his apartment.

Roger Wills answered on the third knock, a bewildered expression on his face. "Yes?"

"Hi, Roger, it's Krissy. From J&E's. We met the other day."

"We did?" He frowned. "At the Banyon Tree?"

"Yep." I smiled and waited for him to recognize me, but that recognition never came.

"Oh, was that today? I haven't been as regular as I once was. I keep forgetting." He stepped aside. "Come on in. I suppose there's something you wish to discuss."

I hesitated on the threshold, worried. Roger hadn't been

super sharp when I'd met him at the Banyon Tree, but he hadn't been this bad. Like Zachary, his condition seemed to have worsened after Cliff's death.

I entered his apartment and closed the door behind me. Roger wandered over to a recliner resting in front of a small television. A black-and-white movie I didn't know was playing on the screen. The volume was so low, I wondered if Roger could even hear it.

"Krissy, right?" he asked, sitting. "We've met?"

"We have." I found a hard-backed wooden chair and turned it to face him. "We talked about Wade Fink."

"Wade." His eyes grew misty. "I still remember Wade. He made mistakes, but he didn't deserve to die."

So, he remembered that. I hoped that was a good sign for the rest of our conversation. "I'm trying to find his killer," I said. "I was hoping you might be able to help."

"Me?" He shook his head. "Oh, I don't think I can help you much. I wasn't there when it happened."

"Do you know who might have been with him at the time?"

"No, no. I'm sure I don't. It was a long time ago." His gaze drifted to the television and he seemed to forget about me.

I sat there, contemplating what to do. I couldn't imagine Roger killing Cliff, but if he did, would he have remembered it? I hated to think it, but it was possible this was all an act. If he and Zachary were working together, they could both be exaggerating their symptoms to throw me—and the police—off their trail.

But looking at Roger's vacant eyes, the way his mouth hung open ever so slightly, I didn't think so.

"Roger," I said. "Do you know what happened to Cliff Watson?"

"Cliff?" His gaze swiveled back to me. "He's a friend of mine. I saw him recently, didn't I?"

My chest tightened. Should I break the news to him that Cliff was dead? If he was faking, I might catch a subtle reaction. If he wasn't, I could make things a whole lot worse.

"I should go," I said, instead.

Roger smiled at me fondly, and I wondered if he suddenly thought I was someone else; a loved one maybe.

The door opened just as I was about to grab for it myself and a man who looked to be in his late twenties, early thirties jerked back, eyes going briefly wide, before narrowing.

"Who are you?" he demanded.

"I'm sorry to intrude," I said. "I wanted to talk to Roger. I didn't realize . . ." I didn't know how to finish that, so I trailed off lamely.

"You know my dad?"

A son? I hadn't known Roger was married, let alone had a kid, but then again, it wasn't like I knew much of the Coffee Drinkers outside of what they'd told me. "Kind of." I stuck out my hand. "I'm Krissy Hancock. I've been looking into his friend, Wade Fink's, death."

If I was hoping Roger's son would open up to me, I was sadly mistaken.

"Leave him alone," he said, taking a threatening step toward me. He was carrying a paper grocery bag, which, depending on what was inside, could be used as a weapon. "He knows nothing about it, and even if he once did, it's unlikely he'd remember now."

"What about you?" I asked, refusing to back down.

"Did he ever say anything about the murder to you?" Roger's son appeared too young to have been around for it, but that didn't mean he hadn't learned something in the years since.

"No." He stepped aside. "I'd like you to go. Dad doesn't need your harassment. He's struggling enough as it is."

I wanted to force the issue, but stepped around him, and outside the apartment, anyway.

"If he says anything that might help . . ."

"I'll call the cops if that happens. But it won't." He closed the door in my face.

I trudged back to my car, defeated. If Roger *had* killed Wade, the memory could very well be lost. Could I really turn in a man who couldn't remember committing the deed?

I wasn't sure. But I did know it was time to tell Paul everything I'd learned.

22

Paul and I decided to meet at Death by Coffee. I was running on fumes and was desperate for a shot of caffeine. Mason was standing behind the counter with Vicki when I arrived. The moment the both of them saw me, they grinned.

"Can't stay away, can you?" Mason asked.

"Nope. You have the stuff of life. I need it."

Vicki rolled her eyes. "One coffee with a cookie inside coming right up."

Mason stuck out his tongue in mock disgust before he leaned against the counter. "How goes the investigation?"

I shrugged. "Could be better. It seems like everyone involved is either hiding something or they're at the point where their memories are hazy, or worse, nearly gone."

"That sort of thing comes with age."

"You should know." I paused dramatically before, "You do remember who I am, right?"

Mason laughed as he pushed away from the counter. "Watch it. I'll have you know I'm as mentally sharp as I ever was."

"Which isn't saying much," Vicki said, handing me my coffee.

"Hey!" Mason's hand pressed against his chest. "That hurts."

Paul chose that moment to enter, which caused Vicki's expression to change from playful to speculative.

"No," I said, forestalling any questions. "We're going to talk about the murders."

"Sure you are." She turned her attention to Paul, an innocent smile on her face, as he joined me at the counter. "What can I get you, Officer?" Behind her, Mason stifled a snicker.

"A coffee is fine." He ran his hand over his face and then used it to hide a yawn before he turned to face me. "You wanted to talk?"

"Yeah, but not up here. Let's wait until we're seated."

He nodded, rubbed the back of his neck, and then sagged against the counter as if his legs could no longer support him. Another yawn cracked his face.

"You look a lot like how I feel," I said, joining him with a yawn of my own. Darn things are contagious.

"It's been a long couple of days."

"Tell me about it."

Vicki returned and handed Paul his coffee. He thanked her, and then led the way to a table in the back corner. He practically fell into his chair, and I didn't manage much better. We spent the next couple of minutes merely sipping our coffees and avoiding each other's eyes.

Upstairs, Beth was picking up books that had been left on the couch. She flashed me a smile that didn't quite reach her eyes before she spun on her heel to put everything back.

It made me wonder how she was doing. She claimed that she was fine, that she was no longer bothered by Raymond Lawyer's verbal abuse, but I seriously doubted that was the case. Once the murderer was behind bars where he or she belonged, I needed to take some time to talk to her. I didn't want to lose her because Raymond was a jerk who couldn't handle losing an employee to a neighbor.

I set my coffee aside and turned my attention back to Paul. "Have you made any progress on Cliff's murder?"

Paul took a slow drink before answering, as if working out what he should say before he spoke. "Not really. No one saw anything, and no evidence was left behind. I'm sure the killer will slip up soon enough, though." He gave me a stern look. "You've been leaving it alone, haven't you?"

I looked down at the bit of cookie bubbling up from the bottom of my cup, unable to meet his eye. "Kind of."

"Krissy . . ."

"I can't help it," I said. "Jay Miller showed up at my place, Paul. I feel like I *have* to do something or else it will keep happening. I can't live like that, not when I know there's something I can do to help."

Paul's face darkened. "You should have pressed charges against him."

"Probably," I admitted. "He scares me. And I think he's the reason Cliff was afraid to talk until the night he died. It wouldn't surprise me to learn that Jay was the one who killed him."

"Let's not get ahead of ourselves," Paul said. "Jay was a cop."

"And cops can go bad. I mean, he *did* break into my house."

It would have been easy for him to take offense, but Paul merely nodded. "That might be true, but you can't go accusing a cop of murder without proof. There are those at the station who wouldn't take kindly to the insinuation that one of their own might be capable of such a thing, even if he did commit other, lesser crimes. Breaking and entering and throwing around threats are a long way from murder."

"Buchannan would be all over me," I muttered, thinking about how he always seemed to look down on me. If anyone would jump at the chance to lock me up for smearing another cop's name, he'd be it.

"Actually, no," Paul said, surprising me. He didn't elaborate on who he was thinking of, however. "Even if Jay Miller knows something about any of the deaths, you have to be careful with who you talk to about him. We can assume Cliff's murder is connected to Wade Fink's, but we can't be sure, not until the killer is caught. And if you anger the wrong person with your accusations, it could make things harder on not just you, but me as well."

"I know." I hated it, but he was right. "I'd already talked to some of Wade's friends before Jay showed up, so I figured I might as well talk to the rest. I'm starting to piece together what happened that day, but I still feel like I'm missing something."

Paul didn't look happy that I hadn't listened and was talking to suspects, but at least he didn't reprimand me. "All right, what do you know?"

I gave him a quick rundown of my conversations with Lester, Hue, Zachary, and Roger. I did my best to lay it out chronologically without adding too much of my own speculation, but it wasn't easy. I finished with, "I'm not sure if they're protecting someone, a friend like Arthur, or if there's some other reason why their stories keep changing, but there's definitely something going on."

"I've talked to most of those men," Paul said. "I didn't get the impression any of them are capable of murder."

"Other than Arthur," I said.

"Possibly." He sighed. "Look, these men are friends. They will protect one another to a point. I wouldn't be surprised if some of their earlier omissions were because they didn't want to paint one of their friends in a bad light. There doesn't have to be anything sinister in it."

"Yeah, but two men are dead." Granted, one of the murders happened over thirty years ago, but still.

"And I don't want there to be more," Paul said. "We aren't sitting on our hands here." Meaning the police. "Buchannan's been keeping an eye on Arthur, even though he does have an alibi for Cliff's murder."

"A good one?" I asked.

"Good enough." He didn't elaborate.

Paul pushed his coffee to the side, hesitated, and then reached across the table to take my hands. "I know you want to help, but please, leave the investigating to us. We know what we are doing."

"So do I." Mostly. "I owe it to Rita to help as much as I can." Paul opened his mouth to say something, but I spoke over him. "I won't do anything stupid. If I talk to anyone, it will be in a public place, and I won't let anyone into my house unless I'm certain of their motives."

"Talking to these men could be dangerous."

I suddenly remembered my conversation with Madeline Watson. I'd forgotten completely about it after my chats with Zachary and Roger.

"Jay's dangerous," I said, which caused Paul to narrow his eyes at me. "I don't just mean because he scared me. I talked to Cliff's sister Madeline on the phone. She told me that Cliff confided in her that he felt guilty for Wade's death. She thinks he knew something, not that he actually did it, mind you. When she told him to go to the police, he said he couldn't. He was scared, Paul. Who do you think he was scared of?"

"That doesn't mean he was afraid of someone on the force," he said, though I could tell he was thinking about it.

"No, it doesn't," I admitted. "But Jay's been involved in this thing from the beginning. Every time something happened that involved Wade, he was there, and that includes the discovery of his body."

Paul sat back, a frown creeping over his features. "He was a cop." This time, when he said it, it sounded weak, as if he was truly starting to wonder.

"Consider it, please," I said. "I know you don't want to believe a cop could have been involved in any of this, but it's possible, isn't it? He threatened me, Paul. Why would he do that if he had nothing to do with either Cliff's or Wade's death?"

He was silent, eyes distant. I let him think it through.

If I was being honest with myself, I knew I was talking to the wrong Dalton. Patricia knew Jay Miller personally. If anyone could tell me whether or not he was dirty, she would know.

But would she tell me? She'd already warned me off talking to him. If I told her that he'd shown up to my house, would she tell me everything she knew? Or would she lock me up for my own protection?

"I'll talk to Jay," Paul said. He didn't sound happy about it.

"Thank you," I said. "Even if he didn't kill Cliff or Wade, I bet he knows who did." Why else threaten me?

Paul stood, leaving his coffee on the table, forgotten. "Go home and get some rest," he told me, even though he looked as if he could use it more than me. "If Jay tells me anything that shines a light on what happened to Wade, I'll let you know."

I rose and rounded the table. It was my turn to hesitate before I stepped close enough to kiss him on the cheek.

It's a credit to how dire things were becoming that he only gave me a strained smile before he turned and walked away.

Why did murder always have to come between us? It would be nice if we could have a day where we got to enjoy each other's company without having death follow us around.

I sat back down and nursed my coffee as I thought about what I should do next. Sure, doing what Paul asked and going home would be the smart thing to do, but just because he was going to talk to Jay Miller for me, didn't mean any progress would be made.

But what could I do? I'd already talked to everyone, and I doubted they'd up and change their tune now, not unless someone suddenly decided to come clean. I could try to pressure Patricia and see what else she might be able to tell me about Jay, but that could wait until I heard back from Paul.

Larry Ritchie's name floated through my mind again. The last time we'd talked, I'd known little about how everyone was connected. Could he tell me more? He knew Jay, knew the Coffee Drinkers. Maybe now that Cliff was dead, he'd be more forthcoming.

I polished off my coffee, and then tossed both my and Paul's cups in the trash. I was heading for the door when it opened and Raymond Lawyer strode through, a storm cloud in his wake.

I flinched back reflexively, but when his eyes fell on me, he didn't lash out.

"Ms. Hancock," he said. There was no love in the address, yet it wasn't full of the venom I'd come to expect from him.

"Raymond."

He cleared his throat and straightened his tie. "I'd like to speak with you a moment."

My gaze flickered to the counter where both Vicki and Mason were watching. Mason took a step toward us, as if he might intercede before things could get out of hand. I gave him a subtle shake of my head before turning my focus back to Raymond.

"Sure," I said. "I've got a few minutes."

Raymond motioned toward the nearest empty table. We both sat.

"I won't keep you," he said.

I crossed my arms over my chest. I knew it was a defensive posture, but I wasn't yet buying this kinder Raymond Lawyer. He was usually yelling by now. I could almost *feel* Beth watching us from up by the books, but I refused to look her way. I didn't want to divert his attention toward her.

"I understand why you are angry with me," Raymond said. "Admittedly, I haven't been happy with you since you came to Pine Hills. Your nosiness has rubbed me the wrong way, and continues to do so now."

"I'm sorry you feel that way," I said. "I've only tried to help."

His jaw tightened and he took a deep breath before he went on. "I don't approve of you running all over my town and getting involved in other people's business."

Your town? I thought, incredulous. What did he think he was, the mayor?

"Regina and I have spoken at great length," he went on,

"and I've come to realize that my antagonism toward you has adversely affected my view of those around me. When I discovered my former secretary was working for you, I came to the conclusion that you coerced her into it. I was wrong."

I blinked at him. Was he *apologizing?* "I . . ." My brain blanked. This couldn't be right.

"Ms. Milner is her own woman. She can choose to work where she wants. It is none of my business. I regret the distress I've caused her, and your customers, and will no longer do so." He stood. "Good day." He spun and walked out the door.

I remained seated, mouth agape. Did that really just happen?

Vicki and Mason approached. Both looked worried.

"He apologized," I said before either could speak. "Well, he kind of did, anyway."

"He what?" Mason asked. He sounded as shocked as I felt.

"He says he's not going to bother Beth anymore."

"Did he say why not?" Mason asked. "Not that I want him to, but this isn't like Dad." He glanced toward the door.

I shook my head. "He said he talked to Regina and he realized he was wrong."

"Really?" Vicki said. "Regina?"

"Something must be wrong," Mason said. "None of this sounds like Dad at all. And to claim Regina as the voice of reason . . ." He shook his head.

When I stood, I found my legs were shaky. "I doubt he'll apologize to Beth directly—talking to me was hard enough on him—but I do believe he was being honest."

"Wow," was all Vicki could say.

"I know." I wondered what had made him change his

mind so drastically. Could Regina Harper of all people be that good of an influence on him? I couldn't imagine it, not with how she'd treated me from the moment we'd met, but I supposed anything was possible.

"Someone should tell Beth," Mason said. "She'll be relieved."

"You two go ahead," I said. "I've got somewhere to be." Just because Raymond apologized, it didn't mean everything else would work out as easily.

Vicki and Mason drifted up toward where Beth was hiding in the books to give her the good news. Maybe now things could get back to normal around here and she'd stop walking on eggshells every time anyone so much as mentioned Raymond's name.

This better not be a ploy, I thought. I wouldn't put it past Raymond to try something like that, just to cause everyone to relax before hitting us with a fresh volley of vitriol once our guard was down.

But if that was the case, I'd deal with it when it happened. For now, I had a pair of murders to solve.

23

"You." Larry spat the word like a curse.

"I'm sorry to bother you again, but I had a couple more questions for you." I was standing on his front stoop, doing my best to look friendly. I realized I was already breaking my promise to Paul, and was talking to someone without backup, but hey, life's full of risks, so what was one more?

Larry didn't even try to act like he was pleased to see me. His scowl was deep enough, the lines might never leave his face. "I do believe I've said all I need to say on the matter of Wade Fink."

"What about Cliff Watson?" I asked. "I'm sure you've heard about his murder by now."

There was a flicker of pain in Larry's eyes before he spun his wheelchair around. "If you're not going to leave without having your say, I suppose you should come in."

I entered his house and closed the door behind me. A bowl of soup sat steaming on the table. Larry rolled over to it, but instead of eating, he pushed the bowl away.

"I didn't mean to interrupt your dinner," I said. "I won't take much of your time."

The strained smile he gave me said volumes about how he already thought I'd taken too much as it was. There was absolutely no kindness in the expression.

"You and Cliff were friends, correct?" I asked.

"We knew one another."

"That's all? You didn't join them for coffee every now and again?"

Larry sighed. "I might have. We didn't keep in touch much after I stopped showing up at the Banyon Tree."

"So, you did know Cliff and the others better than you let on the last time we spoke?"

Another sigh, this one annoyed. "Sure, if you want to take it that way, go ahead."

"I'm not accusing you of anything, Larry," I said. "I'm hoping you might be able to help me understand why someone would come after Cliff Watson. I assume it was because I was looking into a thirty-year-old murder."

"I think you've answered your own question."

"Do you believe Wade's killer also killed Cliff?"

He spread his hands. "You tell me."

"I think so," I said. "Cliff called me the night of his death. He was going to tell me something about Wade's murder, but he never got the chance. Someone killed him before he could tell me, which leads me to believe it was all connected."

Larry leaned forward in his chair with a sudden interest. "He knew something?"

"Apparently. And not long after Cliff's murder, Jay Miller showed up at my house, broke in, even. He warned me off investigating."

I might have been mistaken, but I was almost positive Larry paled. "Be careful, Ms. Hancock. You don't want to mess with Jay."

"That's what I've been told." Even though Larry hadn't offered, I sat down across from him so we were at eye level. "Do you believe Jay could have killed both Wade Fink and Cliff Watson?"

Larry looked away, but I don't think he was trying to be evasive. There was a tension in his posture, a wariness that had me on edge.

And I didn't think it had anything to do with me.

"Has he come to see you?" I asked, voice dropping to a whisper, as if I was afraid Jay might hear me. I guess a part of me was.

Larry gave a nearly imperceptible nod.

"Did he threaten you?"

"Jay doesn't know how to do anything but threaten," Larry said. "He's always been imposing, and has always known how to use it to his advantage. If he doesn't want you to do or say something, he has no problem letting you know. Usually, the repercussions for ignoring him are severe."

Like murder? I wondered. "Why would he come to see you?" I asked. "Do you know something about Wade's death you didn't tell me the last time we spoke?"

Larry started to shake his head before his shoulders sagged. "Honestly, I don't know. He warned me not to talk, but what was I going to say? I wrote articles on Wade's murder. I knew his friends. And Jay and I . . ." He made a frustrated sound before going on. "We had a working relationship back then. He fed me information, and I would write an article that would, shall we say, skew things the way he wanted them to be viewed."

"Did he pay you for slanting your articles?"

"Sometimes. Often, it was in favors. I didn't do anything I didn't want to do, mind you. I was against Wade's relationship then, and I'll stand by my opinion on the matter now. Jay didn't have to do much prodding to get me to write what he wanted in that regard."

If Jay Miller was against Wade and Rita dating, and decided to do something about it, could it have resulted in murder? I asked Larry as much.

"He couldn't have killed Wade. I think Jay is capable of such things, but he didn't murder that man."

"Are you sure?"

"Positive. He was with me when it happened."

I deflated. I'd been nearly certain Jay had something to do with Wade's death, and now I was back to square one.

"I wish I could tell you differently," Larry said. "It took me years to realize what kind of man Jay Miller truly was, what he still is. I regret some of what he had me write for him. I even regret giving so much time and thought to him. But despite my less than stellar opinion of the man, Jay Miller did not kill Wade Fink."

I wanted to hold on to the possibility that Larry was wrong about Jay, but it would do no one any good. If Larry was telling the truth and Jay was with him at the time of Wade's death, then I had to move on. That still left a solid group of suspects, any of whom could be responsible for both murders. Cliff had known something important enough to kill him for, which led me to believe it was likely one of his friends committed not just the first, but *both* murders.

"It's funny," Larry said. "But after how Jay derided Wade for dating a younger girl as much as he did, it's shocking he would up and do the same thing."

My breath caught. "Wait. Jay dated a younger woman?"

"Married her, even. He made such a big deal out of Wade and Rita, and then, once that's over, he goes out and finds himself a kid of his own. You can't make this sort of stuff up."

Larry had little else to provide, so I left him to his now cold dinner. My head spinning as I tried to piece things together.

Jay Miller was against Wade's choice in women, asks the local reporter to write scathing articles about him after his death, but then turns around and dates a younger woman of his own, as if he was trying to be contradictory.

Did that mean he was once interested in Rita, like Hue had been? Or did the controversy over Rita dating Wade create problems with his own relationship?

I should have asked Larry when Jay started dating the younger woman, but I'd been so stunned by the news, it hadn't occurred to me to ask until it was too late.

I arrived at the Pine Hills police station just before dark. Pine Hills had a tendency to shut down pretty early—most of the businesses closed their doors by seven, sometimes an hour or two earlier—but the police station remained active all evening. I only hoped Chief Dalton hadn't already called it a night, because I was desperate to talk to her.

I parked and climbed out of my car, just as Patricia Dalton appeared. The top two buttons of her uniform were undone, and she looked as if all she wanted to do was take a hot bath and then crash into bed for a good night's sleep.

I almost regretted spoiling that for her.

"Chief!" I called as she made her way to her car, which was parked on the opposite side of the lot. "Chief Dalton!"

She turned, saw me, and her shoulders slumped. When she walked over to me, she did so under obvious mental protest. "Ms. Hancock."

"I'm glad I caught you," I said. "I take it you were heading home?"

"I'm off duty, so yeah. If this has something to do with an active police investigation, I'll remind you that you aren't an officer of the law, and that whatever it is you have to say can wait until morning."

She had me there, but I wouldn't be deterred. "Have you talked to Paul lately?" I asked. "He went to see Jay Miller because Jay threatened me and I was pretty sure he was involved in either Wade's or Cliff's murder at the time. Now, I'm not so sure, and I was hoping that Paul might have talked to you and told you something of what was going on." I stopped as I realized I was starting to babble. I did that when I got nervous. And tired.

"He went to see Jay Miller?" Patricia asked, her entire demeanor changing. She stood up taller, tired eyes going sharp. "Alone?"

"He was planning on asking him a few questions, that's all," I said, growing nervous by her sudden shift.

"And you said Jay threatened you?"

"Broke into my house and everything. He also threatened the reporter, Larry Ritchie. Larry says Jay didn't kill Wade, but I bet he knows who did. Why else show up to warn us off talking about it if he's innocent?"

"When did Paul go see him?"

"I'm not sure. I'd say it was about an hour ago, maybe a little longer?"

She yanked her phone from her pocket and jabbed at it like it had offended her, before she slammed it up against her ear hard enough it had to have hurt.

I watched her, trepidation growing. Everyone said Jay Miller was a dangerous man, but Paul could take care of himself, right? I mean, Jay was once a cop. He wouldn't hurt a fellow police officer who was merely asking a few innocent questions, would he?

"He's not answering," Patricia said, pointing her phone at me. "You try."

I jerked my car door open and fished for my phone, which was stuffed into my purse. My hands were starting to shake, and I felt like I'd made a huge mistake by telling Paul about Jay.

I hit Paul's number and waited. Four rings, and then voicemail.

"No answer."

Patricia jammed her phone back into her pocket. "Go home. Wait by your phone there. I'll call you when I find him."

"Do you think Jay did something to Paul?" My voice might have come out as a squeak, but I'll never admit it.

"I don't know. Go home." She turned as if to leave me standing there, worried sick about the one guy I'd fallen hard for.

There was absolutely no way I could sit back and do nothing.

"I want to come." I tried to make it a demand, but my voice had yet to resume its normal tone. I sounded like a terrified mouse.

"No."

"Please. I can't sit at home and wonder if I'm somehow responsible for Paul getting hurt. I'll stay in the car, but please, take me with you."

Chief Dalton shook her head, but I could tell she was wavering. She was worried about her son. *I* was worried about him. Together, we'd stop at nothing to make sure he was okay.

"If you don't take me, I'll just follow you," I said.

Patricia closed and rubbed at her eyes, but relented. "Fine. You'll stay in the car and won't say a peep until I've talked to Jay, understood?"

"Completely."

We hurried over to her personal vehicle. I was forced to toss a half dozen empty travel mugs into the back seat before I was able to slide into the passenger seat. Chief Dalton had the car moving even before I was fully buckled in.

"We might be overreacting," I said, clutching at the dash and roof as she spun the wheel hard to turn onto the main road. I may have let loose a half scream, but once again, I would never admit to doing so.

"Jay Miller was suspended briefly for assaulting another officer," she said. "He was reinstated early and nothing I could find explained why. Albie Bruce acted like the command came from over his head, and regretted he was forced to act. I believe him." She glanced at me. "I don't think we're overreacting."

"Oh." I tried to dig my nails into the dash as she took a turn so fast I felt the tires try to lift from the road. It was taking all my self-control not to whimper.

We sped through Pine Hills, and down a long road that alternated between gravel and some sort of pebbly pavement. A broken-down tractor sat at the side of the road, leaning precariously toward us. It looked as if it had been there for a few hundred years.

Patricia spun the wheel hard at a driveway, and this time, I did whimper, as my mind imagined us rolling. Her tires didn't squeal, but I felt them lose their grip on the road as she turned onto the driveway, which led to a house that wasn't much bigger than my own small place. It was well tended, and despite how out of the way it was, it didn't feel isolated.

"No cars," I commented as she pulled to a stop in front of what I assumed was Jay Miller's house. "That's a good thing, right?" Because if Jay shot Paul or was holding him captive, both their cars would be sitting in the driveway.

Or so I hoped.

Patricia didn't answer. She left the car running as she got out and strode purposefully toward the front door. She used the meat of her hand to hammer on it, calling out to Jay, then to Paul. When no one answered, she hammered again, and then tried the door.

It opened silently, yet my mind supplied the ominous creak anyway.

She glanced back at me, and from the looks of it, she was more than worried now. I could almost read the "This isn't good" expression on her face before she turned back to the house.

After a few deep breaths, Chief Dalton vanished inside.

I made it all of twenty seconds before my door was open and I was heading for the door. I kept imagining the worst, that Jay had attacked Paul, had shoved him into his own trunk, and then had driven him off. Or that Paul was left lying, bleeding, on the floor, and that Jay was miles away, safely in Paul's cruiser, lights and siren blaring so that he could speed with impunity.

I burst into the house, but came to an immediate halt when I saw what awaited me.

A lamp lay shattered on the floor beside a couch that had been upended. The television had a fist-sized hole in it, as did the wall beside it.

There was no sign of Jay Miller or Paul Dalton.

Patricia stood in the middle of the destruction, scouring

it with cop eyes. When she turned to me, there was a fire behind her gaze that just about singed my eyebrows. Then, slowly, she bent down and picked up a pair of items that had been lying beside the shattered lamp. I'd overlooked them in my first perusal of the room.

In Chief Dalton's hands were Paul Dalton's phone and hat. There was blood on the both of them.

24

A strange sense of calm washed over me, burying the fear that had immediately welled up in my chest. I didn't know if it was because I'd grown as a person, or if Chief Dalton's own steadiness kept me from freaking out, but I managed not to scream or panic as she turned Paul's phone over in her hand. The screen was fine, and when she tried it, it turned on, showing both our missed calls.

"What do we do?" I asked.

Patricia didn't answer. She took her time and scanned the room without touching anything but the phone and Paul's hat, which she held loosely between two fingers. The phone, on the other hand, she clutched as if she was afraid that if she let it go, it would mean Paul would be gone for good.

I remained where I was and let her work without nagging her for an answer. My involvement had only caused things to escalate, and I was afraid that if I were to poke around Jay Miller's house, or distract Patricia from her job, I'd somehow trigger an explosion that would wipe Pine Hills completely off the map.

Okay, so maybe I wasn't as calm as I'd hoped.

Paul was in danger. If something happened to him . . .

It won't. I wasn't sure how I knew, but I was positive he'd come out of this okay. I couldn't imagine it otherwise.

"There's no indication as to where they went," Chief Dalton said, returning to me. "Did Paul say anything the last time you talked to him?"

"He said he was going to talk to Jay—that's it."

She nodded. "Go back to the car. I'm going to call this in and then drive you back to your vehicle. From there, you're going to go home and wait by your phone. I want you to call me the instant you hear from anyone who might know where Paul and Jay are."

"You think they're together?"

"I hope so. Now, go. I need to focus."

My instincts screamed at me to tell her that I wanted to help, that I would not sit on my hands while Paul was missing, but I realized I'd only get in the way if I did.

"Okay," I said.

Patricia walked me to the car, and then returned to the house to make her call. Now that I was seated and didn't have her eyes on me, I started to tremble. I picked up my phone and almost dialed Paul's number, until I remembered that the phone was currently in his mother's hands.

I mentally ran down every possibility. If Jay attacked Paul and subdued him, where would he take him? I was sure there were abandoned buildings in Pine Hills, but for the life of me, I couldn't bring any to mind. If Jay was working with someone, would he take an unconscious police officer there so the both of them could decide what to do with him?

Of course, we were practically out in the middle of nowhere. We'd passed at least a dozen places where tire tracks led off the road, into fields and wooded areas where Jay could hide away and avoid detection.

My mind refused to consider other possibilities of what Jay might do with Paul in the woods. He *was* going to come back home.

The fifteen minutes it took before another patrol car arrived was the longest quarter hour of my life. Officer John Buchannan got out of the car and, surprisingly, came over to check on me before going in to meet with his police chief.

"You okay, Ms. Hancock?" he asked. He was dead serious, not a hint of accusation in his eye.

"Kind of." Scratch that. I closed my eyes and took a deep, trembling breath. When I opened them again, tears blurred my vision. "Actually, no, not really."

He nodded as if that was exactly what he'd expected me to say. "We'll find him."

Patricia motioned for him to join her at the house. Buchannan reached in through the window, gripped my shoulder briefly, and then joined the police chief inside Jay Miller's house.

I closed my eyes and fought back the tears. Buchannan's gesture was meant to reassure me, but it had the opposite effect. I mean, John Buchannan sometimes felt like my mortal enemy, a man determined to see me tossed in a cell to rot away for the rest of my life. If he was willing to drop every last grievance to try to make me feel better, then things were far more dire than I was allowing myself to believe.

Another ten minutes passed and two more cruisers appeared, filling the driveway with flashing lights. Becca Garrison got out of one. She gave me a single nod before joining the other cops inside. Then, Patricia returned to her car and started the engine.

"I could call someone to get me," I said. "You should be here."

"I'll take you," she said. "I'll do more good back at the station than here." She gripped the wheel tightly. "I've already screwed up by picking up the phone. I need distance."

"He's your son. No one will blame you for it."

She glanced at me. "I will."

We spent the ride in silence, each of us awash in our worries. I kept seeing Paul's face the last time I'd seen him, kept playing over our last conversation in a futile attempt to find a hidden meaning in his words that would tell me where he was.

When we got to the station, I got out of Chief Dalton's car as if in a dream and wandered over to my own vehicle. It took three tries before the engine coughed to life. I turned on the lights since it was now dark, and then drove, car shuddering in a way that indicated that something was wrong, but I didn't head toward home.

Lights were on in the house Vicki shared with Mason and their cat, Trouble. I parked out front, started to open the door, and then reconsidered. I could see them through the window, eating a late dinner. They were smiling and laughing, with Trouble sitting on a chair at Vicki's side, begging for scraps.

Vicki was my best friend. She would know what to say. Her mere presence would make me feel better.

But could I break up their good humor with my troubles? As far as I knew, Paul was perfectly fine, taking a well-deserved nap at home. Of course, that would mean dismissing his bloody phone and hat as nothing, which it most definitely wasn't.

I can't do this to her. I tore my eyes away from the happy couple, put my car in gear, and this time, I headed for home.

Misfit was waiting for me by the door. I scooped him up and carried him to the couch, where I held him tight. The clock ticked the seconds by. Minutes passed slowly, each one feeling like a lifetime. I watched the second hand make its rounds, wishing there was something I could do.

When my phone rang, I screamed so loud the entire neighborhood must have heard it. Misfit shot from my lap—leaving five shallow cuts in my thigh as he went— and vanished into the bedroom where he'd likely hide for the next hour.

I snatched up my phone, and without checking the ID, I answered.

"Hello? Paul."

"Hey, Krissy."

All the air shot from my lungs, and I was struck completely speechless for a long couple of seconds. *It's him! He's okay.* Paul sounded exhausted, but alive.

"Where were you?" I finally managed.

"I took Jay to the hospital in Levington."

Wait. My mind tried to figure out how to process that information. Did Paul beat Jay up? "What happened?" I asked.

He took a deep breath and let it out in a huff. "When I arrived at Jay's place, the door was open. When he didn't answer my call, I went inside and found him on the floor, bleeding. He was just coming to and when I tried to help him and ask him what happened, he reacted violently. I lost my phone and hat before I was able to subdue him.

Earned myself a good shot to the eye as well. When I tried his phone, it was dead. Someone cut the line, apparently."

"He was attacked?" I thought back to Cliff's murder and wondered if it was connected to Jay being assaulted.

Who was I kidding? Of course it was.

"Seems so. Once I calmed him down, I took him to the hospital. He has a pretty bad head wound and his left hand is broken. It wasn't until I got here that I realized I hadn't grabbed my phone on the way out. I should have called as soon as I realized that, but I wanted to get the story from Jay as soon as possible."

"Did you call your mom yet?" I asked. "She's looking for you."

"I did." He laughed. "She ripped into me pretty good for giving her a scare, but was better when I told her what happened."

"You should have called us," I said, unable to keep the reprimand out of my voice.

"I know. I'm sorry about that, I really am. It all happened so fast, I wasn't thinking clearly. Maybe I can blame it on the knock I took to my head. Still have a headache, if it's any consolation."

I smiled. "Maybe a little."

He laughed. "I'll make it right by telling you what Jay told me, if you're interested."

I sat up, all ears. Misfit peeked around the corner in the hall, and then, once certain I wasn't going to scream again, he meandered toward me. He didn't jump up on my lap again, but he lay down near enough that I could pet him if I wanted.

"All right," I said. "Tell me."

"Arthur Cantrell was the one who attacked him."

"What?" My voice rose, not quite to shouting volume,

but loud enough that Misfit gave me a good glare before settling back down. "Arthur? Wade and Cliff's friend?"

"The same," Paul said. "Chief is picking him up now. The way Jay tells it, Arthur showed up roaring mad and came at him. They fought, but Arthur had caught him by surprise and just about knocked him out on the first blow. He beat on Jay, broke his hand, and then bloodied him up real good before Arthur left him for dead. I'm thinking Arthur might be behind Cliff's murder."

"And Wade's," I said. I knew Arthur was a violent man but didn't think he'd resort to attacking his friends.

Then again, he *had* gotten into a fight with Wade all those years ago.

"Once I hang up here, I'm going to the station. Hopefully, Arthur will confess and we can put this whole murder business behind us."

"Yeah, that'd be great." I frowned. "Why would Arthur attack Jay? Jay came here to warn me off investigating, so it wasn't like he was running around telling everyone who killed Wade or Cliff. If Arthur was the one who killed them, what did Jay have to do with it?"

"I don't know," Paul admitted. "Jay wasn't exactly forthcoming in that regard. He claims Arthur just showed up and attacked him. Didn't give a reason as to why, and when I tried to press him, he clammed up, claiming his head hurt too much for him to think clearly."

"Seems fishy to me," I said.

"Krissy, it doesn't have to be complicated. Maybe Jay Miller knew Arthur killed Wade, as had Cliff Watson. Since there's been renewed interest in the old case, Arthur decided to silence anyone who might rat him out. He started with Cliff, and then moved on to Jay. It could be that simple."

"Yeah, but . . ." But what? Just because I didn't solve it myself didn't mean Paul was wrong.

"If Arthur confesses, you'll be the first to know," Paul said. "I only hope he didn't go after someone else after attacking Jay."

I thought of Roger and his diminished mental state, of Zachary and his physical ailment. If Arthur decided to silence all his friends, they wouldn't be too hard to remove from the equation.

"Is someone checking in on his other friends?" I asked, halfway off the couch like I might do it myself.

"Of course. Chief will have someone check on Rita as well. No one else is going to get hurt tonight, I promise you."

I wished I could believe him, but something still wasn't ringing true for me. Why attack Jay like that? Cliff had been killed quickly and without a struggle. Jay's house looked like they'd had an all-out brawl. Cliff had been willing to talk. Jay was trying to keep people from talking.

"I'd better get going," Paul said, breaking into my thoughts. "I just wanted to call and let you know I'm okay. And to say thank you for worrying about me." He cleared his throat. "Mom told me you were concerned."

"Don't ever do this to me again, okay?"

"I'll try." He laughed again, but it died quickly. "I'll talk to you tomorrow. Stay safe, Krissy."

"You too, Paul." I paused, considered what to say, but everything sounded lame in my head. I left him with a "I'm glad you're okay."

He disconnected, but I held the phone to my ear just a few moments longer. Paul was safe; he was really safe.

But why wasn't I comforted?

I rose and found a piece of paper and a pen. I wrote out all the Coffee Drinkers' names, included Wade's, and then added Larry Ritchie and Jay Miller beneath that.

I stared at my list, tried to piece everything together as a puzzle, but not all the pieces went together as cleanly as I'd like. Jay might have been a violent person and a bad cop, but that didn't mean he was a killer.

Maybe Paul was right and Arthur was our man. Maybe he thought Jay knew more than he actually did, or perhaps Jay had put it all together and had shown up to threaten Arthur, just like he had me. Arthur panics, tracks Jay down, and then tries to kill him. End of story.

"Maybe Eleanor can rest now," I told Misfit. Across the way, all the lights were off in Eleanor Winthrow's old place. Jane wasn't there, and I wondered if I'd ever see her again. Nothing said she'd have to tell me good-bye, though it did hurt to think she might have left town without visiting me one last time.

It appeared as if my role in the murders of Wade Fink and Cliff Watson was done. If anyone could get the truth out of Arthur and Jay, it was Chief Dalton and her son.

I tossed my list into the trash. And then, with a yawn that nearly knocked me off my feet, I carried Misfit to bed, where I promptly fell into an exhausted slumber.

25

Morning came and I was up, showered, and on the phone within thirty minutes of my eyes cracking open.

"Hi, Rita, it's Krissy. Would you mind if I stopped by?"

"Krissy?" Rita sounded groggy, but in good spirits. "Why, I suppose that would be all right. Why? Has something happened?"

"I'll fill you in when I get there," I said. "But I think we might have figured out who killed Wade."

"Oh, dear." I could almost see her fluttering her hand over her chest. "I'll get the coffee on."

I hung up and then called Paul. It went to voicemail, and my heart did a little hiccup but calmed quickly. Paul was fine. If he'd spent all night dealing with Arthur Cantrell, he was likely still asleep. I could get the details from him later.

I tossed some bread into the toaster, fed Misfit, and then once my toast was done, I carried it—and a cookie in preparation for Rita's coffee—to my car. I turned the key.

Nothing happened.

"Not now," I muttered, trying the key again. This time, there was a sputter, and then the car roared to life. "Thank you." I patted the dash, while making a mental note to finally look into getting a new car. I'd needed to replace my old Ford for months, but whenever I thought it was time, it would work fine for a few weeks, before something like this would happen. The heat no longer worked, nor did the air conditioner, but I still loved the thing.

I drove to Rita's, mentally prepping myself for everything I needed to say, and *how* I was going to say it. As far as I knew, Arthur had yet to confess to anything. And despite my doubts, he was very likely both Wade's and Cliff's killer. Why else attack Jay?

My mind tried to answer that question in ways that didn't connect to the murder, but I refused to let it. Things were going to be difficult enough already without my brain convoluting everything.

Even though it was light out, Rita had turned on her porch light. I parked beside her car, gathered my meager breakfast, and approached the front door. It opened before I could knock.

Rita looked normal, but her eyes were haunted, worried. She ushered me into her house without a word and then peered outside like she expected someone to be watching us, before closing the door.

"Coffee is in the kitchen, dear," she said. "I made myself a cup already. Help yourself."

It took only a minute or two to arrange my morning caffeine and breakfast to my liking. I carried them to a chair opposite where Rita sat. She held her coffee mug in both hands. I noted she was trembling, and when she'd glance up, she'd look quickly away, like she was afraid of what I had to say.

"Are you all right?" I asked her, concerned. Rita had never shown signs of any illnesses, but she was overweight and middle-aged. I feared too much of a shock might send her in a downward spiral that she might never recover from.

Then again, maybe I was just projecting. I was worried how she might react to me once I started accusing people she knew of murder. Would she be angry? Would she storm out of here looking for Arthur, to exact her own form of vengeance? Or would she throw me out on my ear, vowing never to speak to me again?

"I'm fine, dear." Rita set her mug aside. "It's strange. I've wondered all these years about what happened back then, and now that I might finally discover who killed my Wade . . ." She took a shuddering breath. "I'm not sure I'm ready."

"We don't have a confession or proof or anything," I said. "If you don't want me to tell you what we think until we have something, I understand." Now that I was here, a part of me would almost welcome holding off until some-time later.

"It's not that," Rita said. "I do want to know. But I'm afraid I'm not going to like what you have to say." She laughed. "Of course, why would I like it? Wade was murdered and his killer has spent the last thirty-plus years a free man. At this point, whatever punishment he receives will never be enough."

I leaned forward and took her hand. Rita squeezed, before releasing me. "Now, dear, tell me what you've learned."

I took a bite of my toast and then chased it down with a long drink of coffee to organize my thoughts before speaking.

"Arthur Cantrell attacked Jay Miller last night," I said, deciding to start with something I knew for a fact. "The police are currently working on the theory he did so in order to shut Jay up. They believe he might have done the same to Cliff Watson."

Rita's hand covered her mouth, her eyes wide. "Arthur attacked Jay?"

"Paul had to take Jay to the hospital," I said. "The assumption is that Jay found out that Arthur killed both Wade and Cliff, and then confronted him about it. He might have tried to blackmail Arthur, or threatened him somehow, but instead of getting whatever he wanted, he ended up in the hospital for his trouble."

"Jay said this?" Rita asked.

"Well, no, not as far as I know."

"Then Arthur admitted to it?"

I could feel myself blush. "No."

Her brow furrowed. "So, the attack could have been about something else."

A sinking feeling formed in my gut. "I suppose so. But it would be a pretty big coincidence, wouldn't it? Cliff Watson is murdered after calling me to confess something about the crime. Then, Jay is attacked and left for dead not too long after."

Rita tapped her chin. She didn't look like she bought it. I couldn't say I blamed her. I was still struggling to make all the pieces fit.

Which should tell me something, shouldn't it?

I pushed the thought away, knowing that if I let myself think too hard about it, I'd find even bigger holes in the narrative, and then what? I'd end up on someone else's doorstep, asking them about a murder they may or may not have committed.

"I know you don't want to think one of Wade's friends killed him," I said, "but it looks like that might be the case.

The more I talked to them, the more it seemed as if the
Coffee Drinkers had something to hide."

"But Arthur?" Rita asked. "I know he's had his troubles,
and I can't say he was my favorite person in the world, but
I never believed he could be responsible for Wade's death.
I . . . I just can't believe it!"

"The police should have him in custody by now." That
was, unless he ran after attacking Jay. I really should have
called Patricia to find out if she'd caught him. He could
be on his way to Rita's house by now, if not making his
way out of the country.

Stop it, Krissy. Already, I could feel my resolve
dwindling, and new questions began popping up. What
about Zachary's story? Or Hue's infatuation with Rita?

Rita sat back in her chair and shook her head. "Lordy
Lou, I'm absolutely shocked by all of this. I can't believe
Arthur would have done such a thing." She abruptly stood
and went into the kitchen. She poured herself a water from
the tap and drained it in one go.

I gave her time to work it through. These were people
she knew. Even though they'd treated her badly over the
years, it still had to hurt to find out one of them might
have been responsible for her boyfriend's death.

Key word: *might*.

Rita returned to the living room and sat down heavily.
She picked up her coffee, looked at it a moment, and then
set it aside again.

"Now what do we do?" she asked.

"We wait," I said. "The police will get Arthur to talk.
I'm sure Jay will have a lot to say as well. Even if Arthur
denies everything, there's a good chance they'll get a
warrant to go through his house. There's probably evidence

of some kind there for Cliff's murder. From there, they'll connect the dots."

"Arthur Cantrell a killer." She tsked. "I suppose I should have known." She sucked in a breath. "Did he attack Candace, too? Is she all right?"

"Candace?" I asked. *Why do I know that name?*

"Jay's wife." She frowned at me like I should have known all along. "She used to be my best friend, you know? We used to do everything together, but after Wade died, we drifted apart. I still kept tabs on her over the years. I suppose I was hoping that eventually we'd become friends again, but it just never happened."

"Jay's married?" I thought back to the disaster of his house but didn't recall seeing anything that hinted that a woman lived there.

Then again, I'd been pretty distracted at the time. She could have been sitting in the next room and I doubted I would have noticed.

"He is. Candace married Jay Miller a few years after Wade's death, which came as a surprise to me, let me tell you. I didn't even think she *liked* him, let alone cared about him enough to marry him."

"Hold up," I said, still struggling to piece it all together. "Jay married your best friend?"

"He did. Was she there when he was attacked?"

"I . . . I don't think so." *Candace.* Where had I heard that name before? It bothered me I couldn't figure it out. "When I was at Jay's, I didn't see anything that indicated she was there at the time of the attack. And Paul never mentioned her when he called me."

"Oh, good." Rita relaxed into the couch. "We might have lost touch, but I don't want anything bad to happen to her. You know how it is—you and your friends move on, take different paths, yet you still think back fondly on the good times."

Rita continued talking, but I hardly heard her. Candace's name kept playing over and over in my mind. Had Jay mentioned her? I was pretty sure he hadn't.

But if not Jay, who else would have talked about his wife to me?

"I think someone mentioned a Candace once," I said, cutting off whatever Rita was saying. "But I can't figure out who."

"I might have mentioned her once or twice," Rita said. "Though I don't recall doing so. Gosh, I haven't thought about her all that much in recent years, honestly. Just in passing. I'd see her and think, 'I should go over and talk to her,' and then the moment would pass and life would go on."

"No, I'm pretty sure it was someone else." Or was it? The more I thought about it, the more I kept thinking I'd heard it from a woman, who very well might have been Rita. "How did Jay and Candace meet?"

Rita sat up, the concern returning. "Why? Do you think she's in danger?"

"I don't know," I admitted. But there was something there, something important. I just couldn't seem to grasp it.

"Well, she used to come with me when I'd go to meet Wade at the Banyon Tree, back when, well, Wade was alive." She took a huge gulp of coffee, like she needed the jolt to press on. "Jay was there a few times, lurking about like he was wont to do. Candace never really talked to him, or anyone else really. She was embarrassed, I suppose."

"Embarrassed? Why?"

"Her dad was there, watching her like a hawk."

It was like a comet had come hurtling out of the sky and struck me upside my head.

"Candace's dad was one of Wade's friends?"

"Of course he was, dear." She rolled her eyes like she was talking to the dumbest person alive. Maybe she was right. "She *was* Candace Ross before she became Candace Miller."

The photograph of the girl I'd seen with Zachary and Vera Ross came instantly to mind. I was pretty sure neither of them had mentioned her name, and I know I hadn't seen it written down in the house somewhere, so how had I heard it?

"If Candace wasn't with Jay when he was attacked," I said, "where would she have been?"

"At work, probably," Rita said.

I stared at her. She huffed and gave me another eye roll. "At Geraldo's. She's a waitress there."

Holes in the puzzle of Cliff's death filled in at a rapid pace. Those holes, in turn, completed a picture of what had happened to Wade Fink. It all tied back to one embarrassed woman.

"What?" Rita asked, rising. "Did I say something wrong?"

"Candace was our waitress," I said, slowly standing. "When Paul and I went on our date, she served us."

"She *is* a waitress, dear," Rita said. "Though, honestly, I don't know why she doesn't make Jay work instead. She's been waitressing for years, and deserves a break. I don't think he's doing much of anything these days, now that he retired from the force."

"No, that's not what I mean. She was there, when Cliff called me. She was standing beside the table when I told Paul Cliff was going to talk to me about Wade's death."

"And? I don't see what you're getting at."

"She was *there!*" I grabbed Rita by the arms, willed her to understand. "Someone killed Cliff after he talked to me. I couldn't figure out how anyone could have known about our conversation. Cliff wouldn't have told anyone he was about to reveal information on Wade's killer, so how did they know?"

"But Candace wouldn't have hurt him. She's not that type of woman."

I opened my mouth to object, but she was right. Candace was at Geraldo's at the same time Paul and I were there. Even if she'd left almost as soon as she heard me tell Paul about my conversation with Cliff, she wouldn't have had time to get to his house, kill him, and escape before Paul and I arrived.

"She called someone," I said. "She told someone that Cliff was going to tell. *She knows who killed Wade!*"

I released Rita from my grip and scrambled for my phone. Rita was babbling behind me, but I didn't hear her. I dialed Paul's number, got voicemail, and then, frustrated, ran out the door.

"Krissy? What's going on?" Rita followed me into the driveway.

"I'll tell you later," I said as I climbed behind the wheel of my car. This time, when I turned the key, it started up beautifully.

Rita was waving her hands at me. I rolled down my window and leaned out as she asked, "What about Arthur?"

"Forget about him." There was a chance he was still tied to the murders, but I was truly beginning to doubt it. "I'll call you and tell you what Candace says."

Rita leaned against her doorframe, hand going to her

forehead, as if she felt faint, before she waved for me to go ahead and leave.

I didn't need to be told twice. I put my car in gear, backed out of Rita's driveway, and with a grinding of gears, went in search of Candace Miller.

26

I tried Paul again as I pulled up in front of the Miller home, but once more got voicemail. A car sat in the driveway this time, an old beat-up Beetle. I didn't know if the car belonged to Jay or his wife, Candace. I was hoping for the latter.

I left Paul a quick message, telling him where I was and why, and then got out of my car.

Something thunked inside the house. It was followed by a loud, feminine curse, and then another thump.

I waited to see if anyone else spoke up. As far as I knew, Jay was still in the hospital, but it was possible he'd been released. I had a feeling he wouldn't be happy about me showing up on his front doorstep, not after warning me off the investigation.

When no other voices joined the woman's, I approached the front door and knocked.

Everything went silent. I waited a handful of heartbeats, and then knocked again.

"Who's there?"

"Candace?" I called through the door. "My name is

Krissy Hancock. You served me at Geraldo's the other night."

"Why are you here?" Her voice was closer to the door now. "I don't put up with stalkers. I'll call the cops."

"They know I'm here." Or would, once Paul checked his voicemail. "I want to talk to you about what happened to Jay."

There was another long stretch of silence. I wondered if Candace had wandered away from the door, intent on ignoring me. She had no reason to talk to me. To her, I was just a nosy woman who'd shown up on her front doorstep.

"Candace?" I pressed a hand to the door. "Please. I just want to talk."

"Go away. I've got cleaning to do." Something thumped. It sounded like she was breaking more than she was cleaning.

I didn't want to stand outside, yelling through a door, but I didn't want to walk away, either. If Arthur didn't confess to the murders, and if they didn't find evidence in his home, then the police wouldn't have him on anything but Jay's assault. Candace might know more, and I intended to find out what it was.

"You called someone that night, didn't you?" I asked. "After Cliff Watson called me, you overheard me talking to my date about it and you made a call. A few minutes later, Cliff was dead. That can't be a coincidence."

All sounds ceased. Even the birds fell silent, as if they'd been listening in and were shocked by what I was insinuating.

I waited and wondered what could be going through Candace's mind. She might not have intended for her call to get Cliff murdered, but I was almost positive it had. The only question was: Would she tell me who she called?

The sound of a dead bolt being unlocked was followed by the door opening.

Candace Miller looked disheveled and exhausted. She wasn't wearing her waitress uniform, but rather, a pair of worn pajama bottoms and a ratty T-shirt with a faded Aerosmith logo on it. Her feet were bare and her hair was pulled into a messy bun atop her head.

She stared at me with red-rimmed eyes for a good couple of seconds before turning and walking into the house. She left the door open for me to follow.

With some trepidation, I did.

The house was still a mess, but the floor had been swept of most of the debris. A new lamp sat where the old had been broken. The television was on the floor, a few more cracks in it as if she'd tossed it to the ground in disgust.

"Came home to this and thought that it was over," she said, plopping wearily down onto the couch. "Took Jay half the night to call me and tell me what happened. Guess I didn't rate too high on his list of priorities."

She didn't sound surprised about coming home to a wrecked house. It made me wonder if it happened often. I scanned her arms and neck for bruises, but there were none. Of course, that meant little, since a lot of abusers made sure the marks they left were hidden beneath clothing.

"I didn't recognize your voice when you knocked," Candace went on. "But after you mentioned the call, I realized who you were."

"You called someone that night, after my call, didn't you?"

She looked down at her hands. She wore fingernail

polish, but it was badly chipped and one of her knuckles was bleeding. I couldn't tell if she'd punched something, or if she'd caught her finger on something sharp. With the mess Jay had left, it could have been anything.

"Candace, a man is dead." Two, actually, but I didn't want to lump Wade's death on top of Cliff's quite yet. "Your call might have caused it. Who did you call?"

"You were talking about people I knew," she said, glancing at me with one eye before returning her gaze to her hands. "It freaked me out a little."

That wasn't an answer, so I pressed. "Did you call Jay? Could he have killed Cliff? Or maybe he passed word on to Arthur Cantrell, who then killed him." And then, later, realized he needed to silence Jay to tie up loose ends. Could Arthur have made plans to come after Candace next?

"Arthur did this." She gestured around the room. "What do you think happened?"

"I think you made a mistake," I said. "No one will blame you for worrying about your friends and family. If you made the call just to warn someone about what was happening and then they took it too far, it's not on you. But if that person did kill Cliff, then they do need to face justice."

Candace picked up a piece of ceramic that was lying next to her. I couldn't tell what it once was. She turned it over in her hand once, fingers flexing on it.

"I didn't do anything."

"Are you saying you didn't make a call?"

She shot another glance at me out of the corner of her eye, and then abruptly stood, dropping the ceramic piece onto the floor, where it broke in half.

"Excuse me a moment." She spun and headed for the bathroom.

I let her go. If she needed a moment to calm her nerves, then I'd let her have it. Whether she intended for Cliff to die or not, this had to be hard on her.

I took the time to wander the room. There were a pair of photographs on the floor beside a chair, tossed among broken glass and plastic. I picked up the photos and looked at each in turn.

The first was of Candace and Jay on their wedding day. She looked happy, though Jay's smile looked a little forced. I wondered if the man knew how to smile correctly, or if he was always scowling and sneering. There was a crease along the middle of the photo, one that had been added before it was framed, as if it had been bent in two and kept that way for a time. *Marital troubles?* I wondered, before setting it aside.

The other photograph was of Candace with her parents. It was a recent picture, not like the one I'd seen in the Ross home. It couldn't have been more than a year old. The family was sitting at a picnic table somewhere, enjoying the outdoors.

Yet something about it bothered me. Candace was sitting beside her mother, with Zachary sitting somewhat apart from the both of them. He was smiling, but his eyes looked sad, as did Candace's. It was as if they shared something between them, something they both were struggling with.

I returned the photograph to the floor just as Candace returned. Her face was damp, telling me she'd likely splashed it with water from the sink, either to mask her tears, or to merely wake herself up.

"I don't have anything to say to you," she said, voice stronger than it had been before she'd retreated to the bathroom.

"Arthur Cantrell attacked your husband," I said. "Are you protecting him?"

"I didn't call Arthur. I didn't call Jay. Cliff's death had nothing to do with me."

"But you told someone, didn't you?" I asked. "He was dead shortly after he called me. You overheard it, and since you knew everyone involved, it's not too big of a leap to think you called someone about it. It's too much of a coincidence to not be connected."

She shrugged. "I don't know what to tell you." She started straightening up again as if I wasn't still standing in the middle of her living room.

I watched her for a minute, wondering what I could possibly say to make her talk. She seemed perfectly content to ignore me, though there was a tension in her shoulders that told me she was painfully aware of my presence.

She's waiting for something. It might simply be for me to leave, but I had a feeling it was something else.

I considered what I knew of the murders, and what role Candace might have played in them. She was the daughter of one of the Coffee Drinkers, was once Rita's friend. She knew Wade, knew Cliff, but she wasn't friends with them.

But someone she loved was.

"You called your dad, didn't you?"

She froze, halfway to picking up the ceramic piece she'd recently dropped.

"That's it, isn't it?" Of course she'd call her dad. He was Cliff's friend, had been Wade's. "You heard me talking to Paul, so you called Zachary to tell him what was happening, and then he . . ."

He what? Killed Cliff? That seemed unlikely considering his physical state. But I *could* see him calling Arthur.

Candace opened her mouth to speak, but the sound of gravel caused her to snap it closed again. A car door slammed and a moment later, the door banged open, revealing Zachary Ross. He leaned heavily on a cane and was breathing hard, as if he'd pushed himself to the limits to get there. His face was awash with sweat, but there was a determination in his eye.

"Don't say a word, Candace."

"Your friend died, Zachary," I said. "I'm just trying to figure out why."

"He died because he couldn't keep his mouth shut." He didn't look at me when he said it. Instead, he kept his gaze on his daughter.

She must have called him when she'd gone into the bathroom, I realized. I should have expected as much, considering her history.

"Candace called someone on the day of Cliff's death," I said, turning my focus on Zachary. "I know she did. The policeman I was with at the time knows it." Or he will. *Come on, Paul. Call me back already.* "He found Jay here. He has Arthur in custody. It's only a matter of time until he puts it all together."

"Dad—"

"No!" Zachary wobbled as he took a step toward me. He stopped, leaned against the wall, and then poked me in the shoulder with his cane. "Leave my daughter alone."

I took a step back, out of cane reach. "She called you that night, didn't she?" I asked. "Did you call Arthur afterward? Or was he already there with you?" And then, because I wanted to gauge his reaction: "Did he also kill Wade Fink?"

Zachary flinched, and his leg buckled briefly. He looked like he might collapse, so I took a step toward him to steady him, but all I got for my efforts was another jab in the shoulder with his cane. He was so weak, I barely felt it.

"Arthur killed no one," he said, resting the butt of his cane onto the floor before he fell. Candace hurried around me and took his arm to guide him over to the couch.

"Dad, you don't have to say anything to her. She doesn't know anything."

"I know, honey." He sucked in a pained breath as he was lowered down. "But it's time. I'm not going to let another of my friends down on my account."

Candace sat next to her father, took his hand. Her eyes filled with tears as she stared hard at the floor between us.

"Candace called me." Zachary spoke slowly, carefully. His face was crimson, and yet, there was a paleness to his features that worried me. "She told me Cliff was going to talk about Wade's death. I couldn't let that happen."

"So, you called Arthur," I said, even though he'd just said Arthur was innocent.

"I did no such thing," he snapped, clearly annoyed by my insistence. "Arthur wouldn't have known what to do. He wouldn't know why Cliff's confession would be so damning."

"Dad, please—"

"Let me speak," he said, with some force. "This is my story to tell, not yours."

Candace let her head fall.

Zachary, on the other hand, looked up so he could look me square in the eye. "I killed Wade Fink. Cliff Watson knew all about it, kept it a secret all these years. When he threatened to tell, I did what I had to do and killed him as well."

I stood there, stunned. *He just confessed.* He actually confessed to both murders! I could only manage one word. "Why?"

Zachary laughed. It was a tired, bitter sound. "Wade threw away his friendships to be with that woman. I took it badly. That's all there is to it."

I looked from Zachary to Candace. "You knew?" I asked her.

She didn't react. She just sat there, head down, hands clutching at her father's own as if she could somehow keep him from leaving her by sheer force of will.

"She knew enough to call me," Zachary said. "That's all." He struggled his way to his feet, forcing Candace to release him. By the time he was upright, he was sweating profusely again and was short of breath. His daughter remained seated, her face a mask of misery.

"So," he said. "Are you going to call the police? Or shall I?"

27

It was almost disappointing, how easy it was. Normally, when a killer confessed to me, they tried to take me down with them, usually physically. I've been chased, assaulted, held at gunpoint, and even have chased killers down myself.

Zachary did none of that. He calmly waited for me to call Paul, who answered this time, and then went outside to sit on the stoop to wait for him. He practically put himself into the back seat of the police cruiser.

And then, with nothing further to do, I went home.

Rita deserved to know what happened, as did Jane Winthrow, but right then, I just wanted to sit with my cat. I think I was in shock. Zachary Ross's explanation fit with both murders—what little explanation he'd given—yet looking at him, I couldn't make it work in my mind.

Sure, I knew he was healthier when he was younger, so killing Wade Fink wouldn't have been difficult.

But now? Cliff would almost have had to help Zachary kill him or sit passively by while he'd done it. I supposed it was possible he'd realized at the last minute he couldn't live with putting a longtime friend behind bars, so he allowed himself to be murdered by the man who'd killed one of his friends so long ago.

And yet . . .

I sighed as I stroked Misfit's fur. Paul would fill me in on the details once he got Zachary's statement. Hopefully, he'd be able to explain how Arthur Cantrell and Jay Miller fit into all of this, because I was having a hard time making those pieces fit.

I must have dozed off with Misfit in my lap because it was a little over an hour later when there was a pounding on my door. I sat up, bleary-eyed, with fresh cat scratches— and a missing cat—on my legs.

"Sec," I managed through gummy lips. I made a pit stop in the kitchen to get a drink of water. My mouth felt full of cotton, and my head was spinning. I was pooped and ready for a good night's sleep where I didn't have to worry about a murderer coming to visit me.

The pounding came again. I set my glass aside and feeling somewhat rejuvenated, I answered.

As soon as I opened the door, a man barged in, shouldering me aside.

"He didn't do it," Arthur Cantrell said, spinning on me. "I don't know how you managed to convince him to confess, but Zachary Ross didn't kill anyone."

"How did you find me?" I asked, suddenly wide awake.

"How do you find anyone?" he asked, but he didn't extrapolate.

"Okay." I realized I was still holding the door open, so I closed it. "Why are you here?"

"You know why." He paced back and forth twice, before coming to a stop. "You been hounding us for days now. You managed to get Cliff killed, and then you somehow get

Zachary to confess to a pair of murders he didn't commit? What do you have against us?"

"Me? Nothing," I said. "I talked to Candace and she called her dad. He confessed on his own." All too easily, I realized. I'd had nothing on either of them, nothing of substance anyway. Sure, guilt could have gotten to him, but after all these years?

Arthur narrowed his eyes at me like he didn't believe me. "He wouldn't do that. You must have tricked him somehow."

"Maybe he was tired of lying," I said. "It happens all the time." And then, because I was curious: "Why did you attack Jay Miller?"

Arthur resumed his pacing. He rubbed at the back of his head, mussing his hair. He looked agitated, and I wondered if he'd gotten any sleep. He sure didn't look like it. It wouldn't surprise me to learn he'd just been released from police custody and he'd come straight to me.

"Jay . . ." He trailed off, scowled as if the name offended him, and then he cursed under his breath.

"Let me get you something to drink." I slunk around him and put on a pot of coffee. I desperately needed it, and it looked as if Arthur did as well.

Arthur continued pacing, muttering to himself as the coffee percolated. I waited by the pot, hand hovering near my knife block, just in case he came at me. Arthur was known to have violent tendencies, and while he might not have killed Wade or Cliff, he *had* attacked Jay Miller. No one was disputing that.

The coffee finished and I poured us each a mug. I fished out some sugar, and since I didn't have creamer in the house, I got out a half carton of milk, which was getting close to its expiration date. I set everything on the counter between us.

Arthur muttered a thanks and filled his mug the rest of the way with milk, no sugar. Since I didn't have a cookie on hand, I added a little milk and sugar of my own and took a blessed sip. Arthur gulped his down like it wasn't scalding hot.

"All right," I said when he looked calmer. "Tell me."

He put both hands on the island counter as if bracing himself. "Jay killed Cliff."

"How do you know?"

"Trust me, I know." His eyes burned hot as he looked at me. "Jay Miller went to Cliff's house that night and murdered him."

"Did you tell the police this?" I asked.

"Of course I did," he spat the words. "But do you think they believed me? They kept coming back to how I was the one who attacked *him*. They acted like I killed Cliff because of some vendetta I had against him, though they couldn't come up with anything that backed their assumption."

"But you didn't."

"No, I didn't. Cliff was my friend. Think of me what you will, but I don't hurt my friends like that. I might knock them around a bit if I think they're being idiots, but I'd never kill one of them."

The funny thing was, I believed him. Despite his aggressive behavior, despite the way he treated everyone around him, I didn't think Arthur Cantrell killed Cliff Watson, nor did I believe he killed Wade Fink. There was simply too much raw emotion in his voice.

"Why did Jay kill Cliff?" I asked.

Arthur's hands went back behind his head and locked

there. The muscles in his arms bunched, veins popped out. He was wrestling with something, some internal battle that had to be killing him inside. And if I didn't miss my guess, it had been digging at him for years.

Thirty-three perhaps?

"Jay was protecting someone," he said, dropping his hands to his sides.

"Zachary Ross?" I guessed.

"No. Jay doesn't care about him, never did." Arthur sat down. "It's taken me years to face the facts. I've always suspected, but after Cliff . . ." He shook his head. "I couldn't ignore it anymore."

"Ignore what?"

A tear formed in the corner of Arthur's eye. "Candace never loved Jay. Jay didn't love her, either, but used her, hung their relationship over her father's—Zachary's—head. He knew." His grin was feral. "He *knew.*"

"Knew what?" I felt like I was becoming a broken record, asking the same type of question over and over.

"Candace did it," he said. This time, more than one tear fell down his cheek. "I believe Candace Ross killed Wade Fink, and Jay, Zachary, and Cliff covered it up."

A horrible clanking sound came from the front of my car, but I didn't take my foot off the gas. My phone was in hand. It rang twice, and blessedly, was answered.

"Paul," I said before he could so much as mutter a hello, "Zachary Ross didn't do it. I mean, he kind of did, but he didn't actually kill anyone. It's his daughter, Candace. And Jay Miller. Get someone on him before he leaves the hospital."

"Krissy?" Paul sounded tired. "What's going on?"

I took a deep breath. Rambling madly wouldn't get my point across. "Candace Miller killed Wade Fink. I believe her dad, Zachary, and her husband, Jay, covered it up. Candace was our waitress when I got the call from Cliff. She made a call, likely to Jay, and he killed Cliff to protect her."

"Where are you?" Paul asked. He still sounded confused.

"On the way to Candace's. She might run."

"Go home, Krissy. I can do this."

"She might get away." And then, because I didn't want Paul to find a way to convince me I was doing the wrong thing, I clicked off.

My phone rang almost immediately, but instead of answering, I shoved it deep into my purse. I was almost to Candace's place. Paul would take an extra ten minutes to get there. She could be long gone by then.

Heck, she might be gone already.

I knew what I was doing was dangerous, but I couldn't help myself. Candace had to know her father's story wouldn't hold up to scrutiny for long. He could claim he killed both Wade and Cliff until he was red in the face, but without facts supporting his claim, and with people like Arthur contradicting him, his story would collapse within a day, maybe two.

Chances were, Candace was already prepping to flee Pine Hills, maybe the country. If I was too late, and she'd already left, she would never face justice.

Thankfully, the old Beetle was still parked in the driveway as I came to a stop. My car coughed, and then abruptly died. Something smelled hot and steam was pouring from under the hood. If it came down to a car chase, I was out of luck.

I'd just opened my car door and was stepping out onto the driveway when Candace popped out the front door, a bulging suitcase in hand. Her eyes went wide when she saw me and my smoking vehicle.

"I know what you did, Candace," I said. "You can't let your dad take the fall." I waved a hand in front of my face to clear away some of the smoke.

"I don't know what you're talking about." She closed the front door.

"Zachary didn't kill anyone, did he?" I took a step toward her. "He's too ill to have killed Cliff, and I have a feeling he didn't kill Wade, either."

Candace eyed me, then my car, before looking toward her own vehicle. Another suitcase sat in the back seat. A scruffy teddy bear sat atop it, which caused my heart to go out to her a little. It looked like a childhood toy that she'd kept into her adulthood, likely a protection against what she'd done.

"What happened?" I asked, moving forward another small step. "Why did you kill Wade?"

"I . . ." She shifted the suitcase from one hand to the other. "I didn't kill anyone."

"I know you killed him, Candace. The police are on their way." I coughed as more smoke plumed from my car and washed over me. "Now's your chance to set the record straight before they get to you. I'm not going to judge you." Much.

Candace eased the suitcase down, never taking her eyes off of me. "It was an accident," she said, her voice barely above a whisper. "I was just so angry with him, I . . ." She bit her lower lip, as if suddenly realizing what she was confessing to.

"He was your best friend's boyfriend," I said. "Why

would you kill him when you knew what it would do to Rita?" And then it dawned on me. "He turned you down, didn't he?"

She closed her eyes, and after a long moment, nodded. "It wasn't fair. She already had everything she could ever want. All I wanted was someone who cared for me like Wade did Rita."

"You could have found it elsewhere," I said. "And eventually, you did."

Candace didn't answer. Her hand rose to her cheek, rested there a moment, and then dropped. I didn't know if she was remembering a kiss or a slap.

Did it really matter?

"What about Cliff Watson?" I asked. "Your dad didn't kill him either, so why lie and say he did?"

"You wouldn't understand," Candace said. "There was just so much going on, then and now. I didn't mean for anything bad to happen to anyone."

Silence fell between us. Candace stood with her suitcase next to her, keys dangling from her pocket. I was closer to her car than she was, so it was unlikely she'd escape that way.

"Turn yourself in," I said. "Explain what happened. This doesn't have to end like this. We can go to the police together, talk about it like adults."

Candance glanced at her car, and then back to me. I could see it in her eyes that she was about to give in.

That was when my car decided to erupt in flames.

Fire shot from beneath the hood, through the dash, and in seconds, my car was engulfed, as if someone had doused it in gasoline. It didn't explode like in the movies, but the sudden rush of heat caused me to scream and scramble away from the inferno.

Candace took the opportunity to run.

Leaving her suitcase sitting on the stoop, she leapt down onto the driveway, legs briefly buckling beneath her, before she found her feet. She started for her car, but quickly realized it was a lost cause, considering my fireball was sitting right behind her vehicle. She veered off and rounded the side of the house.

There was a moment where I was too stunned to react. *My car!* And then sense returned and I realized I couldn't just stand there and let a killer escape. My car was lost—as was my phone and purse, which I'd left sitting in the front seat—but that was a worry for later.

I took off after Candace, and a surge of energy, fueled by adrenaline, had me closing the distance in seconds. She saw me gaining and found her own reserves. She leapt over a small ditch, lowered her head, and put everything she had in running.

My heart was thumping in my chest, and already, I was coated in sweat. My breath came in hitched gasps. I could still smell smoke, and my eyes burned from it, but I refused to take them off the fleeing woman.

A copse of trees sat ahead. If Candace reached them, she might be able to lose me. She might not escape Pine Hills, but the short reprieve might give her time to concoct a story—or another way out of town.

Clenching my teeth, I bore down and ran as hard as I'd ever run in my life. I might not be in the best shape, but I *was* younger than Candace. I cleared the ditch, and before she could reach the small copse of trees, I was on her. I threw my weight into a final leap and tackled Candace to the ground.

We hit hard and rolled twice before we stopped. Candace fought me, of course, but I didn't relent. I held her down until she finally collapsed, eyes squeezed shut against the tears that were spilling down her cheeks.

"I didn't mean for any of this to happen," she whimpered. In the distance, sirens rang out. With every breath, they grew nearer. They'd be there in minutes.

"I know," I told her. And then, because it felt like the right thing to say, "Everything will be okay."

By the time Paul Dalton and half the Pine Hills police force arrived on the scene, I was sitting on the ground, dirt and smoke staining my face and clothes, holding a sobbing Candace Miller in my arms.

28

"I still can't believe it," Rita said with a shake of her head. "Candace? It's unfathomable!"

"And her husband was in on it from the start, too?" Jane Winthrow asked.

We were sitting around my table, cooling cups of coffee in front of us. Paul had given me much of the details, and everyone involved was currently behind bars. How long they'd remain there, I didn't know. There was enough evidence to convict, I was sure, but sometimes, strange things happened, especially with so many years between the first murder and the last.

"He was," I said. "Candace killed Wade in a fit of jealousy. She panicked and called her dad, Zachary Ross, who in turn called a police officer he knew, Jay Miller. Together, they covered up the crime and did everything they could to smear Wade's name." Which included using Larry Ritchie, though I didn't think he knew of Jay's involvement of the crime at the time.

"But what about Cliff?" Rita asked. I'd given her most of the story, but had left out big chunks of it early on since she'd taken the news pretty hard. Only now, a week after the case was solved, was she able to talk about it.

"He was part of the cover-up," I said. "He helped Zachary and Jay. He was there when Zachary received the panicked call from Candace, and followed his friend to the scene. He regretted helping them though, and when I started poking around in the murder, he decided it was time to tell someone what really happened."

"So, they killed him to silence him?" Jane asked.

"Jay did." I learned this afterward, as more of the story came out. "Candace overheard me talking to Paul about Cliff's call, realized what it would mean for her, so she called her dad to see what he might want her to do. He was too weak to do anything about it, however, so he called Jay, who had just as much to lose as the rest of them. If Candace was accused of Wade's murder, not only would he become a suspect in the cover-up, but he'd also lose his wife."

"I still can't force myself to believe it," Rita said, dabbing at her eyes with a handkerchief she'd pulled from her purse. "She was my friend."

"I know." I took her hand and squeezed. "And I do believe she regrets what happened." It wasn't much solace—Wade was still dead—but I thought it helped a little.

Misfit sauntered into the room, saw the somber faces round the table, and then wound his way around our feet before leaving again.

Rita rose from her chair. "Thank you, Krissy. It's been a long time coming, but I finally think I can move on."

I stood as she rounded the table to give me a big hug.

"My pleasure," I said.

"Now, I best get back home." Rita cleared her throat and wiped away a tear. I imagined they wouldn't fully dry for a few days yet. She might claim she could move on, but I knew it would take some more time. These new wounds were fresh, and were tied to the old ones that had yet to heal. You didn't just get over that in a day or two. "I have some thinking to do."

Rita left. Getting over Wade would be hard—she'd spent the last thirty-odd years mourning him—but I thought she'd manage. After a week or so, she'd be the same Rita I'd always known. Or maybe an improved version. She no longer had Wade's mysterious death eating away at her.

"I'd better go, too." Jane rose and clasped my hand. "You've accomplished far more than I ever could have expected. You've done my mother proud."

"I'll miss Eleanor."

"We all will." She smiled fondly. "But she can rest now. I think after everything she's gone through in her life, she deserves it."

That, she did.

I walked Jane out the front door, careful not to catch my skirt in the door as I pulled it closed behind me. It felt strange to be dressed up, but tonight was an important one.

"Will you be back to Pine Hills?" I asked her before she could get into her car. Eleanor's house was dark and empty. Soon, a FOR SALE sign would sit in the front yard. I couldn't imagine anyone else moving into the small house, but it would eventually happen. Change always does.

"I don't know," she said. "Without Mom here, there's really nothing left for me in this town." She looked to the sky, breathed in the evening air. "But who knows? It isn't such a bad place to visit."

"No, it's not."

Jane gave me one last fond smile, and then got into her

car. I waved as she backed out of my driveway. She honked once, and then was gone—likely for good.

I rested a hand on the last remaining car in my driveway. The rental was an upgrade over my old Ford but would need to be replaced soon. I'd already started the process of finding a new car, but I wouldn't rush into the decision. I wanted it to be done right.

Just like tonight.

Before I could return to my house, another car turned into my driveway. My heart hiccupped and I found myself far more nervous than I should be. There was a small scab on my knee from when I'd tackled Candace, and I had a bruise the size of a baseball on my left bicep. Suddenly, I felt self-conscious about the blemishes and was regretting my decision to wear a sleeveless blouse and skirt.

But it was too late to change now. Paul parked his car and got out, looking splendid in a suit and tie.

"Hi," I said, hardly able to take my eyes from him as he strode up to me.

"Hi, yourself."

Crickets chirruped. A dog barked. I recognized that bark and glanced to the side. Lance and Jules were standing outside, Maestro leashed and going about his business. Even from where I stood, I could see Jules's approving wink.

"Are you ready to go?" Paul asked. "Vicki called a little while ago and gave me the address. It'll take us a little while to get there." The triple date was still on, despite the excitement of the last couple of weeks.

"I'm ready," I said, pausing long enough to lock the front door. No purse for me tonight. Everything was lost to my car fire, but none of that mattered. A driver's license could be replaced, as could credit cards and keys.

Looking at Paul now, I knew I still had what was important.

And in the end, that was all that mattered.

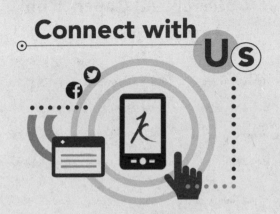

Catering and Capers with
Isis Crawford!